Steven Primrose-Smith was born in Darwen, near Blackburn, in 1970. He managed to escape in 1996 and has since lived in Graz (Austria), Mataró (Spain) and the Isle of Man. He now lives somewhere between the latter and the Costa del Sol. He has a BA in English Language and Philosophy from the Open University and an MA in Philosophy from University of Wales, Trinity Saint David. He is currently in the final throes of a BSc in Mathematics, also with the Open University. His first book, *No Place Like Home, Thank God*, an Amazon Bestseller, described his three-year, 22,000 mile bicycle ride around Europe during which he ate various unsavoury items including a brain, a handful of maggots and a marmot. Steven is currently in the planning stage of a 100-day, 3,700 mile foraging/cycling adventure during which he hopes to survive on only £1 a day. If you're on his route maybe you could give him a biscuit.

Also by Steven Primrose-Smith

NO PLACE LIKE HOME, THANK GOD

GEORGE PEARLY IS A MISERABLE OLD SOD

Steven Primrose-Smith

Rosebery Publications

First published in 2015 by Rosebery Publications
1 Perwick Rise, Port St Mary, Isle of Man

Copyright © 2015 Steven Primrose-Smith
All rights reserved.
steven@primrose-smith.com

ISBN-13: 978-1508697893
ISBN-10: 1508697892

Except in the United States of America, this book is sold subject to the condition that it shall not, by way of trade or otherwise, be lent, re-sold, hired out, or otherwise circulated without the publisher's prior consent in any form of binding or cover other than that in which it is published and without a similar condition including this condition being imposed on the subsequent purchaser.

All characters appearing in this work are fictitious. Any resemblance to real persons, alive or dead, is purely coincidental.

To Mark Hingston,

so he'll stop whining

Monday 28th October

I had only originally gone in for a routine check-up. I did not expect to be told that I was dying.

"Sit down," he said, the charlatan.

He wore his white coat over an open-necked, garish, pink and green Hawaiian shirt, his stethoscope nestled comfortably in his prodigious chest hair. Vince is a handsome man to women, I assume, in his late thirties with a tousled, lopsided hedge of dirty blond hair. I had seen young singers on television sporting such an unkempt mane. On his large desk was a mess of papers and a laptop.

I sat as commanded, my knees creaking. The chair was the white, plastic, garden variety whose legs seemed to buckle slightly despite my slender frame.

"Do you have the results of my test?" I asked.

"I do," he replied, looking grim.

Vince looked me straight in the eye. I waited a long ten seconds for him to provide further information but my wait was in vain.

"So?" I asked.

He pulled a strange face.

"Am I ill?"

He grimaced non-committally.

"What is the nature of my malady?" I asked more forcefully.

"Look," he said, smiling. "We've known each other for ages, haven't we, John?"

"My name is George."

"Is it?" He perused my records. "So it is. But I know you, George. If I tell you what's wrong with you then you'll develop the symptoms. That's what you're like."

"Is it something of a serious nature?"

"Oh yes. Very serious. As serious as a disease can be," he replied solidly and a little too glibly for my liking.

"Is there nothing you can do?"

"What do you mean?"

I was dumbstruck. I shook my head violently to force out the words.

"What do you mean what do I mean? You are the doctor. Is there any available treatment?"

"Not as far as I know."

"Not as far as you know? How far do you know? Maybe there is a new treatment."

"I doubt it."

"Can you not check, for god's sake?"

I was getting frantic now.

"S'pose." He tapped a couple of keys on the laptop on his desk, screwed up his face and then clicked his mouse repeatedly. "No, nothing."

I peered around to see what was on his screen but he slammed it shut.

"So it is fatal then?"

Vince grinned an enormous, inane grin.

"John, John, John. We've all got something fatal. It's called life."

He manufactured a pistol with a trio of fingers and launched an imaginary bullet towards my skull.

"Is that what they taught you at medical school?"

"Look, John. Trust me. You're better off not knowing."

"I believe that is my decision?"

"Not really."

"Did you even go to medical school?"

"I did."

"But did you go inside?"

"Funny one, John."

"If you do not tell me what is wrong with me then what am I actually paying you for?"

He thought for a moment and shrugged his shoulders.

"Take Dave," he said.

"Dave? Cockney Dave?"

"No, Fat Dave."

"What about him?"

"He was in here yesterday. He's got diabetes."

"So you will tell me his results but not mine."

"Listen, if I told Fat Dave he had diabetes then he'd be convinced he was going blind or getting gangrene in his legs or something. Yes, it'd be more work for me, but I've got enough work."

"So Dave does not know he has diabetes?"

"No."

"But I do?"

"Yes."

"Are you familiar with the phrase 'client confidentiality'?"

He appeared mildly pensive for a moment and then waved away my question.

"What Fat Dave doesn't know won't hurt him?" he said. I shook my head sadly. "And it's the same with you, John. If you knew what you had, then you'd probably start to...well, I can't tell you that because then you might guess."

"Give me a clue."

"No."

"Do I have diabetes?"

"I don't know. We didn't test for that. You might have."

"But it is not diabetes that is to induce my imminent death?"

"No."

"Do I have a heart condition?"

"I'm not playing this game, John. There are a million things it could be."

"But it is something bad?"

"It is."

"And it is something terminal?"

"Yup."

"Can you tell me how long I have left?"

"We'll be done in a minute."

"Not this appointment, you moron. My life. Can you tell me how long I have left to live?"

"Weeks."

"How many weeks?"

"Some."

"Could you be a little more precise?"

"OK, I would estimate...seven weeks. Maybe seven and a half."

"My, that *is* precise."

"That's me," he said, arms outstretched, "Doctor Incredible."

I snorted.

"Yes, well, it is certainly incredible that you are a doctor. Vince, you are without a doubt the worst medical practitioner in the entire universe."

"Thank you," he smiled. "But at least I speak English."

"Yes, you do. But today that is of little advantage. Would I have learnt any less about my medical condition had you communicated to me in Estonian?"

"*Sa suremas*," he said.

"What?"

"Yes, you would."

"Yes, I would what?"

"Yes, you would have learnt less. I just told you that you are dying in Estonian and you didn't understand."

I must have looked flummoxed.

"I had an Estonian girlfriend," he offered as explanation.

"Did you have to use that phrase often?"

"Yes." He looked wistful. "She was a very sickly girl."

"Before or after you started courting?"

Vince returned to the papers on his desk. I sat there in silence for a few seconds hoping that he was going to furnish me with at least a hint of information regarding my demise. Instead he wiggled his cheap biro doorwards to indicate in his own subtle way that our session was complete.

"Don't forget to pay Shirley on the way out," he said.

"I am not going out."

"Eh?"

"I am going to entrench myself in reception until your next client departs this office. He is certain to know what is the matter with me."

"Ha, ha," he laughed falsely. "Seriously, John, pay Shirley her fifty euros on the way out."

I waited in reception for a full thirty minutes but I was unacquainted with any of the patients who followed me. The waiting area was full of the usual depressed, middle-aged women pretending to have located a lump. Doctor Vince's soothing hands would alleviate their illusory scare. The service that he offered was as much sexual as it was medical. The ladies appear to like doctors, even quacks.

And then it was two o'clock and lunchtime. I was not going to wait around until Vince re-opened at five. I had things to do, I thought urgently to myself. It was only a few seconds later I realised that, in actual fact, I did not.

I went and purchased a beer, sitting in the sun, contemplating what remained of my truncated existence. All the things I had longed to do would be left undone. I attempted to make a mental list of such ambitions but, despite two beers-worth of meditation, I failed to recall anything except my desire to escape this foetid coastline. I had achieved my three score years and ten. I had precious little left to live for. Maybe it was the right time for me to die.

Tuesday 29th October

I find it difficult to tell you how much I detest this place although I shall of course make a valiant attempt. I abhor this smear of Britain staining shit-brown the Mediterranean's azure. I loathe every cerise-faced, ginned-up tourist cretin that walks this pueblo's faux-cobbled streets, splattered in tattoos and bedecked in football's tribal colours. The local expats here in Merla are even worse. I despise my existence here, or rather my lack of it, with the whole force of my parched and withered soul.

Though my life is concluding in a manner as yet to be determined I feel a great desire to document my final hours, to record any reflections upon mortality. That is the reason for the commencement of this, my life's first ever diary. I hope that you, stumbling upon its pages, enjoy ingesting my thoughts much more than I enjoy typing them into this execrably slow computer. It is a trial already and I am only on Day Two. I hate you too for demanding this of me. I hate everything – everything and everyone except Ambrose.

"Why don't you leave?" I hear you cry like a shrieking child. Would that I could but I cannot. I am a prisoner of the sun, trapped in someone else's paradise by penury, between a rock (i.e., Gibraltar) and a hot place (i.e., Almería's Tabernas Desert). Curse you, Marjorie!

There is only one element of life in Spain that brings a sliver of joy to my weary bones and that is the nation's *denuncia* system. It allows one to make an official complaint about the behaviour of another that must be processed by the local courts. By now I have made so many complaints that I merely have to drop off a written statement at the police station. It must be in Spanish, naturally, but that is what Google Translate is for. The best part of the system is that it is entirely free of charge. There are few of my acquaintances who have yet to experience the pleasure of having the police arrive on their doorsteps to inform them of their denouncement. As their faces crumble at the touch of the law's long arm I am overcome with beatific joy at the justice being served.

*

I took Ambrose for his daily drag along the sea front, sweat soaking through my white Dunnes shirt, rendering transparent its flimsy fabric. I removed my red handkerchief and mopped my greasy brow. How could it be so hot in October? Two young Spanish women walked past, one of them staring open-mouthed at my rosy nipples now clearly visible through the cotton. I may be seventy but I still have it, I thought to myself, but then from behind me I heard her make a gagging sound. I turned to see her miming a retching action to her friend and chastised myself for my hubris.

Poor Ambrose. He has never been the same since I backed over him in the car. Every time I look down at the space where his front leg used to be, a wave of guilt engulfs my heart.

This afternoon he hid in the shadows, avoiding the sun. Little Ambrose had no handkerchief to cool his tiny, white head and he collapsed to the floor, panting like an asthmatic. He eventually stood up lazily and coughed up something pale green. After half a mile or so, my tugging on his lead only resulted in more dry-throated, porcine grunting and so I ceased. He once again tumbled to the floor. I gave him a little nudge with my sandalled foot but nothing was going to reanimate him. I picked him up and carried him. He is getting heavy, too hefty a burden for a man of my age.

Eventually we arrived at my little, flowerless garden and the paint-flaking front door of my tiny, rented house. Inside it was like a furnace. The house is a model of bad design. Until the summer ceases, the temperature of the living room is hot enough to melt a diamond. The second that winter arrives – autumn is an alien concept to southern Spain – my house immediately takes on many of the properties of an industrial freezer. This year's summer had yet to end, another example of global warming, so they claim. I moved to turn on the fan but the electricity was off again. Ambrose waddled drunkenly to his water bowl in the kitchen and fell face-first into it.

I looked around my living room, bored. I glanced at my watch. *Countdown* would start in a minute. If I had electricity. I looked at my watch again. I do not usually visit the pub until after the conundrum. (Yesterday had been a justified exception.) Rules are important. But if I had no *Countdown*, then I had no rule.

The fan suddenly whirled into life and the fridge began to hum, but the seed of an idea, of a cold beer in a frozen glass tankard, had now been planted, watered and sprouted and suddenly *Countdown*'s appeal was vastly diminished, overshadowed by a small beer shrub. Cold Mahou or Rachel Riley in a short skirt? I made the four steps to the kitchen to ponder my predicament. I carefully removed Ambrose's head from his water bowl and returned to the living room. I turned on the television and selected Channel Four. Oh dear, I thought to myself disappointedly, she is wearing a knee-length frock. I switched off the fan and I went for a beer.

Wednesday 30th October

I have a new neighbour. She moved next door a fortnight ago. I know very little about her, but I have ascertained that she is looking for a man. At least this is what her underwear collection tells me. Either that or she fantasizes about being a prostitute. There is always something black and scarlet hanging teasingly from her washing line. These are certainly not the grey, baggy pantaloons so beloved of my Marjorie.

(I realise I must desist from calling her 'my' Marjorie nowadays. I did not form this habit out of love for my now-departed wife. I use it more in the sense of 'my' Dyson, i.e., something expensive that lives indoors and hoovers up every morsel in its path.)

Apparently there is a calculation that one can make to determine an appropriate age gap between a man and his lover. If the gentleman halves his age and then adds seven he is permitted to have relations with a lady of the resulting age. The beauty of this system is that it allows ever greater possibilities the older one becomes. Aged twenty I was only allowed a woman of no fewer than seventeen years. Nowadays however I am permitted access to someone from age forty-two upwards. There is another rule that applies to the maximum age boundary, which is calculated by subtracting seven from your age and doubling the result. This means it would be socially acceptable for me to court a woman up to 126 years of age although, if I am being honest, I do not think I should like that.

I predict that my neighbour is in her mid-40s, which means that if she were to say that I am too old for her, then I can provide a rule as to why she is incorrect.

"There," I can say. "You are wrong. Now have dinner with me."

I have to admit that she fascinates me. I never felt this way about Marjorie, not even in the early days. Marjorie did not possess what might be known as feminine wiles. Her body was particularly unappealing, something I hinted at in a poem entitled *"Your Legs"* in my published collection, *"Poems To Annoy My Ex-Wife"*, a copy of which I am certain sits proudly on your most prominent bookshelf.

Your Legs

I once saw your naked legs.
You didn't know I'd spied them.
The bathroom door was slight ajar.
I'm glad you used to hide them.

My neighbour, on the other hand, has very attractive legs. Today, over our shared terrace wall, I managed to have a conversation of sorts with her. I fear I did not cover myself in glory.

"Good morning to you," I offered as she was about to peg another set of racy briefs on to her washing line.

She looked a little embarrassed.

"Oh, hello," she said.

She balled up the strumpetwear currently in her hand and placed it back into her laundry basket.

"Oh, no," I said. "Do not stop on my account." I smiled charmingly. "You have an extremely interesting range of bloomers."

"Bloomers?"

"Knickers then."

"Yes, I know what bloomers are. I've just never heard anyone use that word before."

"Ah."

"Do you spend a lot of time admiring my panties?"

If only she knew. But with that unnecessary Americanism she had slipped three per cent in my fascination scale.

"Er, no, I apologise." I approached the short, separating wall between our terraces and she cowered backwards. I offered her my hand. "I am George, by the way."

She relaxed a little, realising I was unlikely to vault the wall, and presented her hand to me. Her sleeve rode up and revealed a small tattoo of a rose. Oh dear. That was another three per cent.

"Hi," she said, shaking my hand. "I'm Janet."

She has a lovely smile. And it was only then, standing face to face, that I realised how tall she was, around five foot ten. A tall gentleman like myself looks more respectable with a lady of height.

"Ah, Janet," I said, seeking a connection, "I once had a dog called Janet."

"Really?" she asked. "Was she good?"

She seemed to be suppressing a smirk.

"Yes, she was very good," I said a little uncertainly.

Janet's face cracked.

"She knew a trick or two," I added.

Janet laughed openly.

"Did she swallow?" Janet guffawed.

What a strange question!

"Of course she swallowed." Janet cackled even harder. "If she had not swallowed then she would have been unable to consume her food. Sorry, I do not understand the question. Why are you laughing?"

"Don't worry about it, Georgie Boy. I'm just having you on."

Suddenly I comprehended the meaning of her jape. You fool, George. She made a sexual joke. Now she thinks you a humourless prude. But, on the other hand, she called me 'Boy'. Clearly my maturity will be no barrier to this relationship.

"Oh, ha, ha. Yes, I get it now. You meant a dog as in an ugly woman. And that last bit was about oral sex, was it not?"

"Alright, George, steady on."

"I am certain it was. Well, I feel that I should inform you that I myself am partial to a bout or two of oral sex."

I have never had oral sex. Marjorie preferred not to touch my penis at all. On the evening of our honeymoon she insisted on wearing oven gloves.

Janet looked awkward.

"Well, thanks for letting me know, George."

"Sorry, that was rather forward."

Now she thinks you a humourless pervert.

"Right, George, it's been lovely meeting you but I've got to go inside."

"But you have yet to finish hanging out your, erm, panties."

For a woman with such briefs I am prepared to offer some linguistic flexibility.

"S'OK. I'll do them later. See ya, George."

"Yes, good day."

I felt more than a little despondent as she scuttled away to the security of her house. She turned back towards me.

"Oh, and George?"

"Yes!"

It appeared she wanted some more of her Georgie Boy.

"Is that your car out front?"

"The Vauxhall? Yes."

"You know it's been sprayed?"

I let out a long sigh.

"Why, what have they written on it this time?"

"George Pearly is a miserable old sod."

"Oh." That was disappointing. "Yes, thank you. I will clean it immediately."

Now she thinks you a miserable, humourless pervert-prude with no friends.

I went back inside. Removing the paint from the car would allow Janet enough time to hang out her remaining underwear without worrying that I would pounce on her from the terrace, penis in hand, demanding fellatio.

As usual the paint came off after only an hour of scrubbing. At one point Ambrose hobbled out of the house and slowly approached me. He dipped his head into my forty-one, arriving late for work after a tube strike, he collapsed on the escalator on the way up to his office and became tangled in the machinery, which caused a fuse to blow and a blackout across three blocks of The City. Single-handedly he wiped twenty million pounds off the Stock Exchange in an incident that will be forever known as Black Tuesday Elevenses.

In order to distance herself as far as possible from London, Mary sold up their modest Victorian terrace in Kensington and bought an eight-bedroomed farmhouse on the rural outskirts of Blackburn. This decision was not the first time her sanity had been questioned.

Mary was pregnant when Geoffrey died. It was her first child and, at forty-four, she was a medical miracle but the procedure was not without its risks to the baby, risks that were realised upon birth. Although Kevin was never diagnosed with any particular medical condition it has long been accepted that he is not right in the head.

"How's Spain, George?" she asked.

"Spain is awful, thank you very much."

"That's the spirit, boy. Right, George, I know you're a busy man and so I'll cut to the chase."

"Yes, I *am* a busy man."

I am not a busy man.

"Young Kevin is having a few, well, issues."

"Issues?"

"Some things he needs to work through. Didn't you ever have issues, George?"

"No."

"Well, Kevin does. He has lots of issues. And he would like to work through them."

"Good. He should see a..."

"In Spain," she added.

"Where in Spain?"

"Where do you live?"

"No, that is absolutely out of the question. My house is tiny. There is barely room to..."

"I'll make it worth your while."

"It is not about the money."

"Five thousand pounds."

"Five thousand pounds?" I spluttered.

"For a couple of weeks. Instil into him some of that army discipline."

"I left the army when I was nineteen. I was dishonourably discharged."

"Well, if you don't want it I suppose I could call Richard."

"No! I will do it!"

Gifting me five thousand pounds would permit a comfortable termination to my otherwise meagre existence. More important though it would prevent the same money from reaching Richard, my younger brother. I hate Richard.

"Good. I will book his flight this afternoon. He will be there within the week. Goodbye, George."

"No small talk? It has been ten years after all."

"No."

She put the phone down.

Two weeks of inconvenience would be a small price to pay if it enabled me to live out my remaining weeks in financial ease, forgoing the mostly rice and bean-based diet of recent weeks. Besides, Mary was ten years my senior, which would make Kevin around thirty-five now. I could use a chauffeur.

Saturday 2nd November

Today I was on a mission. If Vince had told Scotch Tony about my ailment then he had surely told others. I would visit what passes as my local and try to winkle it out of one of the dimmer regulars. God knows, there are plenty from which to choose. The bar even has a league table of stupidity. Their weekly quiz offers a bottle of wine for the victors and a round of shots for the losers. Since the value of the wine is in the region of a euro a bottle it is financially prudent to bring up the competition's rear. At least that is their excuse. In any case, each week three or four teams compete to answer incorrectly as many of the forty questions as possible in order to complete the tournament in final place. The overall results are tallied week-by-week on a large chalk board recording a Premier League of remedial quizzing. One week I arrived late, with only four questions remaining and I still took home the wine. I have only once attended the full quiz and I have been sitting at the top of the leader board for the last six months. In many circles my intellect would be a source of respect. Here it breeds only resentment.

I should describe my local. Merla is well-stocked with drinking venues, all much of a muchness, funded entirely by the British and Scandinavians. I visit Bar Wars to support its near constant legal battle with George Lucas over copyright infringement of the iconic film's logo that appears on the sign outside, together with an image of Chewbacca indulging in a once-illegal sex act with an Ewok. Lucas is also not enamoured by the various scenes portraying his other characters on the bar's interior walls. One vignette has Princess Leia being serviced by a stormtrooper. In another, C-3PO is on his knees and providing a willing receptacle for an engorged Han Solo. You have probably deduced that Bar Wars is a refined establishment. Also, and more important, it is the closest bar to my house.

To my utter delight – I am being sarcastic – sitting at the bar was Bullshit Phil. Compared to the typical age of ex-pats on the Costa del Sol, at forty-one years of age Phil is positively foetal. Certainly his brain capacity is. Obviously,

Bullshit Phil thinks that his name is simply Phil and that no one could possibly invent an unpleasant adjective for someone with such a wealth of interesting and plausible tales.

"Hello, Philip," I said, sitting down on the stool beside him. "What is, as they say, up?"

"Eh?"

"How are you doing?"

Phil looked incredulous.

"Get this, Trev," he said to the landlord behind the bar. "The professor wants a conversation."

Trevor looked around disinterestedly and went back to restocking his fridge with blue bottles. That is, bottles of blue liquid, rather than large flies. The fridge already had enough large flies.

"Well, George, thank you for asking." He adopted a mockingly superior tone. "I am doing very well, very well indeed. And how the hell are you, sir?"

I decided to test the water.

"I think I may be a little ill," I said.

"Too right, mate. You're on your last legs."

"So you have spoken to Vince?"

"Vince? No. Mike told me."

"Mike?"

"Morality Mike. You know him. Always wears that daft hat."

"Yes, I know him. And he heard it from Vince."

"Nah, think he said Linda told him."

I despaired.

Trevor the landlord turned around.

"What can I get you, George?"

"Drunk, Trevor. You can get me very drunk."

"Starting with?"

"Since you have nothing better, give me a Glenmorangie."

"Feeling flush, are we?" Trevor said, reaching for the

amber.

"Trevor," I said, "you talk sense occasionally. What is wrong with me?"

"Sorry, mate. That'd take too long. I need to finish the fridges. Talk to Phil. Someone has to."

He poured the whisky into a tumbler and placed it on the bar in front of me.

"Philip?" I said.

"Sorry, mate. We've all been sworn to secrecy. You'll never get it out of me. If the KGB couldn't open my gob then you ain't gonna break me."

Here we go.

"And what information did the KGB want to gather from you?" I asked.

He processed the question for a moment and then settled in for a story.

"Well, I'd stolen...ah, wait a minute. You can't get me that easily."

"Philip, tell me what is wrong with me."

"No."

"Philip, if you do not tell me, then I will have to do something rather unpleasant."

"Nothing you could do would scare me, prof. The Russkies strapped me naked into one o' them fanny-examining chairs. Had me legs in the stirrups. They put me balls in a vice and I still didn't talk."

"Really?"

"They crushed 'em thinner and thinner. Not a dicky bird. In the end my nuts looked like a couple of After Eights."

"I am struggling to believe you."

"Why's that?"

"Because last weekend you were in that corner, unconscious, with your trousers around your ankles and your testicles on show to the whole bar. I did not stare for longer than necessary but your gonads were definitely not reminiscent of a pair of chocolate mint wafers."

He shrugged it off.

"I grew a new pair," he said.

"Of course you did."

"And that, George, is exactly what you need to do. Yes, you're ill. But suck it up. You're alive. That's more than can be said for Scotch Tony."

"Scotch Tony? Why, what happened?"

I took a sip of my Glenmorangie to mask my trembling lip.

"No one knows. He hasn't been in since Wednesday. He's normally in here all the time. I went 'round his place but there's no answer."

"Maybe he returned home to see his children for a few days."

"Nah, he was supposed to be here for the pool league on Friday. It's tragic." He shook his head sadly. "Very tragic. We had to forfeit his game. We ended up getting walloped."

"So what do you suspect has happened to him?"

"I have a theory."

"I bet you do."

"I think it's obvious. It's aliens."

"Alright then."

I knocked back the dregs of the whisky and turned to go. He grabbed my wrist and spoke in a hushed tone.

"I know what they're capable of."

"Does it involve anal probes by any chance?"

His voice was now a panicked whisper.

"Yes, it does. Have you been 'visited' too?"

"Yes, Philip. They arrive every Sunday just in time for lunch. Once they have polished off the Sticky Toffee Pudding we have an hour or two inserting objects into each other's bottoms and then we all jump into their flying saucer and do a lap of the Milky Way."

Phil stared at me.

"You shouldn't joke," he said. "They're watching."

"Philip, you are a moron."

I got up and walked towards of the door before remembering a question I needed to ask.

"Oh, and would you have any idea who spray-painted my car, Philip?"

"Not a clue, mate." He was smiling. "Not a clue."

As I strolled down the street I could hear him calling out after me.

"Get well soon, professor! Best write a will, mate!"

Ha! A will. What use is a will when one has nothing to bequeath?

Sunday 3rd November

It was morning and I was sunk in a trough of despair. I needed to discover the nature of my malady. Vince may be the only English-speaking doctor this side of Málaga but if his medical knowledge is akin to his professionalism he may have misdiagnosed. After all, he once stopped a British tourist in the street and warned her that liver failure was imminent. In reality she was a pasty-faced northerner who had recently enjoyed an overly enthusiastic spray tan. I may not be dying at all. Tomorrow I shall see Vince again.

My mood was lifted when, through the kitchen window, I spied Janet out on the terrace, pinning more naughty attire to her washing line. She must go through three changes of knickers every day. Should I rush out and engage her in conversation? No, I would wait until she had completed the task at hand. If through embarrassment I keep forcing the woman to take her still damp underwear back inside she is likely to end up with an unfortunate case of gusset mildew and I have no desire to be responsible for such a condition. I sat a while and composed a short poem.

Janet's Briefs
Your briefs are briefer than an English summer,
And hot as fire that burns on Spanish hills,
Swaying upon your line like fields of wheat,
If wheat were red and black and trimmed with frills.

I have to admit that it was not one of my better ones.

I decided that I would make a snack to pass the time until I could safely approach my neighbour. I opened the fridge door to find Ambrose inside, sitting on the middle shelf, eating my chorizo. He blinked at me in the light – god knows how long he had been there – climbed out and trotted across the kitchen with the empty sausage packet in his mouth. I have long stopped pondering how Ambrose manages to get himself into such unlikely locations. I suspect that he can teleport. He climbed sluggishly through the cat flap and plodded across the terrace. Noticing Janet he approached the wall, looked up at her and started to bark. Through the open window I could hear Janet talking.

"Hello, little dog. Why are you barking?"

Oh no. A short burst of yaps is usually an indication that Ambrose is soon to defecate. I grabbed a napkin and made for the door. Before I could reach it I heard Janet again.

"I know what you want. You want a biscuit. Hang on a minute."

I quickly opened the door but Janet had already gone a-hunting. Ambrose looked up at me and then adopted the position. Some canines are able to do their business with dignity, taking their weight solidly on their two front legs, raising their rear and delivering a tidy parcel. Since the accident Ambrose has struggled with such daily necessities. Forgetting that he is missing an arm, he puts too much reliance on his missing limb and tumbles forward. Usually it is on his third attempt, and mid-evacuation, that he under-compensates for his lack of balance and instead falls backwards on to the pile he has just deposited. It is a particularly unattractive look for a white dog. I crouched down beside Ambrose, breathing in through my mouth to avoid the unpleasant aroma, and cleaned him as best I could. It had not occurred to me that I was now concealed behind the wall.

"Here, doggy. Have a bicky," said Janet, stretching a hand above my head.

I stood up to my full six foot two.

"Hello, Janet!" I beamed.

She leapt backwards, shrieking like a siren.

"Jesus pissin' Christ! You scared the shit out of me." She held her chest and breathed rapidly. "Why were you hiding down there?"

"No, I was not hiding. I was effecting a cleansing operation. See!"

With an outstretched arm I exhibited the brown-stained towel. Suddenly, now that I had stopped breathing through my mouth, its odour rose and assaulted my olfactory senses. I had to conceal a compulsion to gag.

"Jesus, George. Jesus, Jesus, Jesus!"

"I am sorry."

She breathed out a huge breath to calm herself down a little.

"It's alright," she said. "It's not your fault."

"But I am sorry."

"Apology accepted but please can you do something with that," she said, indicating the soiled napkin in my outstretched hand.

"Oh, of course."

My bin was inside the house. If I disposed of the towel in its correct location, then Janet would depart our tête-à-tête and I would miss an opportunity to woo her. I balled up the tissue and put it in my pocket. Janet winced.

"Have you had a nice weekend, Janet?"

"It's been alright. Nothing special."

There was silence.

"Good, good," I said.

This was not progressing as I had hoped.

"Yeah," she added uselessly.

"Erm, Janet, I was wondering." Go for it, George. "I am having a few friends around soon and I wondered if you would like to come for dinner. I do a mean beef stroganoff."

"I'm vegetarian."

"All diets catered for!"

"I don't know, George. I'm away this week."

"No matter. I will make the dinner for the following week."

"What about your friends? Haven't you already arranged it?"

"My friends are extremely flexible."

Especially since they do not actually exist.

"I don't think I can, George, y'know."

I decided that it was time to play my trump card. My face grew serious, my voice raspy.

"I am dying, Janet."

"What? God. What's the matter?"

"I do not know."

Given the situation this felt like a particularly weak response.

"What do you mean you don't know?"

"The doctor will not tell me. He believes it might disturb me." She looked puzzled. "So will you come?"

"Why won't he tell you?"

"Do not worry. We can talk about that over dinner. It can be a congenial opening topic of conversation. So, you will dine with me, er, with us?"

She had been distracted by my ailment.

"Oh, yes. Yes, of course." Victory! "I won't be back until next Saturday though. Is that OK?"

"Seven thirty?"

"Yeah."

"I will make a note of it in my diary."

I hoped this nugget of life detail gave the impression of a debonair with an overly full social life. I was oozing charm.

"But make sure you've thrown out that shitty rag from your pocket before I come, yeah?"

"Of course. Of course."

I lowered my head and marched back into the house, refusing to make further eye contact lest she changed her mind.

Monday 4th November

"Hi John, come in, sit down."

"My name is still George."

Vince dismissed this comment with a wave of his hand. I sat down.

"What can I do you for?" he asked.

"You can stop acting like an arse and tell me what is wrong with me."

"I've told you. You don't want to know."

"Yes, I do. Look, this is me," I said pointing to my own face, "wanting to know."

Vince shook his head gently.

"Everybody else knows what is wrong with me. Even

Bullshit Phil knows."

"Bullshit Phil. He's unbelievable, isn't he?"

"His stories are."

"He told me he was the first person to swim the Atlantic," he said. I raised my eyes skyward. "Underwater," continued Vince.

"Shut up," I said, determined to take control. "Everybody knows about my illness. Why does everybody know?"

"Word gets out, John."

"Does it? Does it really? But how did it get out?"

"Shirley can be an awful gossip."

"Are you suggesting that your receptionist has been leaking this confidential information all over town?"

He shrugged his shoulders and raised his eyebrows.

"It doesn't really matter *how* it got out, John. It's out there now."

"Right then. I want a second opinion."

"You haven't really had a first opinion yet."

"Can you be serious?"

"Alright then. A second opinion? You can't go around feeding me old set-up lines like that. OK, John, my second opinion is that you're also boring. Ha, ha! I kill myself."

"If only," I said. "I want you to refer me to a specialist."

Vince looked at me for a minute, his eyes dead.

"Fair enough, George," he said calmly. "I'll get you an appointment with Doctor Antonio Garcia as soon as."

"What is his speciality?"

Vince laughed.

"As if I'd tell you that." He smirked as he wrote something in the ledger on his desk. Then he looked up. "Oh, you do speak Spanish, don't you?"

"No."

"Ah. Then I fear it would be a huge waste of your time and money."

"Doctor Garcia is unable to speak English?"

"He barely speaks Spanish. His thick Andalusian accent is impenetrable even for most educated Spaniards."

I stood up.

"Vince, I cannot tell you how much I hate you."

"Go on, give it a go."

"You know something? I do not believe there is anything the matter with me. I have never felt in better health. You are either making it all up or you are so slipshod that you have made a misdiagnosis."

"Classic, John."

"What is classic?"

"You. This. Your denial. Classic first stage of the grieving process."

"You...ARSE!!"

"There you go, John. Stage two, anger."

"Come on, you must be able to do something."

"Whoa. Stage three, bargaining. Keep this up, John, and you'll have worked right through your loss before you leave and I'll have to charge you for therapy too."

"ARGHHH!"

"John, John," he said firmly but calmly. "Sit down."

He looked towards my empty chair with an outstretched palm. I took a deep breath, regained my composure and returned to my seat.

"I can prescribe you something to help."

"To help with what?"

"With the pain."

"There is no pain."

"There will be." He drew a scribble on a thick pad and tore off the docket. "Get these from the chemist now and if things, well, develop then see if they work."

He grinned a charming smile that I suspect is usually reserved for his female patients. I looked at the illegible mess on the prescription. I breathed out deeply.

"I do not want to die," I said shamelessly.

"No, I know." He let out a heavy sigh and then spoke calmly. "Do you believe in god, John?"

"No."

"No, me neither. But there's something I feel really helps in a situation like this."

"What is that?"

"What you need to do is..." An comedy alarm clock on his desk burst forth with an ear-splitting bell. He slammed it quiet with his fist. "Right, time up!"

"No, what do I need to do? Tell me."

"Another time perhaps."

He stood up. I followed.

"Tell me!" I shouted.

"I've got other patients to see. Don't forget to pay Shirley on the way out."

I ripped open the door and marched out into the tiny hallway.

"Put it on my tab!" I yelled as I passed reception and exited the building.

"We don't do tabs," said Shirley.

"You do now!" I shouted before the door closed.

Tuesday 5th November

I had it! I knew how I would discover my illness. Unwittingly, Vince had provided a lead by telling me that he could refer me to Doctor Antonio Garcia. Maybe I could not speak to this medical yokel myself but surely the internet would tell me his speciality.

I made myself a cup of Darjeeling and settled in for a session on the computer. Would I be able to locate a doctor called Antonio Garcia? Well, yes, I would. It was unfortunately all too easy. I found five of them. It appeared that Antonio Garcia was one of the most common names in Spain.

I could eliminate the first doctor from the investigation, a chiropodist in Torre Del Mar, unless of course Vince had discovered a particularly virulent ingrowing toe nail. Likewise, the homeopath in Marbella could be eliminated simply because they all should be.

This left me with three remaining specialists. One dealt with Alzheimer's but after perusing his web page it revealed that he was originally from Barcelona and therefore would not possess an over-enthusiastic grasp of the local patois. Sadly, the remaining two doctors were both oncologists. It looked like my greatest fears were borne out. I would meet my end with the Big C, just as my father had, and his father before him. To be honest, it was little surprise.

I went to the chemist and presented my prescription. The kindly-faced, white-coated servant looked at it closely, smiled uncomfortably and went to fetch the package. He muttered something incomprehensible and when I looked blankly in reply he pointed to the numbers on his till's electronic display.

I am a lazy fool. I have been here for nearly ten years and can still only count to twenty in Spanish. That said, this meagre ability places me well within the top five per cent of the British ex-pat community.

I walked slowly back to the house, feeling low. I opened the door to hear a scuffling sound, wires twisting, something trying to escape. A tiny yap directed my attention to the source. Ambrose was trapped behind the back of the television again. I freed him and went to sit on my only comfortable chair. He trotted to my feet. I patted him on the head. At least I had Ambrose.

The sky clouded over and the rain came down.

"Sorry, Ambrose. No walk today."

Overjoyed at this news he leapt for my lap, his sole front leg slipping between my own, and he walloped his chin on my knee. He rolled over on to his side, unconscious. I went to the fridge to get the only smelling salts that Ambrose knows. The brand new packet of chorizo that I had only purchased yesterday was empty. He had been inside the fridge again. I resolved to get a padlock for my cooler. There was however some cheddar in the cheese compartment. Maybe that would suffice.

With a cube of cheese in hand I walked back into the living room to see Ambrose watching me. He quickly replaced his head on the floor, continuing the pretence at being out cold.

The rain came down more heavily, tropical monsoon style. Water started to leak under my front door.

There have been times when Spain has led the world in innovation. From Averroes to Severo Ochoa, ideas flooded from this peninsula. But despite this entrepreneurial spirit, no one in Spain has ever thought to fit a door frame to prevent the ingress of water during a storm. The Spanish solution is to place a wooden board outside that leans against one's door at an angle suitable to bounce the raindrops away. It only works in the lightest of showers.

Ambrose ran around in tiny, frantic circles desperate to escape the water. I tucked my legs beneath my body and placed Ambrose on my lap. The water poured in. Normally I would attempt to staunch the flow but today I did not feel like doing anything.

It was only three o'clock in the afternoon but with the dark storm clouds outside it felt like evening. Using the remote I switched on the television. David Dickinson grinned back, looking like he had eaten too many carrots. Thunder rumbled overhead.

"One, two, three, four, five and..." I said aloud and clicked my fingers.

The power went off. I curled up in a ball, holding Ambrose tightly and wept before falling asleep.

Wednesday 6th November

Today was a bright, sunny morning, the sort of day that forced one's thoughts outside of oneself and would quickly evaporate my home's dampness. Today I was returning to the mountains.

Since moving to Spain, back in what feels like 1736, there has only ever been one male with whom I attempted to cultivate a friendship. However, shortly after I met Malcolm he decided that his future lay on the oil rigs. As far as I can ascertain, the only reason anybody chooses to work in the middle of the North Sea is for the money. The odd thing in Malcolm's case is that he already had a wealthy estate, a sizeable pension and a massive inheritance to which to look forward. So, in his absence, for occasional company, I have to console myself instead with his wife, Margaret, who still resides here in Merla.

Today Margaret and I would be walking in the splendid hills inland from the town. It seemed unfair to ask a lady to carry Ambrose and so my little dog would have the run of the house today. I expected to return home to find Ambrose in the washing machine.

Margaret is tolerable company but is a little too keen on gossip to be trusted. I like to use her passion for spreading rumours against her. I drop blatant fibs into conversation and then see how long it takes the same information to reach my ears from another source. I once told her that Morality Mike was having an affair – a complete fabrication – and within three days Mike's wife had packed up and left Spain taking their three children with her.

Margaret belongs to each and every ex-pat society in town simply so she can soak up the local news more efficiently and disseminate it later. In more cases than not her membership is entirely inappropriate. For example, despite being a barren woman in her 60s she belongs to two mother-and-toddler groups. She also frequently attends the tennis club despite her withered hand.

Margaret is an absolutely atrocious driver. In order to clear myself of accusations of sexism I need to make clear that this is in no way symptomatic of her gender. Of the thirty or forty women I have closely befriended over the course of my lifetime, at least two of them were capable of driving in a straight line and so it cannot simply be a matter of chromosomes.

I knew that Margaret had arrived outside my house when, from my kitchen, I could hear the squeal of tyres followed by a dull, metallic thunk. As it transpired she had hit my car in exactly the same location as on her previous visit and so no real damage was done.

I gathered my belongings, adorned appropriate clothing and strode out. Margaret wound down her window.

"What's with the crash helmet, George?" she asked.

"Precautions, dear Margaret. Precautions."

"Is that some reflection on my driving ability?"

"Absolutely."

I climbed into the passenger seat and fastened my belt securely.

"Ready?" she asked with the excitement of someone about to launch into space for the first time.

"Yes," I replied nervously.

She turned the key in the ignition and seemed about to set

off without looking around her.

"Mirrors," I offered.

"What?"

"You have not checked your mirrors."

"I'm fine. I'm not wearing any make-up today."

I looked at her hoping to see a half-smirk on her lips to indicate that this was a knowing attempt at humour but it apparently was not.

She set off, lurched left and knocked a small child off his bicycle. She rolled down the window and looked out at the bawling six year-old sprawled on the ground.

"S'alright," she said, less than panicked, "he's Spanish. Let's go!"

She floored the acceleration pedal and squealed out of my street, clipping the wing mirrors of at least two cars and sending an elderly Spanish lady sprinting for the pavement.

"I think we got away with it," she screamed as she tore around the pueblo's streets, spinning the steering wheel at each junction like Starsky and Hutch.

"Please can we slow down now?" I asked firmly.

"How?"

"The brakes?" I offered, sarcastically I thought.

"Which one's the brake?"

Eventually, after a collision with a wheelie bin on the edge of town and the involuntary removal of a Lycraed cyclist from his now-mangled machine, we were nearly there. Margaret removed her foot from the accelerator and allowed the car to slow naturally before coming to a complete stop by nudging the bonnet up against the trunk of a large tree.

"That was OK, wasn't it?"

"Well done, Margaret. You have passed."

We got out of the car and began the long trudge up the hill.

"I suppose you have heard the latest story about me?" I

said.

"Which one?"

"What do you mean, which one?"

"Well, I've heard three things about you this week alone."

"Go on," I said wearily.

Rumours from Margaret are hardly unexpected.

"Well, the first is that you've gone and got yourself a new lady friend."

"I have not!" I yelled but then sheepishly added, "Who told you that?"

"A little bird."

"No, seriously. Who told you?"

"Sarah."

"Sarah who?"

"Sarah Walker."

"I do not know anyone called Sarah Walker."

"She's in the swimming club."

"As are you, I suppose?"

"Exactly."

"I thought that you once told me that you were unable to swim?"

"I can't. I just stand around in the water having a nice chat."

That was no surprise.

"Yes," she said. "Sarah's a friend of Janet."

"Janet. My Janet?"

"Oh, she's your Janet now, is she? I thought you didn't have a lady friend."

"I have only spoken to her a few times."

"Apparently you keep talking to her about her knickers."

"Once! I have mentioned it once."

"Hmm," said Margaret.

"Did Sarah tell you anything else that Janet said?" I asked meekly.

"Yes. She said you were too old. So hands off, granddad!"

"I am *not* too old," I said. "She falls well inside a perfectly acceptable age boundary."

Margaret seemed not to merit my argument with any value. I huffed for a moment or two.

We walked in silence. We came to the edge of an escarpment. Margaret looked over the cliff. I retrieved my camera to record this moment for posterity. I held it to my eye and pointed it towards Margaret.

"Ah, you want a picture of me," she said with a satisfied smile.

"No, I want a picture of the view. Get out of my way."

I feared that Margaret's news about Janet had made me a little grumpy.

We turned around and continued towards the summit.

"So what were the other two rumours that you heard about me this week?"

"I heard that you're dying."

"Yes, that is true," I said sadly. "I fear I have the Big C."

"That's not what I heard."

"What?" I asked, surprised.

"No, it's nothing as everyday as that."

"Who told you?"

"I've heard it from a few people. The entire hand-gliding association was discussing it last night."

I stopped and looked at her.

"Margaret, tell me what it is."

"We've all been sworn to secrecy."

"The whole hand-gliding association?"

"The whole town really."

"You utter bastards."

We continued and made it to the summit, the same spot upon which I had recently had the altercation with Scotch Tony. We looked out at the magnificent view standing side by side. Margaret remained at the edge whilst I went to fetch my water bottle from the rucksack that I had removed moments earlier.

"And the other thing I heard," she said, turning to face me, "was that you killed Scotch Tony at this very spot."

My stomach dropped.

"I did not kill him. There was a misunderstanding. I...who told you that?"

"No one actually. I deduced it myself."

"What?"

"He told me that he was going walking with you. A few days later, his body turns up dead..."

"They have found him?" I interrupted.

"Yes, at the bottom of this very hill that you have led me to."

"There was an accident."

"Nonsense! If it was an accident you would've reported it. And you didn't, did you?"

She looked at me with a steely eye.

"Have you told anybody else?" I asked.

"Not yet," she replied. "Have you been a silly boy, George?"

Not as silly as I was about to be. I bent down to pick up a stick.

"George," she said, panicked, as I took a step towards her. "What are you doing?"

"I'm sorry, Margaret, but you can't live to repeat this to anyone else."

Her scream echoed around the mountains as she tumbled down and down.

Thursday 7th November

"You can't go in there, Mr Pearly," Shirley screamed. "Mr Pearly!"

I crashed through the door into Vince's office. He was sitting there, leaning forward, in each hand a plump breast. The owner, a woman in her fifties with a radiant smile and eyes gently closed, quickly awoke from her reverie and covered her ample chest with a podgy arm.

"What do you want, John?"

"It is not fucking John," I yelled. "It is George!"

"Mind the language, George."

"Who is this?" the woman asked sharply.

"See what you're doing, John? You're trying my patients." He smiled. "Geddit?"

"Shut up, you stupid arse."

"Do you mind popping your top back on, Mrs Backwell, and just taking a seat in the waiting room until I can sort this out."

Vince smiled her his charming smile and opened the door for her. Mrs Backwell left with a harrumph.

"Right, John. What is it?"

"You told me that I should see Dr Antonio Garcia. I checked..."

"Hang on a minute, John," he interrupted. "Is this about your condition?"

"Yes. Of course it is. Why else would I be here?"

"Then I can't help."

"What?"

"You didn't pay your last bill. Ethically I'm not able to discuss your situation until you have paid in full."

"Ethically?"

"Ethically, morally, selfishly, whatever."

"Yes, whatever. I looked up Antonio Garcia."

He mimed the zipping of his lips. He locked an invisible padlock at the edge of his mouth before hurling away its invisible key.

"Antonio Garcia is an oncologist."

Vince frowned. He went to pick up the invisible key, opened the window, loaded the key into an invisible crossbow and fired it outside.

"And yesterday Margaret informed me that you told her, or someone told her, that I definitely do not have cancer."

Vince sat down. He inflated his cheeks and let out a mouthful of air. He looked blankly at me and then started attending to some paperwork.

"Vince, tell me."

"You didn't pay," he said.

"Tell me!"

"You didn't pay."

"So if I pay, will you tell me?"

"I can't tell you that until you pay."

"What? Jesus."

I fumbled in my wallet, extracted a crisp fifty euro note, screwed it into a ball and threw it at his stupid head.

"Thank you." He unfolded the money and flattened it out. "That's better."

"Will you talk now?"

"Of course." He leant back. "So, John, what can I do for you?"

I emitted an exasperated breath.

"Tell me what is wrong with me."

Vince stood up, walked over to his filing cabinet and opened the top drawer. He searched for a file.

"Packham, Paddington, Pastor, Harris...what the hell's that doing in here...Patterson, Pearly. Here we go. Let's see."

"You do not need my file. You know what is wrong with me."

He ignored me and opened the folder before sitting down.

"Ah," he said.

"Ah what?"

"There's a note on your file."

"Well, I assume that you wrote the note."

"Yes, I did."

"And what does it say?"

"It says 'Confidential. Do not tell the patient anything.'"

He folded the file and smiled.

"You bastard." I snatched the fifty euro back. "I am not paying for last time, I am not paying for this time and I will never be here again."

"Oh dear," said Vince, standing up. He pulled a cigarette lighter from his shirt pocket. "Oh dear."

"Oh dear what?"

"Well, if you'll never visit my surgery again then there's little point in me maintaining your records. And if you are refusing to pay for previous treatment I am under no legal compulsion to do so."

He flicked the lighter and held its flame beneath my file.

"What are you doing? Those are my test results."

"You have ended our contract. You said so yourself."

"Yes, but..."

The file was already half incinerated. The flames leapt and licked Vince's fingers.

"Yowch!"

He dropped the burning paper into his plastic waste-paper bin.

"I cannot believe you did that. I will have you struck off."

"Struck off from what?" he laughed. "This is Spain. Your file was taking up valuable drawer space."

"Expect a denuncia very soon!"

51

"Another one?"

"Yes!"

He shrugged his shoulders. I turned to leave.

"I am going to tell the world what a charlatan you are," I said.

"I doubt that'll deter the rich, lonely ladies and their magnificent boobies," he said, beaming widely and jiggling his hands.

I tutted and glanced towards the ashes of my file.

"You do know that your bin is melting?" I said.

"I was sort of hoping you'd have left before you noticed."

I marched through an acrid cloud of burning plastic to the door whilst Vince cried out for assistance.

"Shirley! A little help. Some water please!"

Friday 8th November

It was mid-afternoon. I had spent a busy morning searching unsuccessfully for another English-speaking doctor within a bus ride of Merla. At least it appeared that I did not have terminal cancer. Having terminal Something-Else was little consolation.

I was now reclining on my comfortable chair. *Countdown*'s opening credits had just started. I had a cup of Earl Grey resting on one of the chair's arms and a small saucer of Ginger Nuts on the other. Ambrose was curled up by my feet. I was settled in for a bout of wordplay and top-level ogling. Miserable though it was, this was as fulfilled as my life had now become.

And then, apropos of nothing, my front door was smashed in. It first creaked and wobbled and then crashed to the floor, sending a cloud of dust up Ambrose's snout, initiating a minor asthma attack. I remained seated, frozen in place.

A potato-shaped silhouette was picked out by the bright sunshine outside. I looked towards it. Ambrose regained his composure and did the same. The potato did not move. An eternity seemed to pass.

"Hello, uncle George. It's me," said a voice that sounded like a grown man doing an impression of a small, mentally subnormal child.

"Kevin?"

I stood up.

"Sorry 'bout the door, uncle George. I were stood outside for half an hour. I rung t' bell over and over but there were no answer."

"I do not have a bell."

"What's that then?" he said, pointing to the centre of the door now lying in a position that a door should never be.

"That is the spy hole," I said.

"Ah, fancy. We don't have spy holes in Blackburn. No bugger wants to spy on us."

He laughed to himself.

"I am not James Bond, you know. It is merely a device to allow me to approve whomever is standing at my door and requesting entry."

"Does it work?"

"Of course it works." I did not mention that I had yet to test it. Nobody ever came a-knocking. "Anyway, no matter. Come in, Kevin, let me have a look at you."

Kevin stood in front of the television. His face appeared to be made of dough the colour of a Lancashire sky, his mousy, collar-length hair greasy and welded to his forehead. He was perspiring through a yellow and green, horizontally-stripped t-shirt that exacerbated his lumpy form. Its colour scheme contrasted noisily with his patterned pink shorts. This ensemble was completed with grey socks and brown sandals.

"How tall are you, Kevin?"

"Five two."

"Ah, I doubt anything from my wardrobe would flatter you."

"Eh, I'm fine as it is." He tugged at his shirt and shorts. "I got these in th' airport." Kevin wiped the length of his arm across his nostrils and snorted, leaving a smear of mucus on his wrist. "Shoulda got summat wi' long sleeves."

"In this house, dear boy, we use tissues."

I threw him the box that sat on the table by my chair.

"Ooo, posh. Think I got a cold on t' plane."

"Well, this climate will soon dry you out. Can I get you a drink, Kevin?"

"Have you got any Vimto?"

"No, I have not. Would you care for a cup of tea?"

"Nah, I'll just 'ave a glass o' squash then."

"I do not have any squash either, I am afraid. The only cold drinks that I am able to offer are water and beer."

"Tap water?"

"Yes."

"Mum said you can't drink tap water in Spain."

"Of course you can."

"No, she said it'll gimme the shits."

"It might make you a little loose until you have adjusted to its microorganisms, but that will only take a day or two."

"Its micro-what? I'll 'ave a beer then, please."

"And you are old enough to drink beer?" I asked, before chastising myself.

In the back of my head I knew he was thirty-five but something about his demeanour made him appear to be closer to seven.

"Course I am, silly," he said, smiling like someone to whom a lobotomy was only a recent experience.

"Well then, Kevin, I will find you a beer. And, in the

meantime, if you require the bathroom, it is the first door on the right."

"Smashin'."

He removed his small rucksack from his shoulders and dropped it on to the floor before disappearing. He slammed the bathroom door with such force that the house shuddered.

In the kitchen I started to pour a can of cold Mahou into a glass. From the bathroom I could hear the disturbing grunts of a serious bowel evacuation. From the painful straining that echoed around the bathroom's tiled surfaces Kevin was clearly not consuming enough fibre. I was relieved that I only had to endure this for two weeks. I thought of the money.

The straining subsided. This was followed by ten minutes of silence before a single, high-pitched groan that terminated in a self-satisfied "Get in!"

Kevin departed the bathroom in nothing but a pair of grey Y-fronts, a state of affairs with which I was not best pleased. They were pulled high enough to prevent his prodigious gut from overhanging his underwear's waistband.

"Ah, that's better," he said.

I handed him his beer.

"It might be a little on the warm side now," I said.

"Not to worry," he replied, ensconcing himself in my comfortable chair. "I can't believe I'm really here, uncle George. It's gonna be ace."

I stood between him and the television.

"Well, yes, I am sure it will be 'ace' but we attire ourselves correctly in this household."

"What's that you say?" he replied at the same time as trying to glimpse Rachel Riley through the gap between my legs.

"We do not walk around this house in our undergarments."

"Oh, OK then."

He smiled a big, gormless smile, his fat face creasing in two.

"She's fit, i'n't she?" he said.

"Yes, she is rather attractive."

"Twenty minute wi' me and she wouldn't be able to walk."

"Well, yes, she would certainly be crushed rather flat," I said.

Kevin looked at me coolly.

"Oi, are you sayin' I'm fat?"

"No."

"This is not fat, y'know. I'm on tablets."

"I am sorry."

"I retain water."

I admit that I smirked. Kevin looked hurt.

"Dear Kevin, your mother said that you are here to sort out a few problems. In order for that to happen we need to be honest with each other. And my first honest act will be to state categorically that you may well be retaining an amount of water – humans must if they are to survive – but if all those ripples of blubber contain retained water then you had better be very careful around sharp objects in my kitchen lest you are punctured and flood my house."

Kevin looked at me like a little boy lost. Tears welled in his rheumy eyes. A solitary droplet leaked down his rubbery face.

"I am *not* fat. I retain water." He stood up. "I don't wanna talk about this. I'm goin' to me room."

He stormed off, opening the only door to which he had yet to be introduced, correctly guessing that it was the bedroom, my bedroom, the only bedroom in the house.

*

In the evening I popped to our small British supermarket, delightfully called Food UK International Traders and usually abbreviated to its initials, where I purchased a bottle of Vimto for the same price as two bottles of decent Rioja and a box of Jaffa Cakes well past their sell-by date.

Back at the house I spent twenty minutes using this bait to coax Kevin from my bedroom. The Jaffa Cakes also perked up little Ambrose, who appeared to like them almost as much as chorizo.

For the remainder of the evening we sat and talked. I asked him, given his mother's beautiful English, why he spoke in such an uncouth northern manner. I did not phrase it quite so directly.

"Whadda ya mean I sound stupid?"

"Not stupid. Just, well, regional?"

"I speak Blackburn. This is how people in Blackburn speak. There's nowt wrong wi' it, y'know."

I emitted a snort to demonstrate my disbelief.

"Me mum were rich so I had lotsa nannies an' stuff. They was all local. This is in t' days before they all come over from Latvonia or wherever. And some of 'em were lovely." He guffawed cheekily at his pre-pubescent crushes before returning to the topic of elocution. "Yeah, an' all me mates spoke like this an' all."

"I could teach you correct diction if you like."

"What? Eh, don't say I don't speak proper. Me mum were allus sayin' that. But the more she tried to change me, t' more I spoke like this. I like it. Lee Mack sounds like me."

Good god. And who the hell is Lee Mack?

We talked into the night. During our conversation Kevin listed every single one of the Hollywood movie stars with whom he would like carnal relations as well as his preferred position in each case. I cannot recall a more desperately depressing evening in my entire existence. He would love it at Bar Wars.

Around midnight I popped to the bathroom to relieve myself. Whilst inside I heard Kevin trudge past the other side of the door.

"Night night, uncle George."

By the time I had completed the task at hand Kevin was already fast asleep in my bed, snoring like a contented hog. His had been an exciting day, I thought. Give him a night's peace and tomorrow I will present him with the ground rules. I curled up on the uncomfortable sofa that comes with every Spanish rental and hugged Ambrose close to me, my dreams perfumed by his frequent orangey belches.

Saturday 9th November

I awoke at seven as usual. Kevin did not surface until just after two in the afternoon. Still attired in ashen underpants he rolled down the hallway like a ball of grey plasticine and sought solace in the bathroom until three. Eventually the door creaked open and he shuffled into the kitchen where I was preparing a hot beverage.

"Good morning, Kevin," I said sarcastically. "Did you sleep well?"

"Yeah. Think so."

He rubbed his eye deeply, causing a temporary deformation before his face slowly retook its original shape.

"Would you like something to eat?"

"Yeah, Coco Pops please?"

"Kevin, I have never owned a box of Coco Pops."

"Really?"

From the disbelief in Kevin's tone he would have been less surprised if I had confessed to starting each morning by kicking an orphan to death.

"You should try 'em. They're ace," he said, his eyes wide open. "They turn t' milk chocolatey."

"That is not a property that I require of my breakfast

comestibles. I can supply toast or a ham sandwich."

"I'll 'ave some toast, please."

"Now, tonight, Kevin. I need to ask a favour of you."

"Yeah, OK. What is it?"

"I need you to go out."

"With you?"

"No. Alone. Tonight I am entertaining a lady friend."

"Uncle George," he said, attempting to twist my nipple, "you mucky pup."

I slapped his clammy hand away.

"Less of that, boy." I shot him a steely glare. "I need you to leave me in peace."

"But where'll I go?"

"I can recommend an establishment that I suspect you will find amusing."

"By mesel'?"

"Do not worry. There will be lots of people like you there."

"What," he said with a sneer, "fat people?"

"Do not start that again."

"What d'yer mean? People like me."

I realise that I had dug myself into a hole.

"People like you." I thought quickly. "Entertaining people."

He smiled.

"D'yer think I'm entertainin'?" he said, uplifted.

"Yes. You are the Costa del Sol's Peter Ustinov."

"Who?"

"It does not matter."

If stupidity grew on trees Kevin would be a thicket.

"OK," he smiled. My idle flattery had worked. "But I'll need some dosh."

"I thought Mary was supplying you with adequate funding."

"She said she were gonna do a transfer to yer once I'd

come home. To be honest, uncle George, she's losin' it."

"She sounded sane enough on the telephone."

"She's like that sometimes. Other times she doesn't know who she is. Last Tuesday she spent th' entire mornin' on t' sofa hosting her own edition of *Daybreak*. I had to get t' neighbours in as guests."

"And she has not provided you with any spending money?"

"No."

"None?"

"Nope."

"Well then," I opened my wallet. "Take twenty euros. That should supply an evening of gentle mirth."

"Where's this pub then?"

"It's the Cock and Bull." Kevin guffawed. "Yes, very drole. It is about half a kilometre from here."

"I thought I saw one really close yesterday. Called Bar Wars."

"No, do not go there."

"Why not?"

"It is dreadful."

"It looked good to me. Its sign had an Ewok bein' bummed."

"Yes, I know. Do not go there. Never go there."

*

Evening came. It was already seven and Kevin was still in his underpants. Janet was due in half an hour.

"You will have vacated the premises in the next few minutes, I assume, Kevin?"

"Keep yer hair on, granddad. I'm just poppin' to t' bathroom and then I'm outta here."

At twenty past seven he was still inside. I hammered on the bathroom door.

"Kevin, it is time to leave."

"Hang on, I'm nearly finished. Yer've ruined me concentration now."

Five minutes later there was a knock at my reinstalled front door. I smiled to myself as I verified for the first time the functionality of the spy hole. I opened the door.

"Janet, how lovely to see you!" I said in a rich, charm-filled tone, somewhat reminiscent of Mr. Darcy.

"There you go," she said, thrusting a bottle of red wine into my hands. "Don't drink it all at once."

"Very nice. Would you care to accompany me to the terrace for a glass of chilled cava?"

"Is that where the others are?"

Damn. The others. I had forgotten about the others.

"You are a little early, Janet. The others have yet to arrive."

"Do you want me to go home and come back in a bit?"

"No, no, come with me to the terrace."

Twelve paces from the front door, including the slight detour to the fridge, and we were out on the terrace. Janet took a seat at my plastic table. I poured us two glasses of cava.

"Cheers!" I said.

"Yes, cheers," she replied as we chinked glasses.

I looked at her. My head was uncharacteristically devoid of thought. There was an awkward tension.

"Feels a bit weird, doesn't it? Just us two," she said.

"A little."

"It'll be alright when the others come." She looked at me for reassurance. I am not entirely certain I provided any. "So, who else is coming?"

"That would be telling," I said with a jocular tone.

"Yes, it would. So are you going to tell me?"

"It is a surprise."

"Is it?" she said sternly. "There *are* others coming, aren't there?"

"Of course."

"Because if there aren't then I'll have to leave."

"Of course. Just give me a minute. I think I hear the front door now."

I raced inside. Kevin was finally out of the bathroom and once again sporting his yellow and green t-shirt along with his pink shorts.

"Lookin' good, eh, uncle George?"

"Like a male model," I said.

If that model were Mr Potato Head.

"I'm off out now."

"No, Kevin."

"What?"

"You cannot go."

"Why not?"

"I need you to stay."

"Why?"

"I just do!" I said urgently.

"But I'm all dolled up. The lasses of Merla'll be weepin' into their Lambrinis." Dear me. "I were lookin' forward to goin' out. To meet people like me." He smiled. "Entertainin' people."

"I will pay you to stay."

"Alright."

I fished into my trouser pocket and extracted my wallet.

"Here is another twenty," I said, offering him a note.

"But I were *really* lookin' forward to goin' out."

I searched my wallet anew.

"I have only got a fifty."

He made a so-what face.

"You are not having fifty."

"OK then, I'll see yer later, uncle George. 'Ave a nice night!"

He made to push past me.

"You devious, little shit," I whispered harshly. "Take it."

I thrust the fifty into his gelatinous paw.

"Thank you. Now why d'you want me to stay?"

"I need you to be my dinner guest."

"I thought you was havin' a lady over."

"I am. She is on the terrace. But she is a little nervous and wants some extra company."

With his left thumb and index finger Kevin created a hole and repeatedly inserted his right index finger into it whilst first lolling his tongue and then licking his disgusting hand.

"Threeway?" he drooled.

It took me a moment to comprehend his meaning.

"You filthy animal. No." I thought about it some more. "NO!"

Kevin sniggered.

"So, I'm t' chaperone, am I?"

"Something like that."

"And t' gooseberry?"

"The EU's highest paid gooseberry."

"Alright, uncle George," Kevin said with a big grin. "Show me the meat!"

I grabbed his pudding-like arm and yanked it towards me, yelling in a dark whisper.

"Do not, I repeat do not, talk like that in front of her. Understand?"

He pulled back his arm peevishly.

"Only messin'," he said.

"Well, never, ever mess." I stared at him. "With me," I added as a clumsy addendum.

I exited through the kitchen door. Kevin followed me on to the terrace.

"Janet, dear. My first and, as it turns out, only guest has arrived. Albert and Agnes cancelled whilst I was inside."

"Nothing serious I hope."

"It is too early to say. Albert described it as a minor incident with an industrial lathe," I said in a jocular tone.

I was Jay Gatsby.

"Can you have a minor incident with an industrial lathe?" she asked rhetorically.

"Not to worry. This is Kevin."

I hustled him forward and he caught a glimpse of Janet for the first time. I distinctly heard him say something like "hubba hubba" beneath his breath.

"Hello, Kevin," Janet said.

There was a friendly warmth in her voice.

"Hello," he replied shyly.

He looked down at his feet. Today, it seemed, was Kevin's first day at primary school.

"And are you a friend or a relation of George?"

The idiot looked to me for an answer, his mouth wide open.

"I don't know," he said, seeming entirely vacant.

I looked at him and shook my head sadly.

"Who am I tonight, uncle George?"

I placed my head in my hands, gave myself a moment to adjust and then attempted to recover the situation.

"Janet, this is Kevin. Kevin is my nephew. Quite why he suspects he may be someone else this evening is beyond my comprehension. He is residing with me for a couple of weeks."

"Pleased to meet you, Kevin," Janet said, using just the right amount of condescension to soften his timidity without dislodging the considerable chip on his shoulder. She offered him her hand and he shook it limply. She patted the plastic chair next to her. "Now sit down here and tell me all about yourself, Kevin."

The evening was going to be acceptable, much more than I could have hoped for only ten minutes earlier, as long as I could keep Kevin away from the topic of Hollywood actresses.

Sunday 10th November

Once again I awoke at seven on the couch. Around midnight yesterday Kevin had gone inside, ostensibly to retrieve another bottle of beer, and when he had failed to reappear within fifteen minutes a quick search of my premises located him in my bed again. Janet went home soon afterwards.

His foetid corpse was reanimated at half past one this afternoon and then he spent the next forty-five minutes in the bathroom during which time I got busy with a screwdriver.

"I take it you have found the shower?" I asked as he finally heaved his slug-like body, underpants and all, into the kitchen.

"No. I don't need one." He did. "I'll have one tomorrow or summat."

"Right, Kevin, I know that you have been here for a couple of days already but I feel that it is time to impose a few ground rules."

"Did you get any Coco Pops yet?"

"No, I did not."

Kevin shuffled around the kitchen, opening each cupboard and drawer searching for something artificially sweetened.

"Are you listening to me?" I said. He continued to rummage. "Stop doing that and listen to me."

He turned around to face me.

"Good. Rule number one. No underpants."

"Perv."

"What?"

"You want me naked, you perv."

"No, I do not. I want you fully clothed."

"But you do want me, you perv."

"Shut up. Stop saying 'perv'. How old are you? Six? Do not – watch my lips – do not walk around my house in only your underpants."

"I just like bein' comfy."

"If necessary, I will purchase a dressing gown for you."

"Can I wear my underpants underneath it?"

"No. Yes. It does not matter. I do not want to see your underpants."

"So you just want me to hide me body?"

"Yes."

"Because I'm fat."

I let out a sigh.

"Rule number two. Before going to the bathroom for three hours please inform me so that I have the opportunity to first empty my own bladder."

"OK."

"Why are you even in there so long?"

He shrugged his shoulders.

"Well, you must know," I said.

"I don't. I dunno how long it'll take."

Lord, save me.

"Rule number three. You do not sleep in my bed."

"Fair enough." I was surprised how easily he had conceded defeat on this topic. "Which is your bed?" he asked.

"The bed in which you have slept for the last two nights."

"Eh? Well, where do I sleep?"

"On the sofa."

"That's a bit shit."

"I have only got one bedroom. I told Mary that I only have one bedroom."

"But she's payin' for me to stay."

"She is."

"Well then, I think I deserve a lickle bit o' comfort."

"Do you?"

"Yes. In fact, I think I'm goin' back to bed right now."

"Go on then."

He wandered off. I heard the bedroom door rattle and then he reappeared, looking confused.

"You've put a lock on it."

"Indeed."

"I think I should call mum. She said if I didn't like it here I could go to uncle Richard's instead. I'm sure he'd like the money."

We locked eyes. He smiled a self-satisfied smile. I threw him the key, the little shit.

*

"Errrwww, what's happened to my trainers?"

It was late afternoon and Kevin had emerged from the bedroom after his afternoon nap that had commenced shortly after his breakfast. He was carrying a sodden-looking running shoe at arm's length. Liquid leaked from its heel. He gave it a sniff.

"Errrww, it stinks."

"You should change your socks more often."

"No, it don't smell o' feet. It smells o'...piss."

Oh Ambrose, you little beauty. I am proud of you.

"How can it smell of piss?" he asked.

"Maybe you were sleepwalking during the night."

"I've never done that before."

"New environment. It stimulates parts of the brain that are not normally activated." I said this with full awareness that the only organ usually stimulated by the Costa del Sol is the liver.

He seemed to believe my cover story. I wandered into the kitchen and emptied the fridge of its chorizo.

"Ambrose, come here."

He smelled the meat and flew towards me.

"It is alright. Calm down. You will get it all regardless."

I fed him slice after slice, patting his little, white head.

"Good boy!"

Kevin returned to the bedroom and eventually reappeared wearing only his underpants. He stood in the centre of the living room, with one podgy hand stuffed inside them, scratching himself wildly.

"What was the rule about underpants?" I asked.

"I decided I wanna wear 'em." I was just about to speak when he continued. "Uncle Richard would let me wear 'em."

I saw red. I exploded.

"So that is how it is going to be, is it? Whenever you want your own way, your own bed, your public underpants exhibition, your own marathon masturbation sessions in the bathroom, all you have to mutter is the phrase 'Uncle Richard' and I capitulate. Well, I am sorry, fat boy, but that is not how this house operates!"

His mouth was wipe open.

"Give me the phone!" I demanded.

He passed the mobile to me, still unable to speak. I found Mary's earlier call and pressed Dial.

"You are going home!"

Her phone rang.

"You should pack your stuff," I yelled.

Her phone continued to ring. Come on, Mary, pick it up.

"What are you waiting for?" I asked him.

He did not move from the spot, looking straight at me, his mouth still slack.

The phone was still ringing. And ringing. And ringing.

"She's not in," he said.

"Yes, genius, I know that she is not fucking in," I screamed and threw the phone at his head. It hit him squarely on the chin, sending a fleshy shockwave across his chops, an event he barely noticed.

"You called me 'fat boy'," he said sullenly.

I lowered my mouth to his mucilaginous ear.

"Yes, and do you know why?" I whispered hoarsely. "It is because you are fat. Fat! F-A-T. Mr Blobby Blobby Blobby! Got that?"

He burst into tears and ran into the bedroom, locking the door behind him.

Jesus Christ.

Monday 11th November

Kevin had not emerged from the bedroom by four in the afternoon although the gentle sobbing had stopped in the early hours of the morning. I went to Bar Wars for an afternoon beer and a round of personal abuse. The regulars were there.

"Hey, look, the professor's here," said Bullshit Phil. He was already half cut. "Have you written any good poems lately?"

"Piss off, Philip," was the only appropriate response.

"Hey, hey now," Morality Mike chipped in. "There are ladies present."

I looked around the bar but could see no one of the feminine persuasion.

"Where?" I asked.

Mike and Phil both stole a glance in the direction of Not Gay Alan and then their mouths exploded in giggles, fizzing their beers all over the counter.

"Very funny," said Alan.

"That's just what a woman would say," said Mike.

"Do you three actually live in here?" I asked.

They mutually shrugged their shoulders.

"Give us a poem, professor," said Phil slurring his words.

"No. I am here for a quiet drink."

"Why don't you get one for Alan? He would, you know."

"He would what?" I asked.

"You know."

"What are you talking about, you drunken buffoon?" I said.

"He likes men."

"Phil, you are such an arsehole," barked Alan, who drained his glass and left the bar.

"He wants you." Phil looked at me through squinting eyes, refocussed and then continued, "He wants you to go after him," he said with one eyelid fluttering drunkenly. "Like you would if he was a girl."

"You should go easy on Alan, you should," Mike said. Mike himself was only one pint behind Phil. "You can push people too far."

"I know someone who was pushed too far," said Phil.

"What?" I said, to this non sequitur.

"Scotch Tony was pushed too far. Right off a bloody cliff."

"Aye, did you hear?" said Mike. "They found his body in the mountains. He'd been dead about ten days." I gulped. "His funeral's on Wednesday."

The front door opened and Kevin wobbled breezily into the bar.

"Hello, uncle George. I thought you said I couldn't come in here."

"Who's this?" asked Mike.

I sighed.

"This is Kevin, my nephew. He is here for a few days but will be departing this golden shore shortly."

"Kevin, this is Mike and the turd asleep on the bar is Philip."

"Is that *Bullshit* Phil?" asked Kevin.

"Shhh. Just Phil to you and me, Kevin," I said.

"Is he t' one who told you he invented crisps?"

"Aye, that sounds like Phil," said Mike.

"Smashin'. I want his autograph."

"He didn't really invent crisps, laddie," said Mike.

Phil regained consciousness.

"What you lot on about?" he slurred.

"Can I have yer autograph, Mr Bullshit?".

"Eh?" Phil narrowed his eyes for a better look at Kevin. "Who's this beauty?" he asked.

Kevin smiled.

"Did you invent crisps?"

"I don't remember. I've invented a lot of things."

Trevor the barman returned from a round of glass collecting.

"I'll get you a coffee, Phil," he said.

"No coffee for me. *Cerveza por favor!*"

"You're not having any more beer."

"OK, then I'll have another Soberano."

"You're havin' a coffee or you're going home."

Phil belched.

"A coffee it is then. And a brandy."

"We were just telling your uncle about the mysterious death of our friend Tony, weren't we, Phil?" said Mike.

Phil shrugged.

"But there is even more to this mystery."

"I like mysteries," said Kevin, like a four year-old. He was captivated, moving closer to Mike, with his eyes wide open.

"People are going missing. Maybe there's been a second murder. Margaret hasn't been seen since Tuesday."

He left the sentence hanging in the air.

"Margaret?" said Kevin. "Is that Margaret who is Malcolm's wife?"

How could he possibly know that? I had mentioned neither Margaret nor Malcolm.

"Aye," replied Mike.

"And is Tony that Scotch Tony?"

"Aye, it is. Do you know them?"

"I've read about 'em."

"Where?" asked Mike.

"I read about 'em in uncle George's diary."

"What?" I screamed.

"He writes a diary on his computer."

"When did you see that, you sneaky, little shit?" I stuttered.

"Just now. You really should have a password."

"And what did his diary say?" asked Mike.

"I only 'ad a quick flick through. It's borin'."

"Thank you," I said.

"But he went walking with 'em both."

"When?"

"Oh I dunno. Recently."

"Kevin, I think you should keep your mouth firmly closed," I said, hopefully portraying an air of menace that nestled somewhere above physical punishment and yet shy of actual murder.

"When?" Mike repeated.

"This last couple o' weeks," said Kevin.

"When did you go walking with Scotch Tony, George?" asked Mike seriously.

"A while back. Come on, Kevin, it is time to go."

"And when did you go walking with Margaret?"

"I cannot remember," I said.

"Well, that's very interesting, isn't it? Very interesting indeed. I think the authorities would be interested in this information, don't you, George? I mean, you've denounced us lot often enough."

"No, you must not do that. You would merely be wasting their time and mine. I am sure the police are very busy with more important tasks. Like fining cyclists for not wearing helmets or something. Did you know that cyclists must wear helmets in Spain?" I was babbling. "Come on, Kevin!"

"I wanna stay."

"Come now, Kevin, or I will lock you out of the house."

"If you lock me out I'll smash yer door in again."

For such a mentally retarded character I find Kevin almost impossible to negotiate with. I could have left him there alone and risked having him divulge further secrets or I could have stayed to help navigate the conversation between Charybdis and Scylla.

"Alright then, what do you want to drink?" I asked.

"Have you got any Vimto?" Kevin asked Trevor.

"Do not be ridiculous," I assured him. "They do not have Vimto."

"Yeah, we do," said Trevor. "You want fizzy or still, Kevin lad?"

"Dear god," I said to Kevin, "Why not ask him to sprinkle some Coco Pops in it for you."

Kevin guffawed.

"That's silly," he said.

"If you want a bowl of Coco Pops, Kevin, I can do you Coco Pops," said Trevor.

"You have Coco Pops?" asked Kevin with wonder in his voice and wide-open eyes.

"We have an extensive breakfast menu, Kevin lad. And we serve all day."

"Brilliant. I can have Coco Pops for me tea. Just imagine!" He chuckled to himself. "Aw, uncle George, this is t' best pub ever. I think this'll be me local for now on."

"You have no need of a local, Kevin. You are returning home imminently."

Kevin smiled a knowing smile.

"I betcha I don't."

Tuesday 12th November

Once again I telephoned Mary and once again there was no answer. She was probably in the kitchen hosting an episode of *Ready, Steady, Cook* with one cat dressed as Ainsley Harriott and the other as Antony Worrall-Thompson.

Kevin emerged mid-afternoon carrying a copy of a local English newspaper that he had purloined from the bar yesterday and found me on the terrace sitting in the sun. I am convinced that he only possesses a single pair of underpants. He pulled up the decrepit sun lounger that came with the house and sprawled out his grey blubber upon it, tossing the newspaper to the ground.

"This is t' life, i'n't it, uncle George?"

He folded his arms behind his head, exposing tufty armpits. For a moment I was certain that something rodent-like moved within.

"Life? I prefer to view it merely as existence, Kevin."

"I don't understand you, uncle George. It's lovely down here. Most people'd give their right bollock to live here."

"I am dying."

"Yeah, you said. Anyway, we're all dying." Not you as well. "So before you knew you was dying, was you dancing around an' stuff?"

"No."

Kevin tutted.

"I didn't think so. What are yer dreams, uncle George?"

"I am seventy."

"So?"

"My only dream is that you leave me in peace and I return

to Surrey."

"You don't mean that. You like me here."

"I do not."

"You do. I make you feel young."

"You make me feel nauseous."

Kevin chuckled as though he did not believe me.

"I 'ave a dream, uncle George."

"Thank you, but I was not enquiring."

"I'll tell you anyroad. I'm gonna be a pop star."

Oh lord.

"You are thirty-five," I said. "You are too old. Look at the television today. If you have not achieved superstar status by the age of six then you have left it too late."

"Susan Boyle got famous when she were old."

"She won a talent show."

"So will I?"

"Is there a World's Biggest Moron Contest?"

Kevin laughed.

"You can't get me down any more, uncle George." I bet I could. "I'm a new man. I'm confident. I know my future."

"As I said, I was not enquiring."

Kevin picked up the newspaper and threw it towards me.

"Have a look," he said excitedly.

I scanned the main article on the topmost page.

"You want to get your nails done at Wendy's Salon?" I said.

"Not that page, silly. T' other one."

I turned the newspaper over. Familiar faces beamed back.

"You have got to be joking," I said.

"I'm not. I'm enterin'. It's the first time they've ever held auditions in Spain. So many Brits down here now. I'm gonna win *X Factor*."

I read the details.

"It says the audition is in two weeks' time," I said.

"Yep!"

"You will have returned home by then."

Kevin smiled, his face creasing like a rotten kidney.

"I am going to try Mary again," I said quickly, disappearing into the house to retrieve the telephone. Kevin followed me inside, carrying the newspaper. I selected Mary's number. It started to ring. There was no response. I was about to abandon the call when a voice answered.

"Hello," said a man. He sounded a long way away.

"Hello, where's Mary?"

"Who is this calling, please?"

"I am George Pearly, Mary's brother. Where is Mary?"

"I'm afraid I have some bad news, Mr Pearly. There's no easy way to say this. Mary died. On Friday, we believe. The cleaner only found her this morning."

"Mary's dead?" I said loud enough for Kevin to hear. He looked up from the newspaper article, pulled a face to register acknowledgement of the information and went back to reading the story.

Mary was the second of my siblings to pass away. Charlie, two years older than me, met his end on a yacht in the English Channel. His wife, Elaine, told how he was knocked overboard by a freak wave concealing a particularly buoyant fridge-freezer. His body was never retrieved. What she lost in evening entertainment – Charlie was an aficionado of the ukulele – she more than made up for in life insurance payments.

"Do they know what it was?" I asked.

"We aren't sure yet. There'll be a post-mortem."

"And the funeral?"

"Impossible to say. It depends on the post-mortem. Someone will let you know when it is."

"Sorry, to whom am I speaking?" I asked.

"Detective Inspector Barry Williams."

"Oh. Is there some suspicion of foul play?"

"We don't know, Mr Pearly. It is too early to say. Would you like to speak to anyone else? I believe your brother Richard is here somewhere."

"No!" I spat. I immediately calmed down. "No, thank you. Let me know about the funeral, Mr Williams."

"Someone will be in touch."

I hung up. I stared at Kevin, his head still in the newspaper.

"You do not seem too bothered that your mother is dead."

"Well, y'know," he said, looking up. "She were old."

"Ah well, never mind then," I said sarcastically.

"Yeah."

He went back to his newspaper.

"She died on the day you left."

"Did she?" he replied absently.

"The police have a suspicion it may have been something more sinister."

Kevin raised his head.

"What? Like murder?"

"Possibly."

"Wow."

He started to read the paper again.

"Kevin, did you murder your mother?"

"Me? Nah, there's only one murderer in this family, uncle George."

He sniggered.

"I did not kill those people!"

"Tell it to t' judge."

"I did NOT kill those people, you little shit!"

"And tell it to t' people who sprayed your car."

"What are you talking about?"

"I saw it out t' bedroom window. Someone's sprayed it."

I stormed outside and looked at my car. Those arseholes

had done it again. The bonnet was painted in big, white letters: "We know what you did in the mountains." I stormed back inside.

"Get a rag and the detergent from under the sink!"

"What?"

"You are cleaning the car."

Kevin looked up blankly.

"Uncle Richard wouldn't make me clean t' car."

I smiled him an icy smile.

"You cannot threaten me with that any more. Your mother is dead. She is clearly not going to pay me the money that she promised me for looking after her pet chimp. Clean the car or you are leaving tonight."

He stood up slowly, looking blankly.

"And put some bloody clothes on!"

The balance of power had shifted. I would honour Mary's request of Kevin's two-week visit as her dying wish. And until then I would have a slave.

Wednesday 13th November

I woke up in my own bed for the first time since Kevin's arrival. I made a mental note to change the sheets. I had been too tired last night and Kevin's short stay under my covers had shifted their aroma to one that had a hint of the morgue.

I walked into the living room and Kevin was curled up on the sofa snoring, his belly flopped over the edge. Ambrose stood on the arm of the sofa. He manoeuvred his tail so that its tip lightly brushed Kevin's nose. Without waking, Kevin swatted it away thinking it was a fly. Ambrose repeated the procedure seven or eight times whilst I observed. He actually looked as though he had a smile on his little, canine face.

"Wake up, Kevin. It is morning!" I yelled.

His face slowly uncrumpled as he scratched his head. One eye eventually opened and looked at his watch.

"Eh? It's only 'alf seven."

I opened the curtains. He closed his eyes again expecting the room to fill with light. He sat up and looked outside at the darkness, confused.

"It's still night time!" he said.

"Today, Kevin, we are going on a very important trip."

"Where?"

"I have not yet decided."

"Then how's it important?"

"Because I have been trapped in this house since my ban and today you are going to drive me somewhere pleasant." He laid down again on the sofa. "But first you will cook me my breakfast."

"You want Coco Pops?"

"We do not have any Coco Pops."

"I only know how to do Coco Pops."

"Then you will learn, will you not, Kevin? Two fried eggs, two rashers of bacon, a sausage and two slices of toast, please. Hop to it!"

"Can I have some an' all?"

"Of course you can, Kevin." He half-smiled and rubbed his eyes and belly simultaneously. "If you go and get some more ingredients. Two eggs, two rashers, one sausage and two slices of bread are all that we have in."

"But t' shops aren't open yet?"

"Yes. I know."

"When do they open?"

"Ten o'clock."

Kevin gave a sigh of discontentment.

"'Snot fair," he said, before lumbering into the kitchen. He called out from inside. "I'll prob'ly burn it all."

"If you burn it, Kevin, then I will detach your favourite

ear."

I was enjoying myself immensely. I had not had this much fun since Marjorie had the shingles.

Twenty minutes later I was sitting expectantly at the little table in my living room-cum-dining room-cum-hallway. I had a knife in one hand and a fork in the other. There was a clanking of metal on crockery from the kitchen and then Igor waddled in carrying a plate of cooked breakfast.

"Soz," he said. "I broke one o' yer eggs."

He placed the food before me.

"Oh dear," I said, looking down seriously at the damaged yolk. "This is unacceptable. Give me your hand, Kevin." I took it by the wrist and pressed his palm against the surface of the table. "Spread your fingers, boy." Kevin looked confused but did as he was told. "Now, Kevin, which finger shall I sever?"

"What? None of them. It were an accident."

He squirmed, trying to remove his hand but I held his wrist tightly.

"Tell me which finger or I will choose myself. Eeny-meeny-miny-moe," I said, hovering my knife over each finger in turn.

He closed his eyes tightly and stiffened his body.

"Don't hurt me," he croaked.

"Which finger?"

"T' lickle one."

I let go of his hand. He snatched it back and opened his eyes.

"Kevin, you are a pillock. Now go and make me a cup of tea."

All days should start like this.

After a few minutes he returned from the kitchen and placed the tea in front of me. I immediately stood up.

"I am going out," I announced.

"What 'bout yer tea?"

I merely sneered and shrugged my shoulders. Kevin looked confused.

"I thought we was goin' out," he said.

"We are. But not yet. We will depart in a couple of hours or so."

"Then why did you get me up so early?"

"Because I needed breakfast and because you need to learn how to wake up before News At Ten."

He pulled a face.

"I'm allus up before four in th' afternoon."

"Well done. You must be so proud."

"Where you goin' anyroad?"

"I have a funeral to attend."

*

I have to say that I have enjoyed every funeral that I have ever attended. No one for whom I have cared has ever died. This one would be no different. After all, Scotch Tony was merely transport with an alcoholic male attached.

I entered the long, utilitarian room in which the remembrance service was taking place. About ten people were there, including Vince, Mike and Phil, down at the front of the room. I had no desire to interact with them and so I positioned myself at the rear. A middle-aged woman dressed in black sat on the front row repeatedly dabbing her eyes. I assumed that to be Tony's wife.

The woman in charge of the ceremony mentioned hell a number of times, which annoyed me intensely, and so I rose to my feet and left. I discovered an adjoining room with the door ajar and wandered inside. A coffin was positioned on a table top with its lid removed.

I approached it. Although I have no idea why, it took me by surprise to see Scotch Tony's face peering back at me. The actual burial or cremation must have been after the ceremony.

He was slightly bloated and appeared to be wearing an excessive amount of make-up. With the addition of a few feathers he could have been Danny La Rue.

I watched him for ten minutes. He looked peaceful, content even. I cannot wait to die.

*

By three o'clock we were driving on a country road in the mountains. The ancient Moorish terraces of old were neglected and crumbled and had been mostly replaced by northern European wealth. Some olive trees remained, along with the ground-crawling vines that produce the local, cloyingly undrinkable wine, but for every one derelict *cortijo* of old, two hundred identical white villas with their identical blue swimming pools littered the hillside. The mountains were still beautiful but the British, Germans and Scandinavians were doing their utmost to render it otherwise.

I sat in the back of my car as we trundled through the scenery. I had found an old peaked cap in my store cupboard and Lumphead had agreed to wear it without much fuss. I was born too late. I should have owned a plantation.

"Was your mother still a wealthy woman, Kevin?"

"S'pose. She never bought owt. Well, towards th' end, she'd buy th' odd prop o' two."

"Prop?"

"Yeah, she got one of those sparkly jackets so that she could host game shows. And she bought a dustbin and painted a face on it."

She really was bonkers.

"We won't see any of it. T' money, I mean."

"Why not?"

"She said she were leavin' it to t' cats. She'd allus said that. Even when she weren't mad."

I sighed. My vision of a golden, if foreshortened, retirement was tossed out of the window to join the beer bottles and Coke cans lying in the grass verge.

"So what will you do, Kevin, now that you are an orphan?"

He looked sad for a moment and then smiled.

"I'll live wi' you," he said.

"No, seriously?"

"I am bein' serious. I like you, uncle George."

"You do?"

This was a surprise, even from an imbecile.

"Yeah, you're yer own man. You're in control."

I smiled to myself. I suppose I do possess the outward appearance of a field marshal. Then I looked in the rear view mirror and could see him smirking.

"Yeah, an' you kill people who get in yer way," he said.

"Stop the car."

"What?"

"Stop the car right now!"

He screeched to a halt. A 4x4 that had followed us up the mountain nearly ploughed into my boot. It blared its horn as it swerved past. Kevin turned around to face me and I grabbed him by the lapel of his sweaty polo shirt. I got my face as close as I could to his without smelling his breath.

"I have never killed anyone. Hear me?"

"Yeah," he replied timidly.

"But I am prepared to make a start right this minute if you do not shut your mouth. Never mention this again."

"You're hurtin' me."

"Understand?"

"You've got me skin."

"UNDERSTAND?"

"Yeah, sorry."

I let go of him.

"Now, drive on. You see that village ahead? That is Manzano." He nodded. "We are going to find a bar and I am going to get outstandingly inebriated, and you are going to wait until I am finished and then you are going to drive me home."

"Yes, uncle George."

Thursday 14th November

The next morning I was out on the terrace under a grey sky, watering my herbs that I cultivated in the far corner. Janet appeared with a basket full of clothes and, no doubt, saucy undergarments. I pretended not to notice her. I was playing hard to get.

"Hello, George," she called out.

I looked up and feigned surprise.

"Oh, hello, Janet. I did not see you there."

I missed my calling. I should have become an actor.

"Whatcha doing?" she asked.

"I am just feeding the weeds," I said with a smile. Ah, the charm, the charm!

"Are they herbs?"

"Yes. I have basil, oregano, coriander..."

"Oh, I love coriander. Can I have a look?"

Oh my, keeping my distance was obviously drawing her closer to me. Why had I not used this approach before? She clambered over the small fence between us. Her skirt was rather too short to effect this in a ladylike manner. She walked over to the corner in which I was crouched with my miniature watering can.

"Ooo, coriander!" she cooed.

"Would you like me to take a cutting?"

"Would you? That'd be great."

The gods clearer disapproved of our courtship. At that moment a tumultuous rumble overhead unleashed a sudden downpour.

"Quick! Come inside," I said, standing up and pulling my jacket over my head.

"It's just as quick for me to go home, George. I'll come 'round for the coriander later if that's alright."

"No, I have something to show you," I said urgently.

"Oh, OK then."

She whooped as the rain came down harder and we sprinted the five metres into the kitchen.

"Ah, that is better," I said, shaking my sodden overcoat. A further rumble from the heavens announced a sudden monsoon.

"What did you want to show me, George?"

"What?"

"You said you had something to show me."

"Did I? Oh yes." I had nothing to show her. I looked around the kitchen. "I wanted to show you..." – my kitchen is decidedly dull – "...this!"

I handed her my interesting object.

"It's a tea towel, George."

"Yes, it is. But it is a very special tea towel."

She looked at me, awaiting an explanation.

"This towel was given to me by..." Think of something quickly. "Winston Churchill."

"It looks just like the ones they sell on the Wednesday market."

"Hmmm. Would you like a drink, Janet? Gin and tonic?"

"It's only ten o'clock, George."

"Just a *vino* then?"

"I'll have a cup of coffee if you have one."

"*Carajillo*?"

"What?"

"A coffee with a brandy in it?"

"No."

I switched on the kettle and we wandered into the lounge. Janet perched on the sofa. Kevin choose this moment to emit a loud, sexually satisfied grunt from the bathroom. Janet looked at me awkwardly. Seconds later the bathroom door slung open clumsily and Kevin emerged, a sheen of sweat on his slimy forehead.

"Oh. Hello, Janet," he said shyly. "That's a bit embarrassin'." He looked down at a creased sheet of A4 paper in his hand, a printed photo of Janet. She let out a small gasp. Kevin noticed her reaction.

"Sorry, Janet, I got this off Facebook." He held up her photo. "But you was crackin'," he said.

Janet double-gasped.

"Get out of my sight, you animal!" I barked.

"Where should I go?" he said.

"I do not care. Just stand in the rain for an hour, you filthy pervert."

"George!" interrupted Janet. "Don't be so mean. Boys will be..." she started and corrected herself. "Men will be men."

"He is not a man. He is a mollusc."

Kevin lost his smile and hunched his frame.

"I were just workin' through me pain, Janet. Me mum's just died, y'see."

Never was a problem and its solution more disturbingly juxtaposed. Janet rushed towards Kevin and put an arm around him.

"You poor thing."

"Do not give him sympathy, Janet. He does not care one iota that his mother – my sister – is gone," I said.

Kevin gasped hammily.

"How can you say such a thing?" he replied.

It seems that I am not the only actor in this household.

"There, there, Kevin."

Janet embraced the flabby dolt. She loomed over him,

holding his body tightly. Kevin folded his arms around her. His gargoyle face appeared just below her armpit. He looked me in the eye with a big grin, placed one hand on her behind and gave me a thumbs-up with the other.

There was an insistent knocking at the front door. I opened it to find a young policeman stood there. Those bastards at Bar Wars had dropped me in it. He narrowed his eyes. It was still pouring with rain. I opened the door wide and gestured to him to come inside. He entered, never losing eye contact the whole time.

"Jorge Pearly?" he asked in heavily accented Spanish.

"Yes."

His response was incomprehensible.

"*No comprendo*. Do you speak English?" I said.

He repeated himself in Spanish. I looked towards Janet.

"Do you speak Spanish?" I asked her.

"No. Don't you?"

"No."

"I do," said Kevin.

"No, you do not. You barely speak English."

"I do!"

"Go on then. Ask him what he wants."

Kevin turned to face the policeman and cleared his throat ceremonially.

"What-o do you want-o?"

"Idiot!" I pushed Kevin out of the still open door and slammed it behind him, turning the key in the lock. He hammered on the outside. The new hinges were obviously stronger than the previous ones.

"George!" said Janet.

"It's p-pissin' d-down!" a stuttering, muffled voice came from outside.

The policeman mimed a pen and paper, which I gave to him. He scribbled down a short paragraph and presented the page to me.

"Google Translate," he said. "*Adio!*"

He turned the key, opened the door and left. Kevin splashed inside, his clothes glued to his pork flesh, his hair matted to his forehead.

"What did you do tha' for? I were only tryin' to help. I coulda caught me death out there."

"One can only hope."

We went to my computer and I typed the message into the relevant box and pressed Translate. The reply came back in Russian.

"You have to select English, uncle George."

"Yes, I know that!" I screamed impatiently.

Kevin smiled.

"Uncle George is rubbish on computers," he said to Janet.

Once translated, my instructions were clear. I had to present myself at Merla's police station within three days along with a trusted interpreter.

"So," I said. "It appears that they want to ask me some questions."

"What have you done, George?" asked Janet with a sultry look in her eyes.

"Nothing. Nothing at all," I replied. "Well, not exactly nothing."

Friday 15th November

Today I had an important task. I had to locate an interpreter who operated in both English and Spanish in a town where everyone spoke either English or Spanish and nobody spoke both. Of course I could have paid for a professional interpreter but finances are such that I would have chosen any course of events rather than put my hand into my pocket. I feared that it would be a challenge.

I was on my way out of the door when Humpty noticed that I was departing.

"Where you goin', uncle George?" he asked in his usual whine.

"Out."

"Where?"

"If you must know I am going to find an interpreter."

"I'll come too."

"You will not. You are cleaning the kitchen."

He laughed.

"Who am I? Cinderella?"

"No, you are Shrek."

"I'm comin'. You can't stop me."

"Well, if you join me then we can take Ambrose for his walk."

"I'll get t' lead."

"We will not require the lead. Bring his rucksack. It is in the cupboard."

He retrieved it and looked at it with amusement.

"You've got a bag for you to carry t' dog in?"

"No, I have a bag for *you* to carry the dog in."

I placed Ambrose inside and strapped it to Kevin's back.

"Onward!" I commanded.

Although mid-November it was a warm morning and Kevin was already sweating before we had reached the end of the street. Ambrose took every opportunity to nibble Kevin's ears with his few remaining teeth. Kevin appeared to find this sexually stimulating. I suspect that Ambrose was attempting to chew them off.

We visited all the places that Marjorie liked to frequent: the International Club, the American Club, the three second-hand book dealers and the British-run pie shop. No one spoke Spanish. We had walked the better part of twelve miles.

Finally, defeated, we entered Bar Wars. Bullshit Phil and Mortality Mike were at the bar.

"Can I get a Vimto, uncle George?" squealed Kevin. "I'm knackered."

Thick rivulets of sweat dripped from his greasy brow. With Ambrose strapped to his back Kevin appeared to be a two-headed circus freak, as opposed to the one-headed circus freak he usually portrayed.

"Hey, it's the professor," said Phil. "Killed anyone lately?"

"Shut up, you cretin."

"That's not very PC," said Mike.

I rolled my eyes.

"I know that it is highly unlikely, but are either of you able to speak Spanish?" I asked.

Mike shook his head.

"I can speak Russian, Arabic, Farsi, Hindi, Greek, Turkish and Welsh," said Phil.

"But not Spanish?"

"No."

"Thank you," I said sarcastically. "But go on. Say something in Welsh."

"Llandudno."

"Idiot."

"I know someone who can speak Spanish," said Mike.

"Who?"

"Margaret."

He burst out laughing.

"That's no good," said Phil, joining in the hilarity. "He's already killed Margaret."

"How many more times do I have to tell you?" I said in an exasperated tone. "I did not kill anybody."

"You did," he said smirking. "You're on a spree. Scotch Tony, Margaret and now Not Gay Alan."

"Not Gay Alan?"

"Yes, he hasn't been seen since Thursday. Don't matter. I didn't like him much. Bit of a tosser. He went up to Manzano and no one has seen him since."

"We went up to Manzano on Thursday," chipped in the circus freak.

"Did you now?" enquired Phil. "What an amazing coincidence!"

"Actually we did," I said. "And young Kevin here can confirm that I did not kill anybody. Is that not correct, Kevin?"

"Yeah."

"I was with Kevin the whole duration of our visit."

"Yeah, he were," Kevin said assuredly. Then his face crinkled. "Except for when you wandered off."

"I did not wander off."

"Yeah, you did. You were pissed. You were gone about twenty minutes."

"I did not."

"You did. You were smashed off yer tits. You won't remember it."

"Now that *is* interesting," said Phil smugly.

I had had enough of him. With two hands I grabbed Phil by his t-shirt and pulled him to my face.

"I did not kill anybody!" I yelled.

"Ooo, temper," said Phil in a camp voice. "Hey, Mike. Stick around so there are witnesses this time."

I let go of him. He smoothed his t-shirt with both hands.

"Of course, if you'd started anything proper, I'd have ripped your throat out. I was in the Foreign Legion, y'know."

"You were down the British Legion more like," I said, miming his draining a pint glass, rather wittily I thought. Nobody laughed. "So no one speaks Spanish in here?" I reiterated.

"Bob's lassie probably speaks it," said Mike with a smirk, pointing to an old man, easily eighty, in the dark, far corner of the bar, nursing a half pint of Guinness. I had only briefly spoken to him once before.

"Good. Then I shall speak to Bob."

I ordered half a lager for me, a Vimto for the wide-mouthed frog and an additional half of Guinness. I carried it over to Bob.

"Good afternoon, Robert. A gift."

I presented the beer to him. He raised his head sadly and smiled a half-smile.

"How do. And it's Bob to you."

He sounded like a farmer.

"I am looking for a Spanish interpreter, Bob, and Mike informs me that your daughter speaks the tongue I require."

"Aye, Edith's fluent."

"Do you think she would be able to help me?"

"Aye, I don't see why not."

"Will Edith require payment?"

"Payment?" he laughed. "No, she won't require payment. I'll see her reet," he said in his Yorkshire accent.

Bob was famously well-funded. I was not going to force the money issue. I wrote my address on a beer mat and passed it to Old Bob.

"If Edith could come around for nine tomorrow that would be ideal."

"Aye, she's off tomorrow. I'll sort it."

"Thank you, Bob." I turned to Kevin. "Come on, lardy, drink up!"

I rose to my feet.

"You not staying for this drink?" asked Bob softly.

"No," I said, necking my half pint.

"It'd be nice to have a chat," he said.

"Sorry."

I marched back past the bar and out of the door. Phil, Mike and bar man Trevor all turned to me as I passed, grinning madly.

"And many thanks for telling the police about your insane allegations," I spat at them.

"Didn't tell 'em nothing," said Phil.

"No, it wasn't us," said Mike.

As I left they exploded in fits of laughter.

Buffoons.

Saturday 16th November

It was just after nine o'clock in the morning. I was attired in a well-pressed, white linen suit. The rest of the British community in Merla may prefer to dress like beggars but I would continue to uphold the standard, especially on a day when I needed to make a good impression.

"Bloody 'ell, not again," I heard Kevin rant from the kitchen.

There was a knock at the door. I strolled towards it and looked through the spy hole. There was no one there. Annoyed, I called out to Kevin.

"What is the matter now?"

There was another knock at the door. Once again, the spy hole showed no one was present. Vexed at this infantile behaviour I ripped open the door and proceeded to sprint down my short path to capture whomever was playing the fool. That was not what happened however. Instead I found myself sprawled on the concrete having tripped over a small child, who was now bawling out her eyes.

"Waaaaa! My elbow. You hurt my elbow," she screamed.

"What are you doing in my garden?"

"You hurt my elbow. It's bleeding."

I stood up painfully and helped her to her feet.

"Who are you?" I asked.

She calmed down a little, rubbing her arm and pouting. She could not have been more than ten.

"Who are you?" I repeated.

"Edith."

"Who?"

"Edith. My daddy said you wanted someone who could speak Spanish."

Oh good god.

"How old are you?" I asked.

"I'm eight," she said. "In two sleeps."

"How does your father have an eight...a seven year-old daughter?"

"What do you mean?"

She wrinkled up her nose.

"He is old. Your father is very old. He is, if I am being honest, extremely close to death."

She started to cry again.

"Waaaa! Daddy's dying!"

I was growing impatient.

"Calm down, child!" I shouted abruptly. This shocked her into silence, followed by a stream of dry, staccato sobs. "Listen to me. He is not close to death but he *is* exceptionally ancient. It is not possible for you to exist," I told her pointlessly.

Her sobbing diminished.

"My mummy's young. She's twenty-seven. She's very pretty. She's from Russia," she said proudly. Ah, Old Bob and his money. "My elbow hurts."

"Come inside," I said. "I will get you a plaster."

As we walked through the door Kevin leapt from the kitchen holding a leaking running shoe.

"Your dog has pissed in me pissin' trainers again!"

"Language, Kevin. We have a visitor."

"Sorry, uncle George." He turned to Edith and held out a greasy mitt. "And who are you, lickle girl?" he asked creepily.

"I'm Edith." She smiled and shook his hand. "I'm going to speak Spanish for your uncle."

The pain of her elbow and her soon-to-be-deceased father were distant memories.

"What? This is Bob's daughter? No wonder they was all laughin' yesterday. You can't take her to t' police station."

"The police?" said Edith anxiously.

"I have no other option, Kevin. Do not be alarmed, my dear. The police just want to ask me a few questions."

"I don't like the police. They have guns," she said.

"Yeah, big guns," added Kevin unhelpfully.

I popped to the bathroom and returned with a package.

"Here," I said, peeling a plaster. "For your elbow."

She stuck it on. Unfortunately I had no such bandage for the huge, bloody hole in the knee of my linen trousers.

*

Twenty minutes later Edith, Kevin and I walked into the police station. I would not have chosen to have Kevin present but he had threatened to do mischief to Ambrose in revenge for my dog's beautifully orchestrated campaign of terror against his footwear. I could not bring Ambrose and so I brought Kevin instead. I considered commanding Kevin to wait outside but he does not take kindly to demands and, like a stray animal, he would simply have wandered inside after a few minutes. I spent five minutes looking for a suitable cord with which to restrain him but the thought of his unwilling confinement at the fence of a police station may only have exacerbated my situation.

I approached the desk.

"I, sir, have been requested to present myself at this locality."

The policeman on duty looked blankly.

"Edith?" I said.

"What?" she replied with a laugh.

"Repeat what I have just said."

"Sorry, I wasn't listening. Kevin was pulling a funny face."

I gave Kevin a slap. The policeman looked at me.

"Stop clowning around. This is serious, Kevin. Edith, tell this nice man that I have been requested to present myself at this locality."

"I can't," she replied shyly.

"And why not?"

"'Cos I dunno what you're on about."

I looked blankly at her. The Spanish school system seemed to be performing as woefully as its British equivalent.

"Uncle George wants you to tell this nice policeman that he's been asked to come here by t' police."

"Why didn't he say that?"

She turned to the policeman and spewed forth a confident string of indecipherable Spanish. She certainly was a precocious little creature. The policeman nodded and replied.

"What's your last name?" she asked me.

I told her and she repeated it to the policeman in a Spanish accent. My name is not my name in a Spanish accent. It is my name in an English accent, god damn it! He tapped something into the computer on his desk for a few moments, pulled a few faces and then said something to Edith.

"He wants to know if you met Antony Hingston on..." She asked the policeman to confirm the date. "Between the fifth of November and the ninth of November."

I remained silent.

"Yes, he did," said Kevin quickly. "He means Scotch Tony, dunnee?"

The policeman looked from Kevin to me with narrow eyes. I shot Kevin an angry glance.

"Did you?" she asked, wanting confirmation.

"Yes, I did. We partook of a country stroll together."

Edith looked to Kevin.

"They went for a walk," he said.

Edith confirmed this information to the duty officer. He looked at me with dark, brooding eyes and said something to Edith without removing his glare.

"He wants to know if you killed him."

"Of course not!" I ejaculated.

At that moment the station doors burst open. In came a thick-set, broken-nosed thug, with the waxy skin of an eastern European, flanked by two police officers, who dragged him along roughly. One of the policemen placed his face two inches from the criminal's and screamed something vicious. The captive looked nonplussed and responded in a distant tongue. Edith turned to the prisoner and muttered something in a similarly alien language. The man looked suddenly aghast.

"What did you say to him?" I asked.

"I told him they're gonna fuck him up," she said. My eyes almost popped from their sockets. "What, my mummy's Russian. He's Russian."

"Your language!" I said, still horrified.

"My mummy swears all the time. I bet you swear," she said to me.

"He does," said Kevin. "Like a trooper."

The Russian was hauled into a back room. The duty officer turned to Edith and said something. She relayed the message.

"They're too busy at the moment. They've not enough evidence to arrest you but they're looking," she said. "You can't leave."

"Cannot leave where?" I blurted, imagining a lifetime behind bars, or what little remained of my lifetime.

"You can't leave Spain. They'll want to talk to you again."

I turned to leave. Kevin looked at Edith.

"Ask 'im if they've found Not Gay Alan's body yet?" chimed Kevin.

"Shut up, you fool."

"And Margaret's," he continued. I was forced to hit him in the face once again. The duty officer further narrowed his eyes. Through such tiny slits I would be surprised if he could see anything at all. I endeavoured to rescue the situation. I addressed the duty officer directly.

"Fear not, sir, young Kevin's overly loquacious outburst signify nothing worthy of comprehension."

The policeman looked at Edith. She shrugged her shoulders.

"I don't fuckin' know," she said.

Sunday 17th November

After a mostly acceptable English breakfast prepared for me by my simian butler – the inclusion of a roll mop herring was an unexpected and unwelcome addition – I sat in the comfortable chair reading The Sunday Telegraph, Ambrose asleep on my lap.

Kevin was in the kitchen, washing up and loudly singing a song recently made famous by some bulimic, modern starlet.

"Stop that racket!" I called out. "I am trying to read."

"I'm practisin', uncle George," he replied in a voice dripping with unfulfillable dreams.

"Have you stitched my linen trousers yet?"

"They're just soakin'. I need to get t' blood out first."

Now that Kevin had been partially house-trained it was not an entirely unpleasant experience to have him around. I no longer needed to tidy the house or cook any food, unless of course I desired something of a culinary standard above that of a soon-to-be-condemned greasy spoon.

The music changed to Michael Jackson. Kevin danced out of the kitchen with a mug in one hand and a tea towel in the other. He sang along in a high-pitched, nasal drone, kicking out his legs like someone having a seizure.

"Ready for this bit?" he said.

"No."

"Here it comes. Ready?"

"No."

"Ow!" he shrieked, shooting one arm into the air and grabbing his crotch with his other hand, forgetting that he did not actually possess a spare hand and dropping the mug, which shattered into a thousand pieces. He looked instantly cowed.

"You know what has to happen now?" I said in a low tone.

"Don't, uncle George."

"Adopt the position," I said.

"Uncle George," he begged.

"Adopt!"

"Don't paddle me arse again."

"Adopt!"

He bent over and closed his eyes. I stood up, causing Ambrose to leap to the floor, landing badly and ending up in a heap. He was not unconscious, just angling for chorizo. I rolled up the Sunday Telegraph into a narrow tube, stepped towards Kevin and delivered a single mighty thwack.

"Yow!"

"Do not break my belongings."

"Soz, uncle George," he said, rubbing his backside.

"There is some superglue in the kitchen drawer. Sweep up these pieces and reassemble my mug."

"But that'll take ages."

"Yes, it will. Now hop to it!"

Kevin went to locate the glue. There was a knock on the front door. Imagine my joyous surprise when through the spy hole I could see the delectable Janet. This was the first time that she had ever called around uninvited. I opened the door.

"Hello, George," she smiled.

"Yes, hello. Come in, come in!" I ushered her inside.

She was wearing an impressively tight, white t-shirt.

"So how are you?" I asked.

"George. Up here." She pointed to her face. She had caught me staring inappropriately. "My tits are very well, thank you very much."

"Yes, sorry. It is just, well..."

"I thought I'd come 'round and see how you got on at the police station."

"Not much to report really."

Kevin wandered in from the kitchen.

"Uncle George, I've stuck me hands together." He stood there with his palms securely joined and the backs of his hands encrusted with various pieces of pottery. "Oh, hello, Janet," he beamed.

Janet adopted a sad face.

"How are you, Kevin, y'know, with your mum an' all?"

Kevin cunningly adopted a timidly brave half-smile.

"Well, y'know. I takes each day as it comes."

"Yes, of course."

"Some days are better than others."

"Yes."

He held up his adhesive-bound hands.

"Like today, fer one, this isn't such a good day."

"Don't worry, Kevin. I've got some solvent for that at home," she said.

"Leave him be," I said. "Perhaps it will reduce his enormous capacity for self abuse."

"Fair enough," he said, "but I won't be able to wipe me

arse either."

Once again I had been outsmarted by a retard.

"I just came over to see how your uncle got on yesterday, at the police station."

"They think he killed Scotch Tony."

"Do they?" she asked excitedly.

"They have no evidence," I said dismissively.

"'Snot just them. Everyone thinks so."

"No, they do not," I said. "I do not believe anyone honestly believes that."

"And he killed Margaret. And Not Gay Alan. He's like Jack the Ripper."

"Stop being a clown."

Janet was viewing me with a strange look in her eye, one I had not noticed before. Maybe she found my criminal allegations in some way sexually arousing. I had heard tell of such women. Admittedly, they generally preferred successfully dangerous bank robbers to superannuated murderous poets but her mood had definitely altered.

"So you didn't kill them?" she asked.

Now, what was the correct answer? My decision here could determine my future with Janet. I decided to play it coy.

"Who knows?" I said.

"Uncle George," Kevin said, eyes and mouth wide open, "you *did* kill 'em!"

I shrugged my shoulders.

"I am saying nothing unless my solicitor is present," I said jokingly.

I smiled at Janet. She smiled back. Now what should I do? And, in any case, how would this role continue? Would she desire me indefinitely for the murder of three people or would I be compelled to add to my tally, perhaps knocking off another poor sod on a weekly basis? Within a few years I could have wiped out an entire village just to get within touching distance of her whorish drawers.

"Have you ever been in trouble before, George?" she asked.

Ah, this was a much better strategy. I would reveal my dangerous past in bite-sized morsels to keep her baying for more George.

"Well, we were all young once," I said.

"What did you do, uncle George?"

"I once ran over a dog," I said.

Janet's smile weakened.

"It is true," I added.

Janet's smile dissipated entirely.

"Yes, it is," said Kevin. "This dog!"

He pointed to Ambrose and his missing leg.

"Ah, poor thing," she said.

Ambrose had partially recovered from his earlier fall and Janet bent down to scoop him up. Her recently discovered affection for me was now receding in the opposite direction. I attempted to rescue the situation.

"I once took a large amount of money from a bank," I said.

She turned to look at me.

"Go on," she said.

What was I doing? No one gets danger points for obtaining a mortgage.

"No, forget that. I was done for drink-driving."

"That's disgusting," she said. "No concern for other road users."

Bloody hell!

"Alright, I confess. I killed Tony, Margaret and Alan."

"Really?" both she and Kevin said at once.

"Yes, I did."

"Why?" asked Kevin.

I gave him a steely glare.

"They got in my way," I said wickedly whilst drawing my finger across my throat.

Janet's smile returned. What was wrong with this woman?

Monday 18th November

It was mid-afternoon. *Countdown* had recently completed its demonstration of words, numbers and short skirts and since I had apparently managed to go nearly the whole day without killing anyone I thought I would descend upon the septic tank that is Bar Wars and have a celebratory beer.

As I entered I noticed a small huddle of people clustered around a table just off the end of the bar. Unless I was mistaken the slippery Doctor Vince sat with his back to me. Around his table, four middle-aged women giggled at every word he uttered. His confident voice could be heard echoing around the otherwise empty bar. I decided to hang back and listen in to his conversation. I felt a little like James Bond.

"Deirdre, look at your beautiful green eyes," he said. "If it wasn't for your Geoff I'd whisk you off to somewhere exotic."

"The Seychelles?" Deirdre offered hopefully.

"Steady on, love. I was thinking more like Torremolinos."

I caught a glimpse of his smile in the distant mirror. He cackled like a hyena at his own inanity. Deirdre laughed too.

"Oh, Vince. Get away with you."

She slapped him on his arm. He grabbed her hand and held it there. He looked directly into her eyes.

"But your Geoff won't be around forever, will he, Deirdre? Not with his condition."

"And what is his condition?" asked a portly, grey-haired hanger-on.

"We don't know," said Deirdre. "Doctor Vince won't tell us."

"He told me," said a black-haired harridan.

"Now, now, girls. These matters are confidential." The women all nodded as though Vince were infallible. "I was saying only the same thing to John the other day."

"Who's John?" asked Deirdre.

"Y'know, the poet, the tall fella, about seventy."

They all frowned quizzically.

"Everybody hates him," Vince continued.

"Ah, you mean Loathsome George," chipped in a lumpy trollop.

Everyone else nodded in agreement.

Loathsome George. Hell, I *do* have an adjective! My adjective is Loathsome.

"Yes, he has a dreadful illness. But will he listen when I tell him that he's better off not knowing what he has? No, he won't."

"And what does he have?" asked the harridan.

"Well," said Vince.

This was it. I was about to learn my fate.

The bar door swung open noisily.

"Hello, uncle George!"

Vince swivelled around in his seat in time to see me strike Kevin in the head. Kevin gasped and held his cheek.

"My, that was close, wasn't it, John? I nearly spilled the beans," he said chuckling to himself.

"What did I do?" asked Kevin, hurt.

"This fraud was just about to tell me what is wrong with me and you have ruined everything. Just like you always do."

"I'll make it better," he pleaded. "I promise."

"What can you possibly do?"

"Watch me."

Kevin strolled over to Vince's table like a nine year-old about to ask for his football back.

"Hello, Mr Vince," he said.

Vince looked up, as though trying to determine the species that he was addressing.

"Hello, thing," he said. "And who are you?"

"My name is Kevin and you are being a meanie." Oh lord, Jean Claude van Damme had come to my rescue. "My uncle is very upset because you won't tell him what's wrong with him."

"He's your uncle?" asked Vince, pointing towards me.

"Yeah."

"You two are related?"

A smirk brushed Vince's face.

"Yeah."

"Wow."

"Tell him what's wrong!" said Kevin in the toughest voice he could muster, like a particularly aggressive gerbil.

"No. Go away."

Kevin leaned in towards Vince, resting his elbows in the centre of his table and whispered in a voice clearly audible to me twenty feet away.

"Uncle George is dangerous. You should be careful."

"Yes, I've heard," said Vince unconvinced.

"Very dangerous."

"Yes, I've heard that too."

"Very, very dangerous."

"And that."

"He has killed people."

The women gasped.

"Right!" I said, marching over towards them as swiftly as I could. I grabbed Kevin by the wrist. "Enough of this nonsense. Kevin, go home."

"Don't worry, uncle George, I'm sortin' this."

"No, you aren't," said Vince.

"I will 'sort' this when I finally organise myself and denounce this failure for burning my medical records."

"C'mon," said Vince, smirking. "I didn't burn your records."

"Yes, you did. I saw you. Stop trying to act sincere in front of your, in front of your..." I was searching for a word.

"Biatches!" offered Kevin.

"What the hell is a biatch?" I asked. I gave Kevin a glare. "Hussies. I meant your hussies."

"Same thing," said Kevin.

"I didn't burn them," said Vince.

"Yes, you did. I saw you."

"What did you see?"

"I saw you burn my medical records."

"What did you really see?"

"You burnt my records."

"I burnt a file."

"Well, I, you..."

I was flustered.

"What sort of doctor do you take me for?"

"One who burns medical records."

He laughed.

"But I saw inside the file," I said. "There were medical records."

"Yes. Not yours though."

"Then whose?"

"That Harris bloke's I found while looking for yours. He's been dead for five years. I was trying to shit you up."

"Well done. So you still have my records?"

"Of course."

"I should still denounce you."

"You are free to denounce whoever you like. You've done it often enough before."

"But you are still not going to tell me what is wrong with me?"

"John, let me buy you a drink."

"Are you going to tell me or not?"

He shrugged his shoulders. I turned and marched towards the door. Kevin followed but not without first fixing Vince with the gravest stare that he could manage and drawing his finger across his throat. We made our departure like Laurel and Hardy attempting to make a very serious point.

We walked back to the house. I was still fuming.

"I know what you should do, uncle George."

"What should I do? And before you suggest it, I am not going to kill him."

"No, I wasn't gonna suggest that."

"What then?"

"You should break into his surgery and steal yer records."

"That is the most brainless suggestion I have ever heard."

Tuesday 19th November

"You should break into his surgery and steal your records," said Janet.

She was perched on the edge of the uncomfortable sofa.

"Under no circumstance am I going to become a cat burglar."

"I'm not an expert on human behaviour..." said Kevin.

"We were under no such illusion, Kevin."

"...but I reckon Janet'll convince you to break in."

"No, she will not."

"Betcha she does."

"No, she will not."

"Betcha she does."

"No, she..."

"C'mon, children. Stop fighting. If George doesn't want to find out what is wrong with him then that's his lookout."

"Your cheap reverse psychology will not work on me. And

I do want to discover what is the matter with me."

"What's the problem then?" she asked.

"I do not want to break the law."

"But you've already killed three people," she said. "Unless of course you haven't."

"He has," said Kevin. "Definitely. It's written all o'er his face."

I refuse to become this woman's criminal slave!

"It'd be easy," said Kevin. "I've already worked out a plan."

"And why would you do such a thing?" I asked.

"'Cos Janet's gonna make ya."

"No, she is not."

Kevin rolled out a sheet of A3 paper on the living room floor and smoothed it flat with his greasy palms.

"Here are the plans of Vince's office," he said.

"Those are not plans."

"Yes, they are. They're blueprints."

"They are not. You have drawn a picture of a building in blue biro."

"Same thing."

"I think you should go easy on Kevin. At least he's showing some initiative," said Janet.

"Kevin would not know initiative if he went shopping in Lidl and found a packet of Cheese and Initiative Pies."

"That's stupid," said Kevin peevishly. "There's no such thing."

"Go on then, Danny Ocean," I said. "Explain your break-in."

"This," he said, "is the front door."

"Good."

"You smash it in, go to his filing cabinet and steal your records."

"Very good," I said sarcastically. "And how long did it

take you to formulate this masterpiece of criminal genius?"

"I've been workin' on it pretty much all day."

"Vince has a burglar alarm."

"How do you know that?"

"I once arrived just as he was opening up and he had to type in a code before we could enter the building."

"Maybe he was pretendin'," said Kevin.

"Yes, of course, maybe he was pretending."

"Yeah."

"Yes, he had assembled for himself a little, plastic box that he had to open up and then cause six beeps to sound in the off-chance that one day someone would be there to hear it."

"Yeah."

"If that is a risk you want to take, Kevin, then be my guest."

"They're not my medical records, uncle George. I'm not gettin' busted."

"Well that is that then. I suppose that you should get a magnet and use it to stick your lovely drawing to the fridge, as is the norm for artwork of such quality."

"You're wasting your time," said Janet. "He's not going to break in, Kevin."

"No, he is. I'll find another way." He thought for a moment. "OK, how 'bout this? Here is the filin' cabinet in his office." He pointed with his pen to the location I had described earlier that morning. He had been interrogating me on every aspect of Vince's lair all day. "So all we need to do is to start from this point outside his back window and tunnel into his office."

"A tunnel?"

"Yeah."

"There is a car park outside of his back window."

"So?"

"A car park made of tarmac."

"We need a digger."

"I admire your capacity for reimagining the scale of this project but you are an idiot. Do you not think Vince would notice a digger outside his window?"

"This is Spain. There are diggers everywhere."

"I cannot tunnel into someone's office," I said. "I am not a fucking mole."

"You're so negative, uncle George."

"Shut up."

"It's such a shame," said Janet. "You would've cut such a dashing figure dressed from head to toe in black. Like the Pink Panther."

"The Pink Panther was a diamond," I corrected.

"No, it wasn't," she said. "He was the burglar."

"It was a diamond."

"Uncle George, you think you're clever but you don't know nuffin'".

"Alright then. Would I cut such a dashing figure dressed from head to toe in pink? You know, like the Pink Panther?"

"The Pink Panther didn't wear pink," she said. "He wore black."

"So why was his moniker not the Black Panther?"

"Because all panthers are black," she replied.

"So why not just the Panther."

"That's too borin', uncle George."

"Oh for Christ's sake. If you think I would look dashing dressed from head to toe in black then I can easily arrange such a sartorial extravaganza but I suspect it is not my attire that would prove so alluring as the fact that I was about to commit a serious crime."

"Not as serious as killing someone," she said.

"Admittedly."

"You didn't kill anyone," she stated solidly.

I remained silent.

"Go on," she said. "Admit it."

"I already told you I did."

"Someone who indiscriminately murders doesn't get the willies about breaking into a doctor's office."

Kevin giggled.

"She said 'willies'."

"Shut up, imbecile. It depends what his speciality is."

"Whose?"

"The killer stroke burglar."

"And which are you then?"

I could not have people wandering around this town saying that I was a murderer. I was silent for a moment.

"I am neither," I replied sadly.

I hung my head.

"Uncle George!" cried Kevin. "That was th' only thing that made you interestin'."

"I knew it. I don't like being lied to. I'm off," said Janet.

She made for the door.

"Do not leave," I begged.

She turned around.

"Why do you want me to be a murderer or a thief?" I asked. "Why do you want me to be a criminal?"

"I don't want you to be a criminal, you silly, old sod."

"What is it then?"

"I want a man who knows what he wants and goes and gets it. And if the law just happens to stand in his way then so be it."

I slumped.

"You want your medical records. Vince won't give them to you. A real man would go and get them."

I hesitated a little too long.

"I'll get 'em," said Kevin.

"What?" said Janet and I together.

"I'll go and get 'em. I'm a man who knows what he wants.

And I'll do that for you, uncle George."

"No, no, you will not."

"I will. I think I'll look dashin' dressed head to toe in black."

He smiled widely at Janet. She smiled back.

"You are not doing it," I said.

"Why not?"

"Because you are not."

"That's no reason."

"Alright then. Because I am doing it! Happy now? I will go and steal my medical records."

Janet smiled.

"Told you so," said Kevin.

Wednesday 20th November

I may have foolishly agreed to don the mask of a burglar and purloin my own medical records but were I to discover my malady before this unfortunate event then it would be impossible for Janet to deny that I am a man who knows what he wants and goes out to get it.

Via the internet I had finally located an English-speaking doctor, Doctor Garside, at the other end of the Costa. For the fee of one can of Monster, Kevin agreed to drive me there. I wish he had refused.

We left at midday and had not been moving for more than a few minutes when Kevin uttered an ominous pronouncement.

"Yer car feels a bit weird today, uncle George."

"What is the matter?" I asked from the back seat.

"T' brakes. They feel all spongy."

"Well, just drive slowly and everything will be alright."

"Can I take this cap off? It's makin' me head all itchy."

"No. Leave it on."

We turned on to the A-7 motorway, often referred to as the Road of Death. The traffic thickened as we approached Malaga. I heard a click and a fizz.

"Kevin, do not drink your can whilst you are driving."

"But I'm thirsty, uncle George."

"Put the can down."

"There's nowhere to put it." He looked around. "Can you hold it a mo? I just want another bite of me butty."

"I will not hold your can. And do not eat at the wheel. Concentrate, boy!"

Kevin raised the sandwich to his lips and attempted to take a mouthful whilst holding the can in his other hand. A car ahead pulled in front of us. Kevin quickly grasped the steering wheel with his elbows and effected a clumsy swerve into the next lane. A series of horns sounded from all around us.

"Oops! That were lucky," he said.

"Put down the food!" He was clearly going to ignore me and so I continued, "Go on then, give me the can."

"In a sec. I've nearly finished."

He took a last slurp. Ahead, three lanes were narrowing into two, a fact that took Kevin by surprise.

"Oooooh shit," he said.

He grabbed the wheel clumsily and we swerved into the hard shoulder, grazing the barrier before careening back across the other two lanes. A multiple screech of brakes accompanied the symphony of hoots. In the furore Kevin dropped his can.

The motorway descended down a steep hill to the tunnel at the bottom on the outskirts of Malaga.

"You are going too fast," I said. "Slow down!"

Kevin hammered his foot on the brakes.

"'Sno good," he said. "It's stuck!"

"What do you mean it is stuck?"

"The can's rolled under t' pedal."

We were approaching 80 miles per hour on a stretch limited to 60. There was a flash.

"Have they got speed cameras 'round here?" asked Kevin with impeccable timing.

Down the steep hill we continued to accelerate. The rest of the traffic was not moving as rapidly. Kevin swerved around each car that we passed.

"Get hold of the bloody can!" I yelled.

"I can't." His belly prevented him from reaching the pedals. "You'll have to get it."

I squeezed my torso between the passenger and driver's seats, wedging my hips.

"I am stuck!" I shouted.

We had hit 90 when we entered the tunnel. After the bright winter sunshine we were blinded inside the poorly illuminated hole.

"I can't see nuffin'!" screamed Kevin, still pumping the brake uselessly.

I kept moving, trying to release my waist. With a gargantuan effort I squeezed through and reached down to the brake pedal.

"Stop stamping the pedal or else you will break my fingers, you moron!"

I reached down and grabbed the can.

"Shiiiit!" cried Kevin.

He stomped the pedal, crushing my thumb.

"Arrrgghhh!"

"Grab it!" he said.

I pulled the crushed can away.

"Do not slam on. Just brake slowly," I ordered.

Kevin floored the pedal, causing the car to skid uncontrollably, first into the side of the tunnel and then, with a deafening crunch, into the back of the lorry in front of us. We came to a juddering stop. Kevin ended up with a faceful of airbag whilst I was flung into the stereo. I opened my eyes with my head in Kevin's lap. An unpleasant odour greeted my nose.

"I told you there were summat up wi' yer brakes."

"Yes, they were being operated by a cabbage."

The traffic had come to a standstill, horns blaring, indecipherable insults hurled in a multitude of European languages.

I shakily climbed from the car and held up my hand in supplication. Walking around the Vauxhall my heart sank. There was not a single panel without damage and the engine had concertinaed. Kevin arrived at my side.

"We were lucky, weren't we?"

"You owe me for this."

"But I ain't got no money."

"You will work until you have paid every penny for this to be restored to its original condition."

"It were a shit car anyway."

I attempted a death glare but its power had been reduced since telling him I had killed no one.

The police arrived and took down the details. They breathalysed Kevin and came to the conclusion that, whilst not over the limit or high on drugs, there was definitely something the matter with him.

A tow truck appeared and loaded my nobbled Vauxhall on to its back. I asked the operator how much he thought it would cost to repair. He did not understand my English. I held up my wallet and pointed at the car. He laughed heartily.

"*Dinero* no! Eeez dead," he said depressingly.

The police gave us a ride to the coast road from where we began our long walk home in silence.

"Why don't we just get a taxi?" Kevin asked.
"Do you have any money for a taxi?"
"No."
"Then we will walk."
"But me feet are hurtin'."
"Good."

We arrived home at close to three in the morning. The last six hours had consisted of Kevin howling about his blisters and my administering frequent slaps to quieten him or at least transfer the pain elsewhere.

*

As it turned out our trip down the coast would have been futile. I called the surgery the next day to apologise for missing my appointment. The receptionist answered.

"Ah, not to worry, Mr Pearly. Unfortunately Doctor Garside passed away yesterday morning."

It looked like I would be the Pink Panther after all.

Thursday 21st November

I had set the date for my break-in, the evening of this coming Sunday, the only time of the week that the surgery would be guaranteed to be closed all day. I had even cased the joint, as I believe we criminal folk call walking around in the street outside a building pretending to be lost.

I had developed what I considered to be a well-thought out plan. Vince's surgery closes at lunchtime on Saturday and does not reopen until Monday. I would arrange to occupy his last appointment of the day and distract him upon leaving to ensure that he failed to set the alarm. As well as the window in Vince's office there is a small pane in the lavatory looking out into a dark alley that would offer me protection should I make a hash of entry. Once inside, I would find my results and make my escape.

Janet visited in the evening. She was led into the house by Kevin, who wore for the first time a second-hand dinner suit that I had found for €3 in one of the local charity shops. If he was to be my manservant then he could at least dress the part. The suit did not even nearly fit him – it was so tight it appeared to be slicing him in two – but that merely added to my sense of dominance over this brain-dead human sausage.

"Lady Janet of Merla, m'lud!" he barked in what he believed to be an upper class accent.

"Thank you, Kevin."

"Looking very smart, Kevin," said Janet as she ambulated into the interior.

"Ta. Uncle George, but I need a butler name," he said.

"What do you mean, a butler name?"

"Well, Kevin i'n't very butlery, is it? Like Jeeves or summat. But not Jeeves."

"Any suggestions?" I asked.

Janet looked blank.

"Rhodes!" said Kevin excitedly.

"Why Rhodes?"

"He plays for Blackburn. But it's a good butler name, i'n't it?"

"Yes, alright. For your final night you can be Rhodes the butler."

"What do you mean my final night?" he asked sorrowfully.

"Tomorrow you will have been here for two weeks. That was what I agreed with your mother."

"But..."

"It has been fun and everything but it is time for you to leave."

"But I want to stay," Kevin said, his voice cracking with emotion.

"Don't be so mean, George," said Janet.

"I am not being mean. My meagre funds can only stretch so far and I cannot afford another mouth to feed."

"But I have my *X Factor* this weekend," he pleaded.

"You will just have to go for an audition back in England."

"But all the auditions in England have finished," he sobbed.

"That is hardly my fault, is it now?"

"George!"

"Now fetch us a cup of tea, Kevin" I ordered. Kevin did not move. "Rhodes, we require refreshments."

He stomped off sulkily. Janet shook her head.

"You're the talk of the town, George," she said.

"And why is that?"

"Where to begin? Your mystery illness, all of your murders and now your car crash."

"I have told you. I did not kill anyone."

"Yes, but the police suspect you over Scotch Tony. It's only a matter of time before they link you to Margaret and Not Gay Alan's death."

"Who says they are even dead? They are just missing."

"They've found their bodies. Margaret's was up in the mountains and Alan's was in an orchard on the edge of Manzano. He'd been battered with a rock."

Kevin's head emerged from the kitchen.

"That bar we was at was near an orchard," he said, before retreating to his tea-making.

This was not looking good.

"I've brought you something," she said. "Here." She handed me a paper package tied up with string. "It's just a little something I made for you."

"A surprise," I said. "I like surprises."

I tugged at the string and the package fell open. Inside was some black cloth.

"It's your cat burglar suit."

"Ah."

"I used to make all my ex-husbands' outfits."

Oh, the vagaries of the spoken word!

"Where is the apostrophe in that sentence?"

"Eh?"

"Is it 'husband' apostrophe 's' or 'husbands' apostrophe?"

"What are you on about?"

"How many ex-husbands? One or many?"

"Many. Well, five."

"That *is* many, i'n't it, uncle George?" said Kevin, returning from the kitchen empty-handed. "Soz," he said. "I couldn't be arsed to make you any tea if you're chuckin' us out tomorrow."

"Five ex-husbands?" I asked.

"Yes," she replied, sounding slightly guilty.

"And you made criminal outfits for them all?"

"Pretty much."

"Was all your husbands dodgy, Janet?" asked Kevin, his eyes full of wonder.

"Well, yes. They were nice though. Well, some of them were. Well, one of them was."

"Is this a subject on which you would care to enlighten us?"

"I don't mind but it's boring. Let's talk about how you're going to break in."

"What sort of crimes did your husbands commit?" I asked.

"Robbing mostly. One or two were a bit violent."

I did not want to become involved with a woman who was involved with a psychopathic ex-partner ready to slit the throat of any man who touched her.

"Do they still contact you?"

"Nah, I haven't seen any of them for years. Three are dead and the other two got remarried."

"To each other?" asked Kevin.

"No," replied Janet.

"Idiot," I said. "So they have moved on?"

"S'pose."

"And they would deem it acceptable if you were to find a new mate?"

"George, you talk like you're from the nineteenth century."

"He is," said Kevin with a self-satisfied guffaw.

"Hang on a minute. How did they die?"

"They were criminals. Criminals die. Are you going to try on your outfit?" she asked.

"Yeah, uncle George. Try it on."

"I am not a fashion model," I said, but a tingle of excitement crept up my spine at the thought of what was to come. I would steal what was rightfully mine and then claim the buxom Janet as my prize and become her sixth dangerous husband. I picked up the package and headed to the bedroom. Three minutes later I returned.

"Wow," said Janet.

"Yeah, wow, uncle George," repeated Kevin sarcastically. "You look like the Milk Tray Man on hunger strike." He started to sing. "And they painted matchstick men 'n' matchstick cats 'n' dogs..."

"Shut up," I said.

"You could do with a little development in the upper body, George," said Janet.

"Look, I am not Bruce Willis. I never pretended to be. I am just going to steal my medical records so that you will sleep with me. That is all."

It was rash, I know, but it was spat out without a thought for the sentiment behind it.

"Oh, you are, are you?"

"I am sorry, I am..."

"So you steal a piece of paper and then I go all weak at the knees, open my legs and welcome you inside, do I?"

"Probably not now, no."

"No. You're right!"

"Uncle George, you have no idea how to talk to t' ladies, does he, Janet?"

"No, he doesn't, Kevin."

"I am sorry. It is just...I am attracted to you."

"Really?"

"Yes, ever since I saw you hanging out your knickers."

"My knickers?"

"Yes."

"Yeah," said Kevin. "He even wrote a poem about yer pants."

Janet's face wrinkled.

"Is that true?" she asked.

"Erm, yes," I said. "It was not very good."

"It were shit," said Kevin.

Janet and I both looked at the ground and shuffled our feet. I would have to get some other footwear. These brown brogues clashed terribly with my black outfit.

"This is awkward," she said. "I should leave."

She got up.

"Please stay," I pleaded.

She made for the exit.

"Soz, m'lady, that's my job."

Rhodes the butler sprang into action and opened the door for her.

"Lady Janet of Merla is departin' the buildin'!" he shouted.

"Good luck with the break-in, George," she said.

"Thank you," I said sadly.

She looked at me with a determined stare.

"Don't do it for me, George. Do it for yourself."

She gave a half-smile and then she was gone.

"That went well," said Kevin with an enormous grin.

It was hard to determine whether he was being sarcastic or not.

"Oh shut up, you silly bastard."

Friday 22nd November

"Hello," said the voice. "Is that George Pearly?"

"Who is calling please?"

"It's Larry Baker from Gracefield's Funeral Directors. I'm calling to inform you of the funeral of Mary Bamford née Pearly, your sister, I believe."

"Yes, that is correct." The police had obviously completed their investigations. "So what did the post mortem reveal?"

"The verdict was death by misadventure."

"What does that mean?"

"I'm sorry. I don't have any more details than that. I'm just calling to let you know the funeral will take place this Monday at 11am at Blackburn Crematorium."

Kevin wandered in from the bathroom as I completed the phone call.

"Bloody 'ell," he said. "Why didn't you stop him doin' that?"

He ripped his running shoe from Ambrose's slavering, gummy hold and sat on the edge of the uncomfortable sofa trying to shape it back into something reminiscent of a foot.

"Your mother will be buried on Monday," I said. "I trust you will be attending the funeral."

"No," he said resolutely.

"And why not?"

"It's my audition this weekend, uncle George."

"Your audition?"

"*X Factor*. Remember?"

"What is more important? Entering a talent show or

paying your final respects to your mother?"

"That's easy, uncle George. T' talent show."

"But, but..."

"She's dead."

"I know she is dead."

"She's not in heaven lookin' down on me, is she, uncle George?"

"No, she is not."

"She's gone. Whatever me mum was – doddery old duffer or game show host – she's gone."

"Yes."

"She's not in that coffin, is she? In that coffin is just some bones 'n' stuff. Some stuff that ain't me mum no more."

"True. But I am surprised, and slightly amazed, that you take such a naturalistic view of death."

"Eh?"

"Saying that your mother, the woman who raised you, is no longer really inside her coffin."

"No, she's not in t' coffin," he said. "Nah, it's obvious. She's a ghost, i'n't she?"

"Ah."

"She can be anywhere she wants. So I can pay me last respects all t' same from here as I can from Blackburn."

"I suppose so."

"And I'll pay me last respects by singin' 'Staying Alive' by the Bee Gees."

"Is that not an inappropriate choice of song given the circumstances?"

"I'll let Simon Cowell be t' judge o' that, uncle George."

"You will not meet Simon Cowell. You will be singing to a lacky unless someone decides you are worthy of a television appearance."

"Eh?"

"Do you think those millionaire judges sit through

hundreds of thousands of auditions?"

"Yeah."

"They do not. They have people who perform that desperate task on their behalf."

"Really?" he said, momentarily crushed. "You mean I won't get to meet Cheryl Cole?"

"Who?"

"I was gonna see if she wanted to be me girlfriend." He stared out of the window for a moment, his thoughts elsewhere. "So are *you* goin'?"

"Where?"

"To t' funeral?"

"Of course."

"Even though me mum i'n't in that box?"

"Yes. It is the proper thing to do."

"When is it again?"

"Monday morning."

"So I can stay a bit longer?" he asked.

"No."

"Who's gonna look after Ambrose?"

He had a point. It was difficult to see how he could do any more harm here and if he stayed for the weekend it would be cheaper than placing Ambrose in kennels. Besides, the kennels around here had a bad reputation. I had heard a rumour that, such were the poor conditions, a Labrador had recently hung itself.

"Yes, you can stay."

"Wha-hey! Thank you, uncle George!"

"But only until I come back."

"Whatever. So when are ya flyin'?"

"I will travel on Sunday."

"Ah," he said knowingly, waving a snaking finger. "I know what you're up to."

"What, pray tell, am I up to?"

"You're just tryin' to get out o' breakin' into Doctor Vince's surgery."

"Look, Kevin, if I did not want to break into his surgery I would not do so."

Kevin looked doubtful. He was correct though, god damn it. I did not want to break in and the funeral would give me valuable stalling time.

"It will give me a chance to catch up with the rest of the family," I said.

"You hate t' rest of t' family."

That was mostly true.

"You know uncle Richard'll be there?"

"I assume so."

I felt a shadow pass over my non-existent soul.

"And Mabel and Gladys?"

"Oh god, I had forgotten about those two."

"And Albert Lovelace."

"Is that old cretin still alive? Well, then, it sounds like I will have a whale of a time."

A thought flashed across Kevin's face resulting in a smirk.

"You won't have a whale," Kevin said, obviously cueing up a joke. "You'll have a – wait for it! – damp squid."

He chuckled heartily to himself.

"It is a squib," I said, stony-faced.

"It's a squid, uncle George."

"Squib."

"Ah, uncle George. You know nuffin'."

These arguments were futile. Only the other day I had corrected him when he asked for 'a bockle of pop'. He would not have it that 'bottle' contained 't's. Even showing him the dictionary entry was not enough to persuade him of his mistake. He merely claimed it to be a printing error.

"Why d'you hate all our family, uncle George?"

"I do not hate them all. I did not hate Mary."

"But you never saw her."

"I did."

"OK, when was t' last time you saw her then?"

I thought about this deeply. Mmm, it was indeed a considerable time ago.

"We were in New York together on September the eleventh."

Kevin sat there, gawping. He raised his podgy arm, pointing an accusatory finger.

"No, you fool, we did not carry out the bombings."

"There's summat very dodgy 'bout you, uncle George. Wherever you are, there allus seems to be trouble." And then, like a six year-old child with ADHD, he jumped to his feet. "D'ya fancy a bockle o' beer?"

Thankfully, I thought, he will be gone soon.

Saturday 23rd November

I had not been back to the UK since Marjorie and I moved here in 2005. I had very nearly been tempted to return in 2007 when my son Edward got married to that traveller girl, but since he had left home aged twenty-two claiming that he would rather "eat shit" than spend one more minute in my company I assumed that my presence was surplus to requirements. I contemplated a reconciliatory meeting where I would present as an ice-breaking gift a comedy wedding cake that I myself had baked that consisted primarily of dog faeces but Marjorie counselled against it fearing that it may have been interpreted incorrectly. Besides, she did not want to waste a full bag of sugar on a joke when she could eat it by the spoonful watching Strictly Come Dancing instead. In the end she went to the festivities on her own. Edward only learnt of my non-appearance during the ceremony itself, causing him to break down in tears at the "blatant and typical disregard for his own son's happiness", which caused a chain reaction of misery amongst the entire congregation resulting in hysterical wailing throughout the whole church. Apparently, without even interacting with the proceedings in the slightest, I had ruined his big day. As luck would have it, the newly-weds were divorced within six months, although, according to Edward, the blame for this mishap also lay squarely at my feet. There has not been a single episode in his life for which he has taken responsibility rather than shift the burden towards me. As far as I can recall, the only instance for which he was justified in his accusations was when I accidentally killed his beloved pet rabbit, Mr Fluff, whilst performing an ill-advised magic trick during Christmas lunch in 1979. I made rather a mess.

Times and technology had moved on since 2005. The only travel agent in town had closed down three years ago, pummelled out of business by the brute force of the internet. I would have much preferred to interact with a human in my procurement of a flight ticket but instead I visited the web page of the newly formed and recently successful budget airline, LibraAir. As you probably know, they operate a unique and fiendishly complicated pricing model. The company weighs your luggage at check-in as well as your body and hand baggage at the gate and this is multiplied by a per kilogram-mile factor. The less that you and your baggage weigh, the cheaper is your flight. This pricing structure has resulted in passengers resorting to crash diets in the weeks running up to their flights. One passenger flying to Istanbul actually starved himself to death. LibraAir has also had to implement a strict No Nudity policy as passengers were arriving at the airport in nothing but a pair of Speedos in order to achieve the cheapest possible pricing.

At their current rate of £0.00023 kilogram-per-mile I

completed the transaction with an estimated price of £55 for a return trip to Manchester with my seventy kilogram frame and five kilograms of luggage. A bargain!

"Whatcha doin', uncle George?" said Kevin emerging from a winter sunbathing session on the terrace, grey sweat dribbling down his porcine flesh.

"I am printing out my boarding card for tomorrow."

"I betchave done it wrong."

"No, I have not."

"Let's see then."

He raced towards the printer and grabbed the sheet as it emerged. He looked at it quizzically.

"See!" I said smugly.

"I thought t' funeral was this Monday," he said.

"It is."

"Monday t' 25th November?"

"Yes."

"But you've booked it for December, you wally."

"Do not be ridiculous!"

He folded the ticket into a paper aeroplane and threw it towards me. Its sharp nose cone collided painfully with my Adam's apple. I unfolded the paper and perused its contents.

"Damn!" I yelled upon seeing my error.

"Haaaaa ha!" wailed Kevin, demonstrating his maturity. "Do ya want me to do it for ya?"

"No, I do not."

Back on the LibraAir web site I discovered that corrections were only possible upon payment of a £300 Amendment Fee, the most blatant profiteering. My rage was compounded when I discovered that the kilogram-per-mile rate for flights this weekend was £0.00132 meaning that my new flight's estimated cost would be £296. It looked like I would be living on rice and beans after all for my final weeks upon my return. Maybe I could lop off all unnecessary limbs between now and departure.

Each kilogram saved would reduce the cost of my flight by nearly £4. I would pack as lightly as humanly possible. I was flying out on Sunday and returning on the Tuesday. Clearly for such a short trip I would not need a change of clothing. Also my teeth would survive without a brushing for a brief journey such as this one. It became clear to me that, wallet aside, I did not need to carry anything at all. Normally I would take a book with me to counteract the tedium of three hours squeezed into a battery cage surrounded by plebeians, perhaps a copy of something by Hegel or something lighter like Heidegger, but on this occasion I would have to be content reading and re-reading the instructions on the vomit bag. At least it would be more entertaining than Heidegger.

I looked at my wardrobe. The dark suit that I would normally wear for such a serious occasion was far too heavy. I selected a simple black, cotton shirt and black, lightweight slacks from which I removed the belt. I would wear my dark canvas shoes as a cost-saving option instead of my heavier brogues. I calculated that by my cunning choice of outfit I have shaved £1.17 from the cost of my ticket.

"You wanna be careful if you're flyin' with LibraAir," Kevin said, after I had selected my clothing.

"And why is that?" I asked.

"There was an English bloke flyin' wi' 'em from Barcelona last week. He'd made all o' t' cuffs 'n' collars o' his clothes airtight and then filled 'em with hydrogen to make himsel' lighter."

"That did not happen."

"It did. It were in t' Sport. Anyway he backed into a fella wi' a ciggie. Poof!"

He demonstrated a giant explosion with the full extent of his acting ability.

"I will bear that in mind."

This was clearly an invention of Kevin's over-active imagination.

"It were worse for t' fella next to him. Blew his cock off."

"Really? Well, such an injury would save me a pound or two and, besides, it would appear that I no longer have any need for mine."

Sunday 24th November

"You are aware that this is highly illegal?" I said.

"No, it ain't," replied Bullshit Phil.

"Yes, it is. You have no insurance to do this sort of journey."

"It's just two mates driving to the airport together."

"No, it is not."

"Me and my best mate George," he said.

"If we are 'mates' then why did I pay you fifty euros?"

"To cover me costs."

"It does not cost fifty euros in petrol to get to Malaga Airport."

"And to smooth over some other considerations."

"Like what?"

"Like having to listen to your bleedin' whinging. Zip it, professor."

For the hour long ride to the airport I had finally felt it necessary to engage Phil in a topic of conversation other than his exploits in Afghanistan, his covert espionage work against the Stasi and his illicit and ultimately child-bearing tryst with Carol Vorderman. We finally approached the terminal.

"Right, prof, we've gotta do this a bit sharpish."

"What do you mean?"

"If those taxi drivers recognize my reg I've got a massive problemo."

"For heaven's sake, how often do you do this trip?"

"Three or four times a week. I'm just saying I can't stop."

"You *are* going to stop."

"No, I'm not. I'll slow down but you've gotta jump out."

"I will do no such thing."

"Then it looks like you're coming back to Merla with me. It's another fifty euros if I have to bring you back from the airport as well."

Phil decided it was safer to drop me at Arrivals. We turned the corner into the covered section of the airport. Several taxis were parked up ahead among the tour coaches and throngs of passengers pushing trolleys piled high with suitcases. Clearly this bunch of tourists had not arrived by LibraAir.

"I thought you were going to slow down."

"I have slowed down. Jump out."

"It is too fast," I said breathlessly.

I opened the door slightly and saw the tarmac flashing beneath the car.

"Jump now!"

"It is too..."

Phil gave me a shove and I was bundled out of the open door, tumbling awkwardly, landing with a jolt and rolling painfully on the oily tarmac.

My dramatic entrance had not gone unnoticed. Two taxi drivers standing by their cars stared hard in Phil's direction and had a heated exchange with one another before jumping into their vehicles and racing after him.

I stood up and brushed myself down. I had a small tear in the right elbow of my shirt and a larger hole in the left knee of my slacks. I held myself high and strolled into the terminal building. I could hear the sniggers of lesser creatures as I passed by but chose to ignore them.

Because of the other items on Phil's daily schedule (i.e. having to be in the pub by noon and inebriated by twenty past) he had dropped me off around eleven despite my flight not being until half past five. Still, he was cheaper than a taxi. It was going to be an interminably long day.

Normally I would have packed a home-made snack – the sandwiches at Malaga Airport are hellishly expensive – but in an attempt to save every last penny with LibraAir I had decided that today would essentially be a day of fasting. I had not eaten a thing since buying the ticket last night.

I sat in a comfortable seat considering how I would fill the next six hours. I bought a cheap biro with the last of my change – less weight for the flight – and found an abandoned newspaper containing advertisements with large amounts of white space that I filled with poetry. If I am being honest, what I produced was of little value. My mind was distracted by the funeral, my clumsy conversation with Janet, the impending surgery break-in, my implication in several murders and my imminent and mysterious death. Many artists would argue that turmoil produces their best work. I prefer silence, comfortable slippers, a large glass of fine whisky and the warming presence of my little Ambrose.

My knee was beginning to smart. Looking at the wound I realised that it needed to be cleaned and covered. It was still bleeding profusely and tiny pieces of gravel were embedded in my leg. I needed to wash my knee and apply a plaster. I got up from my seat to visit the airport's chemist shop. I was suddenly light-headed, obviously a result of my lack of food. I grasped at a nearby pillar until proprioception returned.

"99 cents, *caballero*," said the sweet Spanish till girl after she had electronically scanned my small box of plasters. I fished inside my pocket but knew it was devoid of change. I opened my wallet. All it contained was a single, bright green one hundred euro note.

"I am sorry," I said, as I handed it to her.

She raised her eyebrows to ask whether I had anything

smaller. I shook my head. She prodded around in the drawer of her till. I noticed that there were no notes of any kind.

"Man come take..." she trailed off.

Her English was not up to the information that she wanted to relay. Then she seemed to have a brainwave and reached down to a cardboard box beneath her knees. She pulled out a bag of coins. For the next five minutes she counted out ninety-nine one euro pieces and handed them to me.

"*Lo siento,*" she said. Despite splitting them evenly I looked like I had a large rock in each pocket and wished I had not forsaken my belt as the enormous mass of metal attempted to expose my briefs.

*

I had already been in the airport for several eternities. I am sure that time operates differently within such a building. A budding Einstein should do a PhD on the matter. However, finally, with only an hour before my flight, I passed through security, an event that lightened the otherwise joyless existence of the staff as I unloaded handfuls of coins into the plastic tray bound for the X-ray machine.

Now was the moment of truth. I approached the passport desk. I was not supposed to leave the country. Would the police have put me on a stop list? I handed my burgundy pass to the bored-looking Spanish official. He scanned it, looked me in the eye and nodded. I was through. The Spanish police are no match for such a criminal mastermind.

The flight was due to board soon. I stood in the queue behind a pretty British girl holding a baby.

"He is a cute, little thing," I offered.

"She," she replied.

"What?" I asked.

"She's a she."

I pulled a face.

"Looks like a he," I said.

"Well, she's not."

"He has a moustache," I said, pointing at a large, dark brown patch that covered the infant's top lip.

"That's a birthmark," the woman replied.

I looked more closely. Jesus, what had I said?

"Oh, I am sorry. Very sorry," I said guiltily.

"It's alright."

"No, really."

"Forget it."

She struggled awkwardly with her baggage.

"Here, let me take that for you," I said.

I held out my hand to make amends for my previous faux pas.

"Thank you."

She gave me the surprisingly heavy case.

"Next!" called a woman on the gate. The young girl stepped forward, stood on LibraAir's official scales, her weight was noted and she disappeared through the gate.

"Hey, your bag!" I called.

She was gone. I put the bag on the ground. I am no one's patsy. So what if it may have contained vital, life-saving medicine for her weird baby. An early death would be a blessing for such an accursed creature.

"Next!"

I stepped forward.

"What are you doing, sir?" asked the LibraAir official.

"What do you mean?"

"Your bag. You must be weighed with your bag."

"It is not my bag."

"Then whose is it?"

"It belongs to the lady who just went through the gate."

"Then why didn't she take it?"

"She gave it to me."

"And aren't you going to take it through for her?"

"No."

"Sir, if you leave a bag here unattended then I will be forced to call security."

"Call security then."

"And they will in all likelihood remove you from this flight in order to interview you."

"This is fucking nonsense," I said, grasping my forehead.

A male member of staff leaned forward.

"We do not tolerate any abuse of our staff. I suggest you apologise."

"I am sorry."

I was not sorry, not sorry in the slightest.

"Now pick up the bag, sir." I did as I was told. "My, that *does* look heavy," she said.

"Is there not an upper weight restriction?" I asked, hoping that they would refuse the bag on a technicality.

"Not here, sir. LibraAir loves heavy luggage!"

I winced.

"Stand on the scale, please, sir" she said before reading the digital output.

"Ninety-five kilos, Sammy," said the woman to her assistant. My heart sank. Between the metal in my pockets and my kindness to this confidence trickster and her mutant child this flight had cost over £400. I was not happy.

Monday 25th November

I woke up in a strange bed. Had I used my devilish charm to worthwhile effect last night after arriving in Manchester? My eyes slowly focussed on their unfamiliar surroundings. In the room there was an attractive middle-aged woman dressed as a nurse. A uniform? Had we been playing saucy games, my lover and I?

"Who are you?" I asked, immediately regretting my question. If we had indeed made the beast with two bad backs last night this approach to her interrogation was sure to discourage further intercourse.

"Ah, that's better, Mr Pearly. Back in the land of the living? You're in Manchester General," she replied.

"What?" I was shocked. "You are really a nurse?"

"Of course. Why do you think I'm dressed like this? I'm not modelling for Ann Summers, y'know," she said, cackling a hideous, Sid Jamesesque laugh. She approached me, tickled my chin and said in a soppy voice, "Did you fink I was your girlfwiend?"

"Do not be ridiculous!" I slapped her hand away as she cackled some more. "Silly girl!" Why am I mocked wherever I go? "What am I doing here?" I felt a natural compulsion to rub my forehead. "Ouch!"

It was tender in the extreme.

"It seems you took a tumble, dearie. Apparently you were at the airport waiting for the bus into town. It arrived, you stood up and then you just went over."

"Ah, low blood pressure."

"Yes, it was very low."

"I had nothing to eat all day."

"I see. Flying with LibraAir, were you? We get two or three like you every day since they started. They should be banned."

"But everything is alright, is it? I mean, with me, my head? I have a funeral to go to."

I looked at my watch. It was eight o'clock. I still had time to get there.

"Yeah, you're just a bit bruised, that's all."

"So I can go now?"

"Let me have a word with the doctor."

She disappeared.

I waited, and waited. After half an hour I arose on wobbly legs to look for her. I found her in the staff area chatting to two other nurses whilst dunking a Hob Nob into a plastic cup of coffee.

"I need to leave," I said urgently.

"Doctor will be with you in a minute, dearie," she said.

"I need to leave now."

"Just a minute. He's doing his rounds."

"Please can I have my clothes?"

"You sure you want 'em? They're a bit tatty."

"They are all that I have."

"I can let you have something from Lost Property if you like, dearie."

"No. Definitely not!"

"Alrighty. You can have them just as soon as the doctor has seen you."

Needless to say the doctor did not arrive until a quarter to ten. He shone a light in my eyes, said, "Yup, that'll do" in a East African accent and allowed me to be released into the wild.

I raced through the doors of the hospital's reception area to a row of waiting taxi cabs. My plan had been a leisurely train ride into Blackburn but there was now no time for that. I opened the door of the first car in the queue and leapt into the back of the cab.

"Where to, mate?" asked the driver.

"Blackburn."

He sucked air in through his teeth.

"S'gonna be sixty quid for that."

"Whatever. Just go."

"And I'll need to see the spondulicks up front. You look a bit rough if I'm honest, mate."

"Whatever do you mean?"

I caught a glimpse of myself in the rear view mirror. Two

purple-black eyes stared back at me. Add to this the tattered slacks and shirt and I too would have been wary of me. I showed him the contents of my wallet – I had got enough from a cash machine at the airport upon arrival – and he drove off.

I sat in the back and closed my eyes. The car's rhythmic trundle was like an anaesthetic. I think I nodded off for a few minutes.

"Always like it this time of year. Very Christmassy. My mum and dad used to take us there as kiddies."

"To where?"

"Blackpool," he replied. I had a deep sense of unease.

"Why are you talking to me about Blackpool?"

"'Cos that's where we're going."

"I said Blackburn, you idiot!"

"You definitely said Blackpool. And don't get shirty wi' me, mate, or I'll dump you right here on the bleedin' motorway."

"Ah, Christ, Blackburn! Take me to Blackburn!"

*

I arrived at Blackburn Crematorium at a quarter past eleven, eighty pounds poorer.

"You wanna speak more clearer next time, mate," the taxi driver said as he sped off.

I galloped through the main doors and located the hall in which the ceremony was taking place. Grabbing the handles of the double doors with all ten fingers I flung them open to be greeted by forty faces. The congregation were all on the verge of departing the now completed event. Upon seeing my bruised and battered visage the woman closest to the door screamed lustily, a second fainted and a sharp-dressed man whose face I had not seen leapt on top of me and started to pummel me. I curled up into a protective ball.

"Stop that!" I said. "Stop that at once! I am here for the

funeral." The man continued his assault. "It is me, George. Mary's brother."

The man stopped hitting me. He disengaged himself from my back. I unfurled myself and stood up to my full height.

"Ah, Richard," I said curtly. "Thank you for the beating."

"You're late. Still, arrived just in time for the wake. You can always sniff out the booze, eh, George?"

"I wanted to pay my respects."

"Well, it's the thought that counts."

"You will not believe the trouble that I have endured to get here."

"To get here late," he said bitterly.

I shrugged my shoulders.

"You certainly look a mess," he said.

"C'mon, you two, let's get a drink," said Celia, Richard's wife. I have no idea what an attractive woman like her could see in this pompous buffoon.

*

I stood at the bar alone and took a long slurp of creamy Old Speckled Hen.

"Hellooooo, George. How's ya doin'?" sang a familiar voice.

"Yes, hello, Albert. Long time no see."

Albert Lovelace is the most boring man in the world and yet he is entirely unaware of this accolade. He is older than Hades and will no doubt be visiting the place soon enough. No one knows his exact age but most suspect it requires at least four numbers to transcribe.

"I've got one for ya, George."

"Oh, goody," I said coldly.

"What d'ya call a man with a paper bag on his head?"

"If it prevents inane conversations like this one then I would say 'lucky'."

"Russell!" he beamed.

"Yes."

"Geddit?"

"Of course."

"Rustle like paper and like Russell the name."

"Yes, I understand. Are you not aware, Albert, that when you explain the mechanics of a joke it tends to lose some of its inexplicable magic?"

"Suit yourself, you sarky sod."

I walked away from the bar with my pint in hand. I was quickly pounced upon by Mabel and Gladys. Mabel and Gladys are an interesting pair, Mabel the doe-eyed sap and Gladys the sabre-toothed tiger. Mabel employed the overuse of initial vowel sounds so beloved of Lancastrian septuagenarians.

"Eeeeee, George. It's been a while," said Mabel.

"Yes, I am a captive of the Costa del Sol."

"Oooooo, I bet it's nice."

"It is awful."

"Eeeeee, geddawaywithya," she said, slapping my stomach. "Do you get many visitors, George?"

"It is not allowed in my rental contract," I lied.

It is amazing how popular one becomes when one resides in a country with actual sunshine. So I have heard.

"Oooooo," said Mabel, disappointed. "Rental, eh? Not doing so good?"

"Things could be better."

Gladys was suddenly interested.

"Suppose you're hoping for a slice of the pie?" she snarled.

"What pie?"

"Mary's money."

"Of course he is," said Richard, butting in. "Hasn't seen her in years. She dies and he turns up with his begging bowl."

"I am not here for any money. I..."

"How's the poetry world, George?" Richard said.

"So so."

"Shame, shame," he said, shaking his head sadly.

He left a conscious silence to tempt me to return the question. I took the bait.

"And how is it for you, Richard?"

"Fabulous!" He clapped his hands together, smiling angelically. "My twenty-fifth collection is published next week. And" – he leaned forward conspiratorially – "there's talk, some of which includes words like 'laureate'."

Bastard.

"Well, I am sure that will be lovely for you, spending eight hours a day composing dirty limericks for Prince Philip," I said.

"It's not like that and you know it."

Inspiration hit. I cleared my throat and adopted the pose of an orator.

"Dear Philip, it feels like each week,
There's a gaff ev'ry time that you speak,
But you've nothing to fear,
The Queen wants you near,
'Cause the saucy old minx likes it Greek."

"You despicable shit," said Richard, turning on one heel and marching away.

"Eeeeee, that's clever," said Mabel.

"Where's Kevin?" roared Gladys.

"He is paying his respects in his own way."

"Should be here. It's his own mum."

"What actually happened to Mary, Gladys?" I asked.

Gladys raised a lip into an impressive sneer.

"Didn't you hear? Reckon she was hosting *It's A Knockout* in her bathroom. Musta dropped the mike or something. Electrocuted, the silly bitch."

"Eeeeee, can you write a limerick about that?" asked Mabel without a hint of sarcasm.

Tuesday 26th November

I arrived home at six in the evening, eight hours after I had landed, via a patchwork of buses. I did not want to risk further damage to my fragile bones by hurling myself through Bullshit Phil's passenger window as he screamed through Arrivals at seventy miles an hour.

During a long bus ride with which to contemplate my predicament I had come to an important conclusion. I was not dying. The mysterious symptoms that Doctor Vince had forecast had not appeared. In fact, I had never felt fitter. The man is a quack.

I knocked on my own front door but there was no answer. I had left my only key with Kevin. Where could he be? I gave a quick rap on Janet's door but she was either out or ignoring me, as she probably should have done. I sat on my little wall and waited, not really knowing what for. An hour later my front door creaked open and a grey blancmange with the eyes of a turtle peered out, its naked shoulders evidence that my dogsitter had once again reverted to living in his underpants.

"Where the hell have you been?" I yelled.

"Oh, it's you, uncle George. I thought I heard a noise a while back. Soz. I was in t' bathroom."

I stepped into the living room and gasped in horror. It appeared that my dwelling had recently been host to a wrestling tournament in which the pugilists were first smeared in gateau and diesel oil.

"Soz about the mess, uncle George," Kevin said.

There was despondency in his reedy voice.

"Yes, you will be. Where is Rhodes the butler when you

need him?"

"Rhodes is dead."

"Clean this mess up, man!"

"I decided to kill him off."

"Come on! I do not expect to come home to this sort of thing."

Then he burst into tears.

"And put some bloody clothes on! What are you crying for? Man up!"

Kevin collapsed on to the sofa, his pudding face buried in his hands, and wept inconsolably. I came to the conclusion that he had been far from victorious at his silly *X Factor* audition.

"I thought I 'ad a good back story," he wailed.

"A what?"

"A back story. You need a back story. Dead kids and stuff."

I was none the wiser.

"Why do you need dead children?" I asked.

"To make people like you."

No. I was still clueless.

"So what was your, er, back story?" I asked.

"Y'know, me mum an' all that. And you."

"What about me?"

"You're dying."

"Am I? It does not feel like it. I wish it would just hurry up and finish me off."

"They said it weren't enough. They said loadsa people have a dead mum. And no bugger gives a stuff 'bout uncles. They said it had to be a brother or a kid or summut, and it had to be somethin' horrible like a tumour. And t' kid had to be good lookin' too. Or else it don't count," he said, his head still encased in his fat fingers.

"Well, not to worry. Not everyone has a back story."

"An' it didn't help that me trainers stank o' piss!"

I looked over to Ambrose, sitting quietly in the corner, and gave him a smile and a subtle salute. He grinned back toothlessly.

"Well, did you not impress them with your vocal talents?"

He looked up quietly, a loop of mucus dangling from his rubber nose. Upon making eye contact, his forehead wrinkled and collapsed and then he bawled open-mouthed, like a baby pterodactyl awaiting delivery of a small, child-shaped snack.

"Ah, so I will not be seeing you on television then?"

His wailing increased in volume.

"Fret not. Fame is not all it is supposed to be. As a poet..."

He suddenly stopped crying and looked me in the eye.

"I *will* be on television," he said, trying to hold himself together.

"I do not understand."

"I *will* be on television," he repeated. "'Cos I'm one of t' freaks!"

He wailed again.

"The freaks? Talk sense, man."

He calmed down.

"Have you never seen it? They laughed at me." He was slightly more collected now. "I 'ad a first audition in front of a normal bloke an' he sez I can definitely be auditioned by t' judges."

"Well, that is excellent, is it not?"

"No, y'see, they put through the good ones but also t' freaks. An' I were a freak. Louis Walsh laughed so hard I think he 'ad a stroke. Doctors had to come in an' everything. It were horrible."

I attempted to find a positive.

"Never mind. Once you return to England perhaps you can get a job and put all this behind you."

He once again looked me squarely in the face and started to bawl.

"I don't wanna go back to England."

"Well, that is a shame because..."

"I wanna stay here wi' you."

"Impossible, I am afraid."

"I'll be yer butler again."

"I am not in need of the services of a manservant."

He grabbed my lapels and looked pleadingly into my eyes.

"Please," he implored me.

"I am sorry that you have had a disappointing weekend but I cannot afford to keep you here."

"Pur-leeeease!"

"I will buy you a ticket for Thursday."

"I don't wanna go."

I looked at this sweaty lump of man-child.

"One thing is for certain. You will not be flying LibraAir."

Wednesday 27th November

"What's up wi' you, uncle George? You look rubbish."

I did not feel well at all. I had been up most of the night vomiting and now I felt deeply congested.

"I have a lump in my throat," I said.

"Is that 'cos I'm goin', uncle George?"

"Definitely not."

Whatever was the matter with me I was certainly not in any mood for a leaving party. That said, I would not let a little thing like imminent death get in my way. I would soldier through as always.

"Have you packed up your things, Kevin?"

"No. I'm hopin' you'll change yer mind."

"Pack up your things, Kevin."

"It won't take long. I've only got a few bits 'n' pieces."

"Tomorrow we go to the airport whether you have luggage or not. Even if I have to take you in those dirty underpants I will take you."

"Perv."

Ever since I had returned and insisted that my contract with Mary had been successfully completed and that Kevin would actually be leaving, our master-slave relationship had disintegrated. He had returned to his slovenly ways.

"You want to take me. Perv," he said.

"Shut up or I will give you a thrashing."

"Perv."

Tomorrow could not come soon enough.

*

It was early evening and I was lying in bed, creased in agony. My heart was thumping and my now empty stomach ached terribly. I remembered Vince's advice to take the pills when the pain eventually arrived. Quack or not, it was worth the possibility that they might offer some relief.

Fortunately a slot in the bathroom's busy schedule had come available. I stumbled inside and opened the medicine cabinet. It contained products that I definitely did not purchase. I lifted out a green tube and read the label. Oh dear god. What is wrong with that boy?

I found the pills at the back of the cabinet. Vince had not informed me about how many I should take and the packaging and instruction sheet were in Spanish. I decided on two of the little, red pills, knocking them back with a glass of cold water, and immediately felt a little better. I closed the cabinet doors and looked at its mirrored front. I ceased my self-pitying slouch and pulled myself up to my full height. Breathing deeply through my nostrils I filled my lungs with life, looked myself in the eyes and said out loud, "I will fight this thing!"

There was a hammering on the bathroom door.

"I need to use the bathroom, uncle George!"

"Wait a minute, boy. I am not done," I shouted.

"Quick, quick," he said, panic-stricken, "it's comin' out."

Oh for the love of god. I flung open the bathroom door. Kevin was hopping around outside like a Native American performing a rain dance.

"Does your cream work?" I asked.

"What cream?"

"The green tube in the cabinet."

"Dunno. Think so. Lemme in."

He pushed his way past me and I was thankfully in the hallway looking at a closed bathroom door before I heard the horror that ensued inside.

Twenty minutes later he reappeared with a grin on his melon head. I was sitting in the comfortable chair. I had become increasingly bored reading Schopenhauer and had turned on the television. An old episode of *Moonlighting* was being repeated. I do not normally watch such drivel but I felt I needed some lessons in the art of love-making.

"That was close," Kevin said.

"I do not want to know."

"Really, *really* close."

"Be quiet."

"Have you ever shat yersel', uncle George?"

I stared hard at him.

"Do I look like a man who has 'shat' himself?"

"I have," he said.

"Filthy creature."

"Loadsa times. Doctor said I've got an unpredictable bowel."

"I do not need to know this."

"You do. If summat happens you know it's not my fault."

"You are leaving tomorrow. Do you plan to soil yourself between now and then?"

"Well, it's a party, i'n't it? I might go a bit mad."
"Thank you for the warning."

*

Two hours later we were in Bar Wars for Kevin's extravaganza of a leaving party, the volume of the music far exceeding the capacity of the party-goers to absorb it. I had expected an attendance of four, five if we counted Trevor the barman. We stood against the bar, looking at the door.

"I'm gonna welcome people as they come in," said Kevin.

"This is not the Oscars, you know. No one is coming."

"There's loads comin'."

"How are there 'loads coming'?"

"This weekend when you was away I came in here a coupla times."

"I told you never to come in here without me."

"Yeah, whatever. Anyroad, I met loadsa new friends. It's nice in here."

I looked around at the décor with its various depictions of Star Wars-based pornography. In the corner I noticed a new painting that I had not seen before. Darth Vader was inserting R2D2 into the capacious rear end of Jabba the Hut. Delightful.

The door opened and in walked three people I only knew vaguely: Thick Rick, Peter the Tool and Whale Mary. As a woman, or maybe two women – it was hard to tell in that dress – Mary was honoured to have been assigned an adjective.

"How do, Kev. How's it hanging?" said Peter, patting the dough ball on his back.

"Oh, it's hangin' alright," Kevin replied with a snigger.

They spoke a language that I could barely comprehend.

Peter looked at me and nodded.

"George," he said, tight-lipped.

"Peter," I replied.

"So Kev," Peter continued, mock-punching him in the

stomach, "how many's coming tonight?"

"Quite a few. There would've been more but uncle George killed some of 'em."

Kevin looked at me and laughed. So that was how it was going to be, was it?

"How come you haven't been arrested yet?" Peter asked.

I remained silent.

Whale Mary opened her chins.

"Police don't care if it's only us English getting knocked off," she said, probably imagining eating an enormous pie.

More people streamed in. There was Jackie and Mad Dave, alcoholic Purple Ronnie with a nose like a bruised strawberry, Billy the Fish, Devon Mark and even Little Tithead. Faces appeared that I had never seen before in my life. I have lived here for ten years and cannot name a single friend. Kevin has been here for two minutes and has a bar full of them. For a moment I considered the possibility that there was something wrong with me but, as the saying goes, only hogs are friends with hogs.

Suddenly the door opened just as the current song stopped playing. A slender figure stood in the shadows. All eyes turned towards the entrance. Silence reigned. And then she stepped forward, like a vision of the perfect woman, or rather an almost perfect woman who had fallen on hard times and turned to prostitution. What was Janet wearing? A short, black leather skirt, fishnet stockings and tall stilettos. Her top was torn and white and did not reach her navel. It hung off her shoulder, clearly displaying a red brazier beneath. She strode across the floor just as a song started to play that contained the frequent line "I Want To Sex You Up". Three more paces and she reached Kevin and planted a firm kiss on his pastry lips, smearing them with her scarlet lipstick.

"I'm going to miss you, little fella," Janet said to him.

Kevin blushed and covered an enormous grin with the

back of his hand.

"Awww," was his eloquent reply.

"George," she said soberly.

"Janet."

I remembered this afternoon's episode of *Moonlighting* and tried to give Janet my most charming Bruce Willis sideways smile. She suddenly looked concerned.

"Are you alright?" she said.

"Yes. Why?"

"God, I thought you were having a stroke or something."

Perhaps it is better if I do not impersonate Bruce Willis ever again. Janet's face changed.

"What's that smell?" she said, sniffing the air. We all emulated her actions.

"Eurgh," said Kevin. "Smells like shite."

"Kevin, did you do what you warned me you might do?" I asked.

"It's not me," he said. "Mine doesn't smell like that."

Kevin and Janet leaned in towards me.

"I think it's you," said Janet with a look of disgust before taking two steps backwards.

"Uncle George's shat himself," sang Kevin with a little too much triumphalism in his voice. "Filthy creature," he added, laughing heartily.

The room took note. The laughter increased and spread from face to face. I leapt into the nearby urine-flavoured bathroom to survey the damage. I had made a mess. How could that have happened?

I frantically tried to clean myself up as well as I could. There was a knock on the bathroom door.

"John, is that you?"

"It is George, Vince."

"Did you take those pills I prescribed?"

"Yes, this afternoon."

I heard an explosion of laughter outside.

"It's a side effect, John. It says so on the instructions. If you can read Spanish."

He walked away, laughing.

My trousers and underpants were ruined. I had even got it on the bottom of my shirt. There was another knock on the door.

"Uncle George, are you alright?" came Kevin's whiny voice.

"No."

"What can I do?"

"Go home and get me a change of clothing."

"Nah, it's started to rain. I'll find summat here."

Two minutes later he knocked again.

"Uncle George?"

"Yes."

"I've got summat for yer. Open the door a bit."

I pulled the door slightly to reveal the flash of a thousand phone cameras, the miserable bastards.

"Leave me alone!" I screamed.

"Here, uncle George."

Kevin passed me two bar towels and then closed the door.

"And what am I supposed to do with these?"

"Wear 'em like a skirt," he shouted through the door. "One at t' front and one at t' back."

"You are a cretin. Get me something more appropriate!" There was no response. "Kevin!"

A song with a thumping bass-line started up outside. At least it drowned out the laughter.

I fashioned the bar towels into a rudimentary skirt, pinching them together at my hips. It was shorter than Janet's. I had become the world's lankiest transvestite. Opening the door was a challenge. Twice I dropped the towels. Eventually I opted for a foolproof plan of inserting my elbow behind the door handle, pressing down firmly whilst pulling it towards me and opening the door with my foot. There was a creak as I exposed myself to the world.

I was standing in a roomful of people wearing nothing but a home-made mini-skirt. The cameras went off again and the laughter increased. People were literally rolling on the floor. Janet approached and put an arm around my bare shoulder.

"It's alright, George, you couldn't help it."

And that is when it happened. The door's self-closing mechanism stole the back half of my makeshift skirt. In an attempt to catch it before it fell, I let go of the front towel, which floated to the floor, leaving me completely naked. Unexpectedly, the laughter suddenly stopped and was replaced by puzzled frowns. Someone switched the music off. A single camera flashed. After a second's shock I grabbed my manhood to shield it from view. The room was deathly silent.

"George," said Janet, with concern in her voice. "Why is your penis green?"

Kevin suddenly howled with laughter, the only one in the room unhorrified.

"You're not s'posed to use that much, uncle George."

"Shut up, Kevin!" I barked.

"That much what?" asked Janet.

"Do not say a word, Kevin!"

"You're only s'posed to use a bit."

Kevin was rocking on a bar stool and slapping himself with merriment.

"What is it?" asked Janet.

"Knob growing cream," said Kevin. "He's got some in his bathroom cabinet."

"You little..."

I could not retrieve the expletive I required.

The room in unison shook their collective heads sadly.

"Uncle George, you're gonna be hung like a camel if

you're not careful," said Kevin through tears.

I defy any man who happens upon a tube of penis enhancing cream in his bathroom cabinet not to try it at least out of curiosity.

"I am going home," I said.

I walked naked towards the exit holding my luminous crotch. The room was silent except for Kevin's hysterical guffawing. I stole a coat hanging on a hook near the door, hurriedly wrapped it around my waist and ran, splashing shamefully through the rain.

Thursday 28th November

My head was pounding when I awoke. I went to the bathroom. The cabinet was a lot emptier now that Kevin had packed up to leave. I looked at the pills that Vince had prescribed and reached for some paracetamol instead.

Unusually Kevin was already awake.

"I told you not to use that computer," I said as I walked into the living room.

"Uncle George, you've gone viral."

"No, I am certain that it is not contagious."

"Eh? No, look at this. You're all over th' internet."

I peered over his shoulder and then looked on in dismay as he played a video of my departure from the pub bathroom, the dropping of the bar towels and my green nether regions. It had been thoughtfully captioned with the title "George Pearly Goes Green". The video finished with an advertisement for Hercules Penis Enhancement Cream. Yes, very damning but hardly a ratings grabber.

"What is that number there?" I asked.

"That's how many people 'ave seen it."

"A hundred and twenty-five million!"

"Yeah, it's a lot, i'n't it?"

"That is twice the population of Britain!"

"Yeah, yer famous, uncle George. You an' yer green willy."

Is it not enough that I am the laughing stock of this town? I should now be ridiculed by the whole world.

Kevin looked up from the computer.

"Has it grown yet?" he said with a snigger.

"Shut up, you fool," I replied, rubbing my head.

"Still ill, uncle George?"

"No, I am fine."

There was silence for a moment.

"Y'know, I could nurse you, uncle George."

"No."

"I could look after you when you get proper ill."

"That is very kind of you. But no. I am not getting 'proper ill' and you are leaving." I looked at my watch. "In thirty minutes."

*

We were approaching the airport.

"If you park on the short stay car park the taxi drivers will not recognise you this time," I said to Bullshit Phil from the passenger seat.

"I ain't scared of 'em. My S.A.S. training an' all that."

"Of course. But park on the car park – I will pay – come in with us. I will ensure that Kevin boards the plane and then we can drive home again without any car chases and without my having to roll around on the tarmac at any point."

"Alright," he said sheepishly.

"You were in th' S.A.S?" said Kevin.

"I can't talk about it."

"For one very good reason," I replied.

Phil shot me an angry look but did not take the bait. He was not acting with his usual bravado. I could see a slight bruising escape from just beneath his sunglasses. The taxi drivers had obviously got their man on our last visit here.

Ten minutes later we were inside the terminal and Kevin had checked in. We stood in Pablo Picasso Airport's vast hangar facing each other.

"Right, well, s'pose I should just go through security now then, uncle George," said Kevin sadly.

"Yes."

Kevin turned to leave. Then he stopped and looked at me with miserable eyes.

"I wanna stay, uncle George."

"I know."

"I've got nuffin' in England. I've got friends here."

I nodded.

"No job, no money, an' no skills to get a job. Nuffin'."

I gave him a look that I hope suggested that he should have applied himself more at school.

"An', uncle George, I've got nowhere to live."

"You can go home until the estate is liquidated."

"An' then what?"

He was close to tears.

"Why can't he stay with you, George?" said Phil. "You ain't got long left anyway."

I stayed silent.

"Well at least chuck him a few quid to tide him over."

"Very well," I said.

My funds were limited but if it would smooth the departure of this fatuous blob I could spare a little.

We walked together to a cash machine, I inserted my card, stabbed in the PIN number and requested one hundred and fifty euros, just enough to seem impressive and yet not enough to prevent him from starving to death in a week or three. The transaction was refused.

"That is odd," I said.

I inserted the card again and this time asked to check my

balance. I nearly collapsed.

"What?" I screamed. "How is that possible?" The account total that should have been around twelve thousand euros now read zero. "What the hell has happened?" I jumped up and down pointlessly. "It is all gone! All gone! I have nothing!"

"Looks like someone's hacked your account, mate," offered Phil.

"Yes, thank you, Einstein!" I punched the cash machine, which drew the attention of the security staff.

Kevin's phone rang.

"Hello, Kevin speakin', how can I help you?" he said in a ridiculous unknowing parody of a call centre phone monkey. "Really?...Yes, please...Wow!...That *is* good news...Yes, OK then, bye...Yes, bye."

He switched the phone off and grinned widely.

Phil and I both looked at him.

"Well, I'll be off then," said Kevin, gesturing towards Security. His mood had lifted considerably.

We continued to view him, our eyes narrowing.

"Quite excitin' goin' on a plane again, i'n't it, uncle George?"

He turned to leave.

"What was that phone call?" I asked.

"Excuse me, *señor*."

I spun around to see a Spanish policeman with an intelligent face, which was a new experience for me.

"Can I see some I.D., señor?"

"What is this?" I asked.

"I.D.?" he repeated.

I presented him with the passport that I always keep in my jacket pocket, the only I.D. that I possess. He looked it over and nodded.

"I thought so," he said. "I recognize you from the

internet."

Kevin sniggered.

"Were you thinking of leaving Spain, señor?"

"Oh, no. My nephew here is returning to the UK."

"Because you know that you are not allowed to leave Spain until we complete our investigations."

"Yes, I know that."

There was a burst of static and muffled Spanish on the policeman's radio. He turned his back on us whilst he attended to it.

"That phone call?" I said to Kevin.

"What about it?" he replied.

"What was it?"

"Oh, well, it seems that mum's left everythin' to me."

The woman had once again demonstrated her insanity.

"How much wonga, Kev?" asked Phil.

"Seven millions," he said with a huge, gormless smile.

The policeman spun around.

"You have just won the lottery, señor?" he said to Kevin.

"No, no, me mum died, sir, and she left me summat."

"My condolences, señor. You must be upset."

"Yeah, it were a bit upsetting. Couldn't bring mesel' to go to t' funeral. But uncle George went instead."

The policeman looked at me wide-eyed. His eyes matched my own.

"And this funeral was in England, señor?"

"Yeah, in Blackburn. Have you ever been? I wouldn't. It's shit."

"And when was this funeral, señor Pearly?"

"Errr..."

"You may as well tell the truth. We can check flight records."

Damn his eyes!

"Last weekend," I said quietly, giving Kevin a glance that

attempted to melt his head.

The policeman said something into his radio. Two police officers appeared from nearby. He unhooked a pair of handcuffs from his belt and held them up in front of me on one finger.

"Turn around, señor Pearly."

I froze. Kevin and Phil looked aghast. Kevin tried to say something.

"Help me, Kevin!" I pleaded as they marched me away. "Help me!"

Kevin looked back, open-mouthed.

I could hear Phil's voice in the distance.

"If I were you I'd abandon the selfish git."

Friday 29th November

It was half five in the evening. All I had been offered to eat since my arrest yesterday morning was a bread roll and a bowl of thin soup. Kevin had evidently followed the advice of Phil and returned home to his millions.

"Welcome, señor Pearly!" hailed the police officer through the bars of my cell, a six foot by six foot space with a tiny bed and a plastic chair. "You are something of a celebrity."

"The green penis incident?"

"Sorry?" He looked confused. "I mean your impressive collection of denuncias. I have never before seen a man denounce so many of his fellow countrymen."

I looked blankly.

"I am Jesús Herrero Herrero, Merla's new chief of police. You cause my men a great deal of work."

"I am simply availing myself of the system your government has installed."

"And now you leave the country when you know you are

not allowed?"

"Yes, but I returned of my own volition."

"That is true."

"And I went to attend the funeral of my own sister, extenuating circumstances I am sure you agree."

"Hmm," he said ponderously. "You have a visitor."

"I do not suppose that it is a small, greasy man who appears to consist entirely of sausage meat?" I asked, resigned to a negative.

"Yes."

"Really?"

Kevin was foolishly loyal. He had not forsaken his uncle.

Jesús opened a door and in walked Kevin carrying a box.

"I will be outside if you need anything," Jesús said.

"Kevin, Kevin, Kevin, how genuinely lovely to see you."

Kevin appeared to be marginally disturbed by my enthusiasm and then looked around suspiciously, seeming to ensure that no one was watching.

"I've got summat for yer," he said in a whisper.

"Happy birthday to me," I said sarcastically.

He opened the box to reveal its contents, an awkwardly folded binder, which he took out and held carefully from beneath.

"What is that?"

He opened the binder to reveal a deformed bun. He looked at me expectantly, as though I was supposed to know what to do with this object.

"What?" I asked, confused.

He looked deflated.

"I thought you'd be excited," he said.

"Why?"

"It's a cake in a file," he said hopefully.

I thought for a moment and then it dawned upon me.

"I assume that you are taking the piss." I looked at him

and it became evidently clear that he was not. "It is supposed to be a file in a cake. And not that sort of file, you moron."

"Oh." He scratched his slimy forehead. "I wondered why it'd be any use."

"Sorry, you are not a moron."

"I am."

"A bit perhaps. But thank you. And thank you for not leaving me to rot in here."

"S'OK."

He shuffled his feet awkwardly.

"I am feeling much better today," I said.

"Smashin'."

Silence. Conversation through the bars of a cell are like those at hospital bedsides. Everyone feels a need to talk about something, anything, no matter how pointless.

"My money came through, uncle George."

"All of it?"

"Yep!"

"You are a very wealthy man. What will you do with your new-found position of financial power?"

"Dunno. Think I might make a song."

"Good idea," I said.

It was a terrible idea.

"An' become famous," he added.

"Yes, possibly."

"Like you."

"I am not famous."

"Oh yes you are, uncle George. Your vid's now up to four hundred million views. They even showed it on telly last night."

"Dear lord."

I covered my eyes.

"They pixelated your todger. You could still tell it were green though. Has it grown much?

"Shut up, Kevin," I said wearily.

"Mine hasn't. I'm not sure it works."

"Of course it does not work."

There was a full minute of blissful silence.

"Uncle George?"

"Yes," I said impatiently.

"I'm sorry for gettin' you into trouble. Sometimes I just sez things wi'out thinkin'."

"No, it was my own fault. I should not have bothered to attend the funeral."

"You know you're only in here for doin' a runner. You've not bin charged wi' owt else."

"I should be thankful for small mercies."

The conversation took a pleasant turn. Kevin was not quite so fat-headed as normal and the bars that separated us meant that any potential threats of violence on my part carried no weight. Besides, Kevin held all the aces. Until I could reach the bank and find out what had happened to my account I would have to rely on Kevin's charity, a possibility that made me feel decidedly queasy. Back at the house he would no doubt be sleeping in my bed and parading around the living room in his underpants at will, probably now jewel-encrusted underpants rather than the otherwise encrusted ones he previously wore. We talked for over two hours. Jesús seemed to have forgotten about us, or perhaps he was listening in to our conversation to collect any evidence that arose. I looked at my watch. It was eight in the evening. I had been in jail for well over thirty hours. It felt like thirty days.

Kevin sat on a chair finishing his story.

"An' that's why we split up. She said she were jealous o' me, well, of all t' girls lookin' at me. She couldn't handle it. So she left. Next thing I know, she's knocked up by t' newsagent."

"Kevin, sorry to interrupt your heart-breaking tale but did the police officer give any indication of when I should be allowed to leave."

"What? Oh yeah, you can go anytime you like."

"What?" I said.

"I paid yer bail before I came in."

"You...you...So why have we been sitting here talking for the past two and a half hours?"

"Dunno. Thought you liked it. Shall I get 'im t' open t' door?"

"If it is not too much trouble," I said.

Jesús reappeared with a large set of jangling keys. I assume this was merely for effect since the police station only possessed a single cell. The barred door creaked as it opened.

"Señor Pearly, Jorge – you do not mind if I call you Jorge, no? – we are treating you more leniently than we would a man of younger years. But do not run away again. We will return your passport when we are certain of your innocence. And you need to visit the police station once a week until then."

Kevin was on the verge of opening his mouth. I had no idea what incriminations would emerge but it was better not to take the risk.

"Do not say a word, Kevin. Not a word."

Saturday 30th November

I woke up on the sofa with a head banging and throat on fire. I am not dying.

Around midday Kevin surfaced, stretching his jelly arms and rubbing his head with eyes barely open.

"Ahh," he said, yawning widely. "Your bed's comfy."

"Yes, I know."

"These are comfy too," he said, gesturing crotchwards.

I hadn't noticed the new addition to his underpants collection. A yellow sponge-like character in red shorts and a badly drawn squid covered their expanse.

"Y'know, I thought they wouldn't be comfy, 'cos I thought they'd be square pants." He guffawed. "But they're not."

What was the idiot talking about?

"Thought I'd treat mesel'."

"Are you going to spend your entire fortune on underpants?"

He laughed.

"You're silly. Anyroad, big day today, uncle George."

"Yes."

"Have you worked out yer plan?"

"I have."

"I betcha it don't work."

"It will work."

"I betcha it don't."

"It will work, I tell you."

"I betcha..."

"SHUT UP!"

My aching brain did not require the incessant squawking of Kevin's negativity. I swung out a clumsy arm but Kevin ducked.

"I think you could eas'ly kill someone, uncle George."

"Not this again."

"You've got a right temper."

"Yes, well, maybe I shall kill you."

"Nah, I'm safe. You can't kill me. You need me. You need me money."

Such truths are hard to stomach with a head that feels like a military band is marching through it.

"I don't think it'll work," he said. "But I'll help yer."

"No, you will not."

"I will, uncle George."

"Do not go anywhere near Vince's surgery today."

*

I was sitting in the waiting room alone, my 13:55 appointment imminent. I could see the top of Shirley's head behind the tall reception desk. From inside Vince's office I had been able to hear feminine giggles for the last fifteen minutes. His door opened and a fifty year-old woman emerged, flushed and smiling. She looked back into the office, made a telephone of her right hand and mouthed the words "call me" before sniggering and skipping lightly towards Shirley's desk.

"That's fifty euros," Shirley said.

"I'd happily pay double," the woman said, smoothing down her hair.

Vince appeared from his office and leaned with one arm against the frame of its doorway.

"Same time next week, Sandra," he said.

Sandra smirked, blew him a kiss and left. Vince visibly shuddered.

"Who have we next?" Vince asked. He saw me and tutted. "You may as well go home, Shirley. John's not a big one for paying."

Shirley scooped up her belongings wordlessly and had departed the building seven seconds later.

"Right then. Come in, John."

I walked calmly into his office. We both sat down.

"What can I do you for?"

"I just wanted to ask a final time if you would tell me what is the matter with me."

"No can do, John." He peered closely at me. "You don't look too good, John."

"I am fine."

"You're not. Don't fight it, John."

"Right then," I said, and stood up.

"Is that it?"

"Yes."

"No yelling? No threats?"

"No."

"Fair enough." Vince stood up. "Well, that looks like me done for the weekend." He opened his office door. "After you, John."

I walked back into reception and hung around. Vince followed and went behind the reception desk, sorting through some papers scattered upon it. He looked up.

"Sorry, was there something else, John?"

"Have you scheduled anything wonderful for the weekend?" I asked.

Vince looked confused.

"No, not really," he replied suspiciously. "Have you?"

"I am participating in a kind of treasure hunt tomorrow."

"Really?" He collected the papers into a pile, opened a drawer and took out a set of keys. "Well, I'm off."

We walked together towards the exit.

"Where's your treasure hunt then, John?"

"Not many miles from here."

He opened the front door.

"Age before beauty," he said with an extended arm.

Vince followed me out, fiddled with the lock mechanism and pulled the door shut behind him.

Success!

"Oh, hang on a mo," he said. "Forgot the alarm." He unlocked the door, stepped inside and punched some numbers into the keypad on the plastic casing. "Better to be safe than sorry, eh, John? Don't know who's knocking about, do we?" he shouted from inside.

Failure!

I attempted to swallow my disappointment but instead

only managed to start a fit of coughing. Vince reappeared.

"Sounds nasty, John. You should see a doctor," he smirked.

"If only I could find one."

All of my carefully laid plans had come to nothing. Suddenly from around the corner Kevin appeared, licking an ice cream, with a small Spanish boy in tow.

"I didn't know the circus was in town," said Vince, noticing him.

"Hello, uncle George. Everythin' sorted?"

"No, not really," I replied grumpily. "Who is your friend?"

"Dunno," said Kevin, giving me an enormous wink. "He just followed me."

Kevin was clearly acting. It was just a pity that the quality was that of a junior school play.

Vince walked up to a push bike fastened to the railings beside the surgery and started to unlock it.

"Is this yer bike?" said Kevin.

"Obviously," replied Vince. He finished unlocking it and put his keys in his pocket before climbing on to the saddle. "So long, saddos!"

"Oh, I forgot, doctor," said Kevin, still in wooden actor mode. "Can you do me a favour?"

"Probably not."

"I've just used up me inhaler and me other one's in England."

"So?"

"Please can you write me a prescription for one?"

"No."

"Me asthma's really bad."

"Make an appointment for Monday."

"Probably be dead by Monday. That's how me mum died. An' me dad. An' three of me brothers. An' me cocker spaniel."

"Bloody hell," said Vince. "Alright then." He climbed back

off his bike, leant it against the wall, fished out his keys and unlocked the surgery door. "Wait here!" he said.

He disarmed the alarm and disappeared inside.

"What are you doing?" I asked Kevin.

"NOW!" he yelled.

The small Spanish boy grabbed the bike from the wall, leapt on to its saddle and pedalled for his life.

"Vince, Vince," yelled Kevin. "That Spanish lad's nicked yer bike. Quick!"

Vince reappeared with his keys in his hand.

"What?"

"Look, he's halfway down the street," said Kevin, pointing towards the thief.

Vince sprinted after him, turning around after a couple of seconds.

"Just pull the door to. It locks automatically. I'll get this little bastard."

The bicycle disappeared around a corner shortly followed by Vince.

Kevin smiled the smile of a victor.

"Good, eh?"

I was impressed.

"Yes, well done."

He reached for the door handle.

"No, do not shut..." I said.

He pulled the door, closing it with a satisfying click.

"An' that's how you get someone to leave wi'out settin' t' alarm," he smiled with his dumpling arms outstretched.

"Idiot," I said, thumping myself repeatedly on the forehead.

"What?"

"You closed the door."

"Yes. An' th' alarm's not on."

I shook my head.

"We could have simply walked into his office and taken my results."

Kevin thought about this for a moment.

"Oh yeah," he said, rolling his eyes.

"Oh yes," I repeated.

"I didn't think o' that."

"Obviously."

"Still, it's more fun this way, i'n't it?"

"For whom?"

"Fer everyone."

Sunday 1st December

I was standing in the alleyway around the back of Vince's surgery dressed like a stick insect at a funeral. I had crept here under cover of darkness, unseen by anyone. I shone my torch through the surgery's bathroom window. The toilet was directly beneath it and – perfect! – the lid was down.

I covered the entire surface of the glass with thick, brown adhesive tape and then gave the centre a firm tap with a small hammer. The window cracked almost noiselessly. With a long knife I found a crack in the centre of the glass and pierced the tape, sliding the knife to the right until it would go no further. I flipped over the knife and did the same to the left. With my gloved fingers I pressed the lower half of the window, slipping my fingers into the gap that I had made, and pulled out as many taped shards as possible.

"Wow, uncle George. That was cool," said Kevin in his normal day-time, definitely-not-down-a-dark-alleyway-breaking-into-a-building voice.

I flipped around with the speed of a leopard.

"What are you doing here?" I said in a panicked whisper.

"I came to help."

"Go home. And keep your voice down."

"I wanna help. I wanna be t' Pink Panther."

"Go home. This is *my* problem. Or go back to the pub or wherever you have been this evening."

"I've got somethin' to tell yer."

"Go away."

"It's important."

"It can wait."

"Bullshit Phil said..."

"I do not give a solitary fuck was Bullshit Phil said. Disappear!"

"Alright then." He paused. "You sure?"

"Now!"

He shrugged his putty shoulders and wobbled off into the darkness.

I returned to the window, carefully picking out the remaining glass pieces. The frame was now free of skin-piercing danger. It was only two feet square but large enough through which to squeeze my narrow hips. Beneath this new entrance into Vince's surgery I up-ended the black bucket that I had brought with me and stood upon it. I inserted my upper body through the frame, taking my weight on my lower stomach and then I inched my way inside. My fingers reached the lid of the toilet and I steadied myself with my flattened palms. When my knees eventually reached the frame, gravity and the mass of my body collided to spill me on to the bathroom floor with a dull thud. I was inside. I was a burglar. My stomach danced with excitement.

I opened the bathroom door, my torch sending a search light across the otherwise black surgery wall. I padded through the corridor. Perhaps I should have headed directly to Vince's office and to my paperwork but I was inebriated on criminal power. I slunk into reception. Maybe I could find some evidence to assist in Vince's downfall.

Shining my torch on Shirley's desk all I could discover were her knick-knacks – a photograph of a child, a small frog and a mug that said Life's Shit, Have A Coffee. I approached the filing cabinet and opened a couple of drawers but they merely contained old patient invoices. I felt my hand down the back of the drawer and located a stuffed envelope, but this simply held more receipts and – oh, this was interesting – one of the receipts was for three crates of Glenfiddich. I had no idea Vince had such a problem.

I closed the filing cabinet and examined the drawers of the reception desk. The bottom one was labelled Vince's Stuff. I pulled it firmly but it would not give. It was locked. Damn! But I had an idea. I tested the drawer above it. It slid open easily. I removed the drawer from the desk to permit me access to the contents of Vince's special place. I dragged out a handful of papers, placed them on the desk and perched myself on Shirley's chair.

The pile mostly contained love letters from his patients. I tried to read some but this was an unwise action for a man already feeling nauseous. The bottom sheet was not a letter though. It was a list of women's names with a series of numbers next to them. I scanned the torch up to the top of the page to see that the numbers related to column headings.

Oh dear god.

The headings were labelled Breasts, Arse, Legs and Shag Quality. He had developed his own perverse system to objectify the women that he had lured into his seedy bed. I scanned down the list of names. And that is when I saw Janet's name. Janet Hardarce. That was she. To think that a woman of such quality would sink to such depths. I turned the paper over in disgust.

Hmm. How could he treat women as a number? Only the basest creature would stoop so low. Hmm. I wonder...

I turned the page over to view Janet's scores. She

unsurprisingly attained a ten for Shag Quality. I immediately felt disgusted with myself. Hmm, I wonder who scored lowest? I scanned down the list. Oh no. Mandy Keogh, Bullshit Phil's wife. The man is an animal, sleeping with the wives of his friends, even if it is only a half-friend like Bullshit Phil. But Mandy scored a lowly two. That must be difficult for Phil, what with his being an ex-porn star and everything. I perused the list a little longer before remembering I had a job to do. I replaced the papers and the drawer and stood up, accidentally shining my torch towards the main window. It illuminated a pale face staring in.

Shit! I ducked back down under the desk with the torch switched off and waited a few seconds, breathing heavily. I slowly raised my head in the darkness to see if the face was still there. It was. I ducked back down again. The face looked familiar. Chubby cheeks and greasy hair. Oh no. I looked again. The face's owner rapped on the glass. I ran towards the window.

"Kevin, piss off," I said in a loud whisper. "Piss off now!"

He started doing a mime, beckoning me towards him. I shone my torch directly into his eyes, blinding him. He stumbled around and crashed into a lamp post.

Right, finish the job, George, before Kevin gives the game away. I crept towards Vince's office. I creaked open the door and shone the torch inside. The window had its shutters closed. That meant I could turn on the light to search more efficiently for my reward. I flicked the switch as I entered the room, flooding the space with bright light.

"Hello, John."

Vince sat at his desk.

I could not speak. I felt sick.

"Having fun, are we?" he continued. "Do you think I'm some sort of idiot? That inane ploy yesterday. I'm not happy. And that little shit got away with my bike." He picked up his phone, pressed a single button, waited a few seconds and then said, "*Ahora.*"

"You have been waiting for me?" I said.

"Bingo!"

There was silence for a moment.

"Well," I said, "at least I am not an alcoholic."

"Meaning that I am?"

"Three crates of whisky?"

"Presents, John. For my better patients. The ones that pay rather than trying to rob me."

I could not even hold that over him, the bastard.

Within a minute a police car arrived, two hulking officers handcuffed me and led me outside. Kevin emerged from the shadows.

"I tried to tell yer," he whined.

"You knew about this?"

"Yeah, Vince told Bullshit Phil you was up to summat, an' Phil told me."

"Why did you not tell me?"

"You wouldn't listen."

"You should have told me anyway."

"I can't do right fer doin' wrong."

"True."

The officers dragged me towards the rear doors of their car and a hand forced my head inside.

I looked out of the window at Kevin and shook my head. He did his 'Snot My Fault gesture. It *was* his fault. It was very much his fault.

Three minutes later we arrived at the police station. On the desk was Jesús, the police chief.

"Ah, Jorge. Back again? I fear this time you may be inside for a little longer."

Monday 2nd December

I had once thought that existence on the Costa del Sol was an unending stream of tedium. After spending time in a prison cell I believe that the two experiences share many similarities.

The door to the room outside my cell opened and the head of Jesús appeared.

"You have a visitor, Jorge," he said.

The door opened fully and a smiling Kevin appeared.

"Hello, uncle George."

"Yes, hello," I said wearily. "Do you have good news for me?"

"Like what?"

"Have you bailed me out again?"

"Nah, they won't let me."

"What? You mean...you mean I am stuck in here. Why will they not let me out?"

"Dunno. Just said you can't go."

"Well, ask them again, you moron."

"Nah."

"It is your fault that I am in here."

"It's not, is it?"

"Yes!"

"Who broke in t' surgery? Were that me? No, it weren't. They reckon yer gonna get six months fer this. Even if they don't do yer fer all those murders an' all."

"I have told you, I did not murder anybody!"

"Anyroad, I've got yer a present."

"Another cake in a file?"

"No."

"What then?"

"Have a guess."

"Just tell me."

"Have a guess."

"Tell me!"

"Guess."

I gave up.

"You have brought me a book to pass the long hours inside."

"No. Better than that."

"Have you brought me a jumper to keep me warm at night."

"No. Better."

"If I am to spend six months in jail then there is nothing else I could possibly desire."

"Hey, I just 'ad a thought."

"You never forget your first time."

"You'll die in prison, won't yer?"

"I am not dying."

"Then why did yer try to steal yer results?"

"What is this magnificent gift you have brought me?" I said changing the subject.

"I haven't got it wi' me."

"Where is it then?"

"Outside t' house. It's a car."

"A car?"

"But I s'pose it's not much use to yer now, is it?"

"No."

There was silence.

"Are yer gonna say thanks."

"Leave me alone," I cried.

"If yer gonna be like that."

Kevin turned and headed to the door just as it opened.

"Another visitor for you, Jorge. You are a very popular man today."

Kevin stormed out and Vince appeared. He smiled a reptilian smile.

"What's it like inside, John?"

I said nothing.

"You've treated me badly, John. Why did you break into my surgery?"

"You know why."

"Your results? You do not realise that I'm doing this for your own benefit, John. As soon as you know what's wrong with you you'll succumb to the symptoms."

"I have already succumbed to the symptoms. I am nauseous. I have a pounding headache."

"Those are not the symptoms of your condition."

"Are they not?"

"No."

I thought about this for a second.

"See," he continued. "You believed a headache or whatever to be the relevant symptoms and that's why you had them. Now, I would get you out of here, given your condition. Y'know, drop the charges. But there are rumours you've hurt a few people and so while you're behind bars the town is a little safer."

"Yes, I hurt some people, I did." I fell to my knees clutching the bars. "But it was an accident."

"I don't believe you, John."

"It is true," I said, exasperated.

"Then tell me about it, John."

"I cannot."

"Then you stay here."

"Let me out!" I pleaded.

"Sorry, John."

"Is there nothing else I can say that will persuade you to release me?"

"I very much doubt it."

He turned to leave. I suddenly had an idea.

"There may be one thing I can say."

"Try me, John," he said still walking towards the door.

"Mandy Keogh."

He turned, looking ashen.

"What about Mandy Keogh?"

"It would be unfortunate if Bullshit Phil were to discover your tryst, especially with his background as a ninja."

*

"So you are free once again, Jorge," said Jesús.

I was standing by the main desk completing a form with the help of the police chief.

"It would appear so," I said.

"I hear you like to walk in the mountains."

"Who told you that?"

"It does not matter, Jorge. I like the mountains too. You and I, Jorge, we should take a walk together."

"Why?" I asked suspiciously.

"Because...because I like you, Jorge, and I have a matter I need to discuss with you."

"A police matter?" I panicked.

"Maybe. Maybe not."

After considerable thought I relaxed. If they had collected any evidence relating to the mountains or of my supposed memoryless encounter in Manzano I would have been arrested by now.

"Very amenable, your nephew, Jorge."

"He is an arse."

"Very compliant."

"Why? What has he done?"

"He gave me this," he said smiling and holding up a memory stick.

"And what is that?"

"I believe it is your diary. I asked and he gave."

Sweat beaded on my upper lip.

"Nothing to say for yourself, Jorge?"

I shook my head swiftly.

"We will walk together on Thursday, yes?"

I grabbed my jacket from the desk.

"Am I able to leave?" I asked.

"Of course."

I opened the door.

"Thursday, Jorge. Your nephew told me you have a new car. Pick me up from here at eight. I know a great walk."

I left, closing the door behind me. Jesús called out.

"Try to stay out of trouble, Jorge!"

*

As I approached my house I noticed a new addition to my street. It appeared that Kevin was entertaining a visitor, a lady friend no less. Her pink jeep was parked outside my front gate. And then the penny dropped and I realised that there was no visitor after all. My new car was merely one more weapon in the arsenal of my life's humiliation.

Tuesday 3rd December

Finally, after the weekend and my days in and out of prison I could contact the bank about the fraudulent behaviour on my account. They said they would investigate but it may take some time. What would I have done for money if Kevin had not been here?

That said, had Kevin not arrived in the first place the whole town would not suspect me of multiple murder and my digital diary would not be in the hands of the police. I would also possess a non-pink automobile. On balance I felt that my actions earlier this afternoon had been fully justified.

"Eurghh. That bloody dog's done it again, t' mucky get!"

He tipped the yellow liquid out of his training shoe into the sink. "I dunno how he does it. I even put 'em on a high shelf."

When Ambrose is unable to perform his duty I am only too prepared to step into the breach.

Kevin threw his shoes out on to the terrace to dry in the winter sun.

"I hate that dog," he muttered under his breath.

I looked towards Ambrose, who once again appeared to smile.

"You are conscious earlier than normal today. If one can call it consciousness."

"Yeah, I've got a mission."

"And what is that? To return the car to Barbie?"

"What's wrong wi' it?"

"It is pink."

"So? I like pink."

"Have you ever noticed that the colour pink seldom encroaches upon my existence?"

"Eh?"

"Nothing I own is pink. There is a reason for that."

"I thought you'd like it."

"I do not like it. I hate it."

"That's the thanks I get," he said, grumpily.

"And it is a jeep. I am not Action Man."

"I know that."

"You will take it back to the garage and exchange it."

"Who sez?"

"I do."

"I like it."

"You said you had purchased it for me."

"Maybe it was fer both of us."

"I do not want it."

"Suit yersel'," he said and disappeared out of the front

door in his stocking feet.

*

I heard him before I saw him. I was sitting in the comfortable chair reading Milton. I had enjoyed an almost pleasant day with Kevin absent the entire time. I could hear a conversation outside my front door.

"Wow, Kevin! What happened to you?" It was Janet's voice.

"I was gonna get some new trainers an' then I thought I'd have a change o' look, now I've got some cash an' all."

"Well, you look very dapper. I'm impressed."

The door opened and Kevin entered wearing an expensive silver suit and a top hat. In his right hand was a walking cane and his left a black briefcase. His feet were encased in expensive, black, Italian shoes. Despite the money invested in his outfit, even a Hugo Boss suit could not conceal his lumpen form.

"Good day, uncle George," he said, tipping back his top hat with the end of his cane.

"The oven is on," I said. "Twenty minutes a pound plus twenty minutes."

"Eh?"

"You look like a Christmas turkey that has been kicked around a car park and then wrapped in tin foil."

"Don't be so mean," said Janet, following him in and perching on the sofa. "He looks lovely."

"See," he said, sticking out his pink slug of a tongue. "I look lovely."

"Why?" I asked, gesturing towards the sartorial horror show before me.

"I, sir," he said, "am a gentleman thief."

"Really?" said Janet, leaning forward to hear his tale.

"And what, may I ask, have you stolen?"

"In this very brief case," he said, tapping it with his silver cane, "I 'ave yer results."

"My medical results?" I asked with amazement.

"Wow, Kevin. How did you get them?" asked Janet, eyes wide open.

"Easy. This morning I walked into t' surgery an' asked Shirley for an appointment. She said I'd 'ave to wait. So I did. She popped to t' lav so I hid behind t' sofa in reception. She must a thought I'd got bored or summat and left. Shirley and Vince went fer dinner. I nicked yer results and got back behind t' sofa. They came back, she popped to t' lav again and I left. Piece o' piss."

"So they did not set the alarm at lunchtime?" I asked.

"Nope."

"But what would have happened if they had?"

"I'd a stayed behind t' sofa during t' dinner break."

"Genius!" said Janet. "Very impressive."

"I could get used to this, uncle George. I am t' Silver Panther."

"Yes, very inconspicuous."

"Do you wanna see yer results?"

"Mmm."

I felt nervous. After all this time, did I really desire to understand what would kill me?

Kevin snapped open the briefcase.

"You know that I do not believe that I am dying."

"Let's just have a look," said Janet with a serious, thin-lipped grimace.

He pulled out a thin folder with my name on the front. Flicking it open he stared at the sheets within. His face contorted in confusion.

"I can't read his writin'."

"Give it to me," I said, snatching it from him.

I read the page, a long paragraph of densely knitted scrawl that was all but indecipherable. But then I saw it, three capital letters. And once I had decoded those, I could hazard a good guess at the three words that preceded them.

"Shit," I said.

"What is it?" said Janet.

"Shit," I repeated more loudly.

"What?" said Janet and Kevin in unison.

"I have..."

"What?"

"I have CJD," I said in a hoarse whisper.

"What?"

"It says a virulent strain of CJD," I croaked.

"Shit," she said.

"What's that?" said Kevin. "What's JCD?"

"CJD is Creutzfeldt-Jakob Disease," said Janet.

"An' what's that?"

"It's the human form of BSE," she replied.

Kevin exploded with laughter and then quickly covered his mouth.

"Uncle George..." he repressed a smirk. "Uncle George's got Mad Cow Disease?"

Janet glared at him.

"Stop it, Kevin. It's very serious."

Kevin stood up with his cane in hand, tipped back his top hat and said in his best impression of an upper class accent, "I do not find it in the slightest bit amoooooooosing."

*

I was in shock, a dreaded numbness had overcome me. I had not truly believed my end was near.

I found a medical website to learn the symptoms that I am soon to experience: failing memory, behavioural changes, lack of co-ordination, visual disturbances, hallucinations, involuntary movements, blindness and death. Once the symptoms begin, the end is near.

Was this divine retribution for what I had done, a karmic

penalty paid out before the crimes that I would commit had even been perpetrated?

My neighbour walked into the living room from the kitchen carrying a cup of tea.

"There you go, George," she said grimly.

I looked at her, at her face. Soon I would not be able to remember her name. Her name? What was her name? I thought hard for a second. I could not access it. I started to cycle through the alphabet for first names. A. Abigail, Alison, no. B. Belinda....F. Fiona...I. Irene. J. Jackie, Janet. Janet! I looked her deep in the eyes.

"What are you thinking, George?" she said.

"It has begun," I replied.

Wednesday 4th December

It was late afternoon. Kevin walked into the room sniggering.

"You got any milk, uncle George?"

"There is some in the fridge."

Kevin had burst out laughing before I had even finished my response.

"I do not think you understand how serious my condition is," I said.

"If I believe it's serious, will you give me a..." he left a dramatic pause and guffawed, "a pat on the head?"

I stared at him blankly. He fell on the floor, holding his rolls of flesh and giggling like an infant. After several minutes of hysterics he picked himself up, disappeared into the bathroom and reappeared wearing his silver outfit again.

"Going somewhere nice?" I asked.

He once again adopted his Lord Charles voice.

"I, sir, am going on a dinner date."

"Yes, I heard Susan Boyle was in town."

"Very funny, uncle George."

"Who is the lucky lady then? Let me guess. It must be some poor unfortunate from Bar Wars. Ah, is it Sandra With The Teeth?"

"I'm not desperate, y'know."

"I think you will find that you are. Is it Alison?"

"Which one's that?"

"Alopecia. Missing finger."

"Uncle George, I have a much better lady than that."

"Who is it then?"

"Janet."

"WHAT?" I exploded. "My Janet?"

"She's not your Janet."

"She is not yours either."

"Not yet. But maybe she will be."

"But, but..." I lost my usual composure. I regained none of it when I burst forth with, "But I saw her first!"

"Oh, is that how it works on t' Costa del Sol? First one who bagsies a woman gets to ride her before anyone else?"

"No. Sorry," I replied, although, if I am being frank, in my experience that does indeed appear to be the system.

"I'm taking her to Bar Wars."

"I should have thought that an optimal first dinner date might involve cutlery."

"They don't just do burgers, y'know, uncle George."

"No, they also serve hot dogs."

"Yes, but they also do," and here he began quoting from their menu, "a range of international dishes. They do nachos."

"Finger food."

"They do pizza."

"Served by the slice. Finger food. It is all finger food. I was speaking to Trevor only the other day. The only silverware that they possess is the single spoon that they purchased in case you desired any more Coco Pops."

"Well," he sniggered in a most nauseating manner, "perhaps finger food," he said raising and wiggling his middle digit, "is very appropriate."

"Yes. Perhaps you can wait until you have left the establishment before you attempt to insert anything into her."

"Who knows?" he yerked. "If she's lucky, uncle George."

Poor, poor girl.

First my local and now my woman. He has taken my existence and imprinted upon it his massive, gelatinous arse. I picked up poor Ambrose and offered him to the dolt.

"Here! Take Ambrose. He is all I have left that is mine."

"No, thanks. He's horrible."

There was a knock at the door. The spyhole revealed that it was Janet. I opened up and stepped aside to allow her entry.

"Ready, Kevin?" she said. "You alright, George?"

"Mmm," I said.

"Just need to brush me teeth," Kevin said, rolling into the bathroom.

I turned to Janet.

"I cannot believe you are going on a date with...with that!"

"I'll go on a date with whoever I damn well please."

"Yes, but him."

"He's nice. And he's kind. He thinks the world of you."

I tutted.

"God knows why," she said. "Besides, it's not a date. Just two friends having a meal."

"Kevin thinks it is a date."

"So?"

"I think it is a date."

"George, sometimes you act about seven."

I am not proud that I adopted a soppy, mocking voice.

"Sometimes you act about seven," I said peevishly.

"Bloody hell," she said, shaking her head. "Come on, Kevin! Hurry up!"

"I thought" – I looked down at my shoes – "I thought that perhaps we could, well, you know."

She smiled tightly.

"Yes, I know you did. Sorry, it's..."

Kevin burst from the bathroom and danced into the living room. He tossed a small package into the air with his left hand and caught it flamboyantly with his right.

"I'm all tooled up an' I'm ready to go."

He was holding a packet of condoms.

"You won't be needing those, Kevin," said Janet indignantly.

"Bareback, eh, Janet?" he said. "Mucky." He scowled a mock-shocked expression. "S'OK. I'm only joking. They're not even mine. I just found 'em in t' bathroom. Uncle George, you animal!"

I had given up.

"Feel free to use them, Kevin. I have had them for years."

"I'm still here, you know," said Janet.

"They're still wrapped in cellophane, uncle George," said Kevin, examining the packet.

"I know."

"Use by 2010 it says."

"Lean times," I said.

"Still, they probably wouldn't fit you now, uncle George, what with yer massive, green donkey dick."

"Please go, Kevin."

"Hung like a bull," Kevin said, grinning at Janet. "A mad bull."

"Go now!"

Janet opened the door. Kevin hurled the condoms to her. She deftly caught the packet and threw them rather skilfully into the waste paper bin in the far corner of the room.

*

I am used up, depleted, a geriatric, attractive to no one. Soon, gladly, I shall slip from this foetid Earth, with nothing to prove my erstwhile existence other than the two self-published collections of poetry, selling on Amazon for 99p each. My life's work, the sum total of my worth, has a value of £1.98. I am looking forward to my imminent mental deterioration so that I no longer have the capacity to analyse my uselessness and redundancy.

I pray he did not maul the girl tonight. His fingernails are always shockingly filthy. I hope that she has had a tetanus vaccination.

Thursday 5th December

Kevin emerged from the bedroom uncharacteristically early. He had been in such a good mood before his date yesterday that he had agreed to accompany Jesús and I on our walk today.

"How was your date?" I asked.

He adopted his ridiculous upper class tone.

"A gentleman never reveals," he said.

"Yes, I know, and so how was it?"

He laughed a dirty laugh but changed the subject.

"What time are we meetin' Jesus, uncle George?"

"He is not called Jesus."

"Yes, he is. I saw it on t' charge sheet."

"It is Jesús. You pronounce it Hay-*sus*. Stress the 'sus'."

Kevin thought about this for a second before dismissing it entirely.

"Nah, he'll allus be Jesus to me."

It was another bright and sunny winter's day, the perfect

conditions in which to go for a drive in the Pink Pratmobile and have a delightful outing with a man who wanted to throw me into jail.

Kevin was already standing in the tiny front yard with Ambrose strapped to his back. I left the house and locked the front door.

"You forgettin' summat, uncle George?"

I turned to Kevin.

"No, I do not think so."

"Kecks?"

"What?"

"You've got no kecks on."

"What are you..."

I did not finish my sentence. I looked down to see that I was not wearing any trousers.

"I shouldn't a said nuffin'," said Kevin, tittering to himself.

"This is not my fault," I said with as much dignity as it is possible to muster whilst standing in the street in one's underwear.

"It's the mad cow thing," offered Kevin.

"Yes," I said sadly, "I fear it is."

I returned to the house to attire myself correctly whilst Kevin installed Ambrose on the back seat and climbed into the driver's side. As I emerged from the house Kevin gave the car's horn a couple of blasts resulting in an embarrassingly ineffectual parp-parp.

We drove to the police station. The chief of police was already waiting for us outside. Kevin rolled down his window.

"Come on, Jesus. Jump in t' back!"

Unseen by Jesús I gave Kevin a quick slap.

"I have already told you. It is Hay-*sus*," I said.

"If he tells me to call 'im Hay-*sus* I'll call 'im Hay-*sus*," he said, mocking my attempt at a Spanish accent. "Till then he's

Jesus."

Jesús opened the door and climbed into the back beside Ambrose, who uncharacteristically snarled at him.

"Good dog," said Jesús nervously, patting his head.

"Where are we going?" I asked.

"I will give directions," he said.

We drove through the town, through a cacophony of car horns, obviously attracted by the preposterous appearance of our automobile and it was with some relief that we took the familiar, and empty, mountain road.

"You drive very well," said Jesús to Kevin. "For a British person."

"Yeah, you'd never know I never took a test, would ya?"

"What?" I said.

"Are you telling me that you have no licence?" said Jesús.

"Ah, shit," said Kevin, suddenly realising that he had a policeman in the back of his car.

"You have been driving me around all this time and you have not even passed your driving test?" I said.

"Never really needed to. I was driving all 'round t' farm from bein' 'bout ten. Why should I take a test if I already know how to drive?"

"To get a licence perhaps?"

"Nah."

"I will deal with that later," said Jesús grimly.

"Oi, Jesus, can you gimme a licence?"

"I'm afraid not."

"You not got no special powers?"

"Jesús is only a name," I whispered to Kevin. "He is not the Son of God."

Eventually we pulled up at exactly the same spot as I had the last two times that I had been out walking, a point I noted as ominous. We gathered our respective bags, a small rucksack each for Jesús and I and Ambrose's carrying bag for

Kevin.

"Can I just have the keys a minute?" I said.

"Yeah, what for?" replied Kevin, throwing them to me. I pocketed them instantly.

"So that you cannot leave when you are tired or bored," I replied.

"That's sneaky, uncle George."

"Onward and upward!" I barked.

*

The climb was pleasant but having seen these vistas twice already in the previous few weeks the novelty was wearing thin. All along the footpath I was waiting for Jesús to broach the subject of the murders but he said nothing about it. Curious.

As we reached the summit, Jesús turned to me.

"You are very fit, Jorge."

"Yes."

"Not many seventy year-olds would be able to make it to the top."

"I have had a lot of practice."

"Yes, and that at least answers one of the questions that I had."

"Which was?"

"Were you capable of reaching the point from which your victims were thrown? I needed to be sure."

"So now you know," I said glibly.

Kevin unclipped Ambrose's rucksack, placed him upside down on the ground and plopped his own backside on to a rock. Ambrose's three legs pumped in the air uselessly.

"Well, let him have a little run," I said to Kevin.

He undid the bag's straps and set Ambrose free.

"You see, Jorge, my problem was that I had no evidence. The previous police chief was not very thorough. The bodies were both cremated before we suspected anything was remiss. They were not checked for suspicious characteristics. According to our records, Tony's was a clean fall and, a little embarrassingly, the records for Margaret have disappeared entirely."

"What 'bout Alan?" said Kevin. "I thought he was battered to death," said Kevin.

I glared him into silence.

"Where was this?" asked Jesús.

Unfortunately it was only temporary silence.

"In Manzano."

"I know nothing of this," said Jesús. "Are you saying that Jorge is implicated in this murder too?"

"Aye, he is."

"Kevin!"

"Well, well. I did not read that," said Jesús. "I was only looking for information about Tony and Margaret in his confession."

"What confession?" I said.

"Your diary, Jorge. This," he said, holding the memory stick between his fingers.

"That is ridiculous. It was not a confession of anything."

"I disagree."

Silence fell. I puffed out my cheeks in realisation that my final days on this planet would likely be locked in a prison cell.

"You will come quietly, won't you, Jorge?"

"Of course."

What option did I have? After all he had his police pistol attached to his belt.

"Good." He smiled. "Then I want something to eat."

Jesús reached into his bag and removed a package. He walked away from us, over to the ledge and peered down.

"So this is where you threw them, Jorge?"

"No. I did not throw anybody."

He turned to face us.

"Long way down," he said. "I wonder what my wife has prepared for me," he said, fingering his package and removing a sandwich. "Ah, chorizo! My favourite!"

Ambrose's little ears pricked up, he sniffed the air and then flew like a fat bullet towards Jesús, hitting him squarely in the chest whilst impressively catching a mouthful of sausage mid-flight.

"Aarrgh!" screamed Jesús as the force of my dog's small but dense body toppled him backwards, over the ledge, disappearing from view.

Kevin and I shared a wide-eyed look before we both darted to the ledge. We looked down the mountainside. Jesús was still tumbling earthwards, his flailing body performing a macabre dance as it hit each ledge and tree stump. We looked at each other with a silent grimace before returning our eyes to the free-falling policeman. His body landed at the bottom with a sickeningly dull thump. Ambrose sat on the ledge happily munching the red meat.

"Bloody 'ell," said Kevin. "Ambrose killed Jesus!"

Friday 6th December

"I have told you, Kevin, I am not going to report what happened to Jesús."

"But if they..."

"They already believe I have murdered two people."

"Three."

"I did not kill Not Gay Alan!" Kevin glared at me. "I did not kill anybody."

"Ah!" said Kevin, appearing to have a revelation. "I've worked it out."

"You have worked what out?"

"I know who t' murderer is."

"Who?"

He turned his eyes towards Ambrose and outstretched an arm with an accusing finger.

"Ambrose killed those people. I mean, I witnessed one of 'em."

"You think that Ambrose is a serial killer?"

"Yes, I do."

"And what is his motive?"

"Eminenty, my dear Watson. His motive is...chorizo!"

"Shut up."

"We have seen him fly. He can teleport. He can climb walls."

"When did he climb a wall?"

"He pissed in me trainers when they were on t' highest shelf."

"Ah," I said, keeping quiet about the perpetrator of that particular crime.

"He's a death machine. But unlike you, he ain't written a confession."

"My confession," I said.

It was a strange choice of word from Jesús. What had Jesús read in my diary? I went to the computer, opened up the word processor and scrolled back through to the earlier entries. I settled on 31st October, the day Scotch Tony had disappeared. I read through the entry, laughing at my deceit over the tomatoes, and arrived at the conclusion. I was taken aback.

"Bloody hell!" I said.

"What's t' matter?"

"Someone has..."

"What?"

"I did not write this."

*

I spent the rest of the afternoon perusing my digital journal. The longer I looked and analysed, the more confused I became. They were two passages that I had no memory of writing.

"Which ones?" asked Kevin.

"On the thirty-first of October, I wrote: *A nudge. It was only a small nudge. But, I'm afraid to say, large enough.*"

"What 'bout it?"

"That did not happen."

"You sure?"

I thought about it. My mind was misbehaving.

"No."

"Whaddaya think happened?"

"He was annoying me."

"Who?"

"Scotch Tony. He would not tell me the nature of my illness. I got angry. I threw his car keys into a tree."

"Was this tree hangin' over t' ledge?"

"No. I do not remember. No. It feels like none of it ever happened."

I rubbed my head. My brain felt like it was transforming into porridge.

"And then there is this other part," I said. "On the sixth of November I wrote: *I'm sorry, Margaret, but you can't live to repeat this." Her scream echoed around the mountains as she tumbled down and down.*"

"Ah," said Kevin.

"She fell but I did not push her. She was standing near the edge. I saw a snake moving towards her and so I grabbed a stick to flick it away. She thought I was coming for her. She stepped back and that was when she fell. But she only fell to the first ledge. She hurt her leg and thought she might have broken her wrist but that is all. That is what I remember anyway."

"Can I be t' policeman fer a minute?"

"What?"

"I wanna interrogate you."

"Go on then, Columbo."

"If those things happened like you said, the car keys an' the snake, why didn't you write 'em?"

"I do not know."

"But..."

"Yes, I do. I thought if I left out the detail it would make my diary more dramatic."

"Why does it 'ave to be dramatic?"

"I thought people might read it."

"Who?" he said with mocking laughter.

"My fans."

Kevin guffawed more loudly.

"The people who read my poetry," I continued.

Kevin collected himself together.

"Well, if you didn't write those words, who did?" he asked.

"I do not know."

"But you're sure you didn't write 'em?"

"Yes. I remember. I think."

"Yesterday mornin' you couldn't even remember to put yer kecks on. Are you sure?"

I rubbed my forehead and looked him in the eye.

"I am not sure of anything any more."

I returned to reading my diary. I suddenly discovered something else.

"And this," I said. "I wrote: *I took it by the wrist and pressed his palm against the surface of the table. 'Spread your fingers, boy.' Kevin looked confused but did as he was told. 'Now, Kevin, which finger shall I sever?'*"

"What about it?"

"That did not happen. That definitely did not happen!"

Kevin looked disappointed.

"It did," he said. "I was there."

*

It was three in the morning when I woke abruptly.

"Argghhh!"

Kevin was screaming as though in the process of being slit from neck to navel like an abattoir pig.

"Gedawayfromme! Gedaway!"

I leapt up from the sofa and raced to my bedroom – his bedroom – flinging open the door. Kevin was rolled in a ball at the far corner of the bed with the duvet pulled tightly up to his chins. His sweat had plastered his hair to his forehead. He saw me.

"Uncle George, save me!"

I looked towards the floor and discovered the source of Kevin's terror. Silly sod.

"It is only Ambrose," I said calmly.

"Yeah, I know," he screamed, panic-stricken. "He's gonna kill me."

"Yes, but only when I say the keyword."

"Aargh! Yer workin' as a team."

"Shut up, you clown."

"You are. You're like Fred 'n' Rose West," he yelled.

"Stop shouting. You are hysterical."

"You're Rose an' Ambrose is Fred, t' mastermind."

He closed his eyes tightly, screwing up his face.

"Just get it done," he said. "Say t' word."

"Kevin..."

"Say it!"

"Alright then. Ambrose," I barked. He looked towards me. "Ready...chorizo!"

Kevin screamed a lusty cry that he held for as long as he could before quickly running out of breath and descending into a coughing fit. He slowly opened his eyes, one at a time.

"Well?" he said.

"There is no keyword, Ambrose is not a killer and you are a moron."

"I'm gonna keep me eye on you," he said viciously to Ambrose. "You're up to summat. You won't outsmart t' Silver Panther."

Saturday 7th December

"Are you feeling saner this morning, Kevin?"

"I'll be reet once I've had me Coco Pops."

Now that Kevin was responsible for the household finances – there was still no word from the bank – the weekly shopping list had altered somewhat.

"I were thinkin'" he said, a throwaway remark that hung above the approaching phrase like the sword of Damocles. "Jesus fell off t' same ledge as Scotch Tony?"

"Mmm."

"So someone'll find 'is body in t' same place too."

"I suppose so."

"An' they suspect you o' Tony's murder. So they'll definitely suspect you of killin' Jesus."

"Hay-*sus*."

"Jesus," he repeated smugly.

"An' if they think you killed a copper, they' ain't gonna be hangin' about, are they? They're gonna 'ave yer."

"What are you suggesting?"

"We need to hide t' body."

Oh lord.

"It's th' only way," he continued.

He was correct.

"Get Ambrose's bag!" I said.

"I'm not goin' if he's goin'."

"Do not come then."

"But you won't be able to move 'im by yersel'."

And that is why we climbed back into the car and I headed into the mountains for the fourth time.

*

The pink monstrosity was wending its way through the Spanish brush to the starting point of our mountain adventure.

"Excitin', this, i'n't it, uncle George?" said Kevin.

"What, murdering police officers?"

"We didn't kill 'im. Ambrose did."

"No one in their right mind is going to believe a story like that."

"Maybe he left some muddy footprints on his chest."

"Why? It has not rained for days and Ambrose was on your back for the entire duration of the walk."

"Well then, uncle George." He leaned over like a man about to deliver a plan. "Maybe we could *make* some muddy footprints on his chest."

"As much as I appreciate your input, I do not particularly want my dog to hang for this."

"Then it'll be you."

"Not if we hide the body."

"Where we gonna put it?"

"I do not know. There are some old mine shafts up in the hills. Maybe we can conceal him in one of those."

"Right, we're here," said Kevin tugging on the hand brake. "Let's find Jesus!"

*

It was difficult to decide where the chief of police would have landed. After three hours of searching the base of the mountain I believed that I had found our landing site.

"So you reckon it's here then, uncle George?"

"It must be. I am sure that way up there is our ledge. This

spot is the first place that he would have made contact with the ground. And there is nowhere to go from here."

"But he's not 'ere."

"Have a look in the bushes. Maybe he bounced."

We hunted around beneath the coarse shrubs, the waft of rosemary and thyme filling our nostrils, spiking our hands on the sharp needles of the Spanish broom.

"He ain't here, uncle George."

"I think you may be correct. Which means only one thing."

"'T' cops have already found 'im."

"Alright then, it means one of two things."

"He's bin eaten by wolves," said Kevin enthusiastically.

"There are no wolves up here."

"He's bin eaten by wild boars."

"Alright, one of three things."

"He's bin found by gypsies and had his organs 'arvested."

"Kevin, I think that your final suggestion is highly unlikely."

"Is it? The Silver Panther must consider ev'ry possibility."

"Must he?"

"Yeah, why, what was you thinkin'?"

"That he is...alive."

"We shoulda brought Ambrose to hunt 'im down and finish 'im off."

"He survived the fall."

"Or maybe Jesus died," he said spookily. "An' then came back from t' dead."

"Shut up, Kevin."

"If he's alive, that's bad news fer you, i'n't it? 'Cos now he's gonna dob you in."

"Yes."

"Pity he's not dead."

I thought about this for a minute.

"You have a point," I said.

"Maybe we should kill 'im."

"In for a penny, in for a pound and all that," I said sarcastically.

"Shall we?" he said with eyes wide open and a goldfish mouth.

"I was joking."

"Oh." He looked around dumbly with his hands in his pockets. "What's that?"

He bent down and picked something up.

"What is it?" I asked.

"It's a business card. But it's in Greek or summat."

"Let me see." I snatched the card from his greasy paw. "That is not Greek. It is Russian."

"Can you speak Russian, uncle George?"

"I lived in Moscow for a while."

"Yeah, but you've lived in Spain for a while an' yer can't speak Spanish."

I ignored this comment.

"So what does it say?"

"Why would a Spanish police officer have a Russian business card?"

"You don't know it was his. It coulda been anyone's."

"This is not a footpath, Kevin. Have you noticed?"

"Yeah, it's scratchin' me legs."

"Exactly. Apart from Jesús and ourselves I will wager that no one has ever stood on this spot in the entire history of the Earth."

"So what does it say?"

"No. I have it! He *was* alive! He must have been hurt. His legs must have been broken at least. Maybe he crawled away and perished somewhere nearby."

"Where though?"

I surveyed the area. Miles and miles of dense, coarse

shrubbery lay before us.

"Damn it! He could be anywhere."

"Come on, uncle George. Tell me. What does it say?"

"I do not know. I cannot speak Russian."

"Ah."

"But I know someone who can."

Sunday 8th December

"I thought you said the new police chief speaks English," said little Edith. I had borrowed her from Old Bob again.

"I did."

"Then why do you need me to translate?"

Because there is a distinct possibility that my dog murdered him, I thought.

"I have reason to believe that the police chief will not be present," I said.

"Why don't you speak Spanish?" she asked.

"I have tried to learn."

"How hard?"

"Never you mind, young lady."

I had briefly attended a Spanish class at the local language school but after six weeks all I had learnt was how to greet people in Spanish and tell the time. Until my dealings with the police I had never had to communicate with Spaniards and so greetings were redundant. And as I own a watch I would never need to ask the time in Spanish. If any Spanish speaker were to make a similar request of me I would simply walk on and pretend I had not heard him.

Kevin entered from the bathroom.

"Whatcha doin'?" he asked.

"We are shortly to visit the police station."

"We?"

"Edith and I."

"Whaddabout me?"

"You can stay here."

He looked around quickly and spied Ambrose, who was eyeing him directly.

"I can't stay here by mesel'. Not wi' him. He'll kill me."

"He will not. You are being ridiculous."

"But he's only a little dog," said Edith, approaching Ambrose and stroking his tiny, white head. Ambrose rolled over on to his back in anticipation of additional attention. "Look. He's lovely."

"He's actin'. It's a trap. I'm not stayin' here. Unless you wanna come back home and find him eatin' me innards."

"I cannot think of a sight that I would rather see," I said.

"Why are you so mean to Kevin?" asked Edith.

"I have had a lot of practice."

"But I'm not safe here," he whined.

"You cannot come to the police station. You are a liability."

"Oh, am I?" he said, seemingly a little hurt. "When are you goin'?"

"Two minutes. After this cup of tea."

Without another word Kevin disappeared into the bedroom. Just as I had drained the last of my hot beverage he reappeared wearing his silver outfit and top hat, tapping the tiled floor with his walking cane.

"What are you doing?" I asked.

Edith saw him and burst out laughing.

"Are you going to a fancy dress party?" she asked.

"I am..." He paused for effect, the intended effect being drama whereas the actual effect was pity. "I am the Silver Panther and I will seek justice wherever I can."

"For the love of god, you are not coming."

"You can't stop me." He smiled wickedly. "And you know it."

He was correct. Until the bank returned my money I would have to suffer whatever inanities he exacted upon me.

"Alright. But do not open your mouth."

*

It was eleven in the morning and we were standing at the counter in the office of the police station. The same officer was on duty as the last time that I was here with Edith. It was our turn at the desk.

"I am George Pearly. I have been asked to present myself here on a weekly basis for some unfathomable reason."

The officer looked immediately to Edith. Her face wrinkled but she plucked some sense from what I had said and relayed it. The officer pulled a book from under the desk and made a note in it.

"And whilst I am here, may I speak to Jesús Herrero Herrero?"

Upon hearing the name of his superior the police officer replied immediately.

"He's not here," said Edith.

The police officer said something else.

"He wants to know why you want to see him," she said.

"We wanna know if he's dead or not," interjected fathead.

Fortunately the Spaniard's English was not up to the task of translation.

"Do not interpret that!" I barked at Edith.

The officer was still waiting for an answer. I had not rehearsed a response.

Edith turned to the policeman and babbled away in Spanish. He looked satisfied with her explanation.

"What did you say?" I asked.

"I told him that Jesús had said he could recommend a lawyer to you and that you wanted the details."

I thought for a minute.

"Good," I said. "Well done, dear." I turned to Kevin.

"Why can you not be more like Edith?"

"I'd look shit in a dress," was his glib reply.

"Not as shit as you look in Bacofoil."

If Jesús had not returned after four days he was surely dead and his corpse lay hidden somewhere in the mountain shrubs, a corpse containing a copy of my electronic diary. Whether or not I wrote those words, perhaps he had yet to relay his knowledge of my 'confession' to his colleagues. I would be safe if we could locate him and my memory stick.

We exited the police station.

"Ah, I forgot. Edith, can you read this?" I said, presenting to her the business card that we had collected from the woods yesterday.

"Where did you get this?" she asked.

"We found it," said Kevin.

"Where?"

"It does not matter where," I said. "What does it say?"

She wrinkled her face.

"I think it's bad people," she said.

"Bad people?" I asked.

"It's got words on I don't understand."

"But it is Russian, is it not?"

"Yes."

"Does it have any words on that you do understand?"

"Yes, some," she said.

We went through the card, line by line, translating a useless word here and there. In a jaunty typeface there was a sentence that appeared to be the company's motto.

"This line," I said, pointing to it. "What does this line say?"

"That's why I think it's bad people."

"What does it say?"

"It says, *We Don't Fuck About*."

"Ah."

This was hardly the marketing tool of a legitimate organisation. Perhaps this was some kind of Russian intimidation service. But with what connection to Jesús? Maybe if we found his body we would discover other clues and be able to answer that question.

"Come on, Kevin. The Silver Panther has a job to do."

Monday 9th December

Yesterday's search proved fruitless. We hunted from noon until darkness, around six in the evening, and happened upon nothing more than a dead goat and a sprained ankle. The inability to locate my memory stick was worrying but it was far from the most disturbing thing to occur today.

Kevin was particularly disappointed that the coarse spines of the Spanish broom had shredded his trousers in numerous locations giving him the appearance of a metallic Man Friday, probably how Gary Glitter looked after his first few weeks in Thailand.

"I'm gettin' a message, uncle George," said Kevin, holding his temples and creasing his plasticine brow.

"What?"

"I'm gettin' somethin'."

"What are you talking about, man?"

"I'm a bit psychic."

Oh lord.

"No, really. I am. Like me mum."

"She was not psychic. She was psychotic."

"Hey, she's dead, uncle George" he said, hurt.

"Yes." That was tactless. "I am sorry."

"S'OK. I'm over it."

"It is wonderful to see that you have managed your grief so effectively," I said sarcastically. "So what message are you getting from the underworld, Mystic Meg?" I asked.

He frowned.

"Somethin' has happened."

"Really?"

"Yeah, really."

"Well, I cannot tell you how impressed I am."

"I haven't told you what it is yet."

"Oh sorry. I thought that was the totality of the knowledge that you had gathered from the spiritual realm."

"No."

"Have you used your magical powers to locate my memory stick?"

"Don't be daft."

"Why is that daft?"

"Your memory stick's not a person."

I felt that the best way to conclude this conversation was to remain silent.

"Somethin's happened to t' car."

"A car is not a person either."

"Dur."

"Dur what?"

"The something that happened to t' car was done by a person."

"Ah. So what has happened to my beautiful car?"

"Let's go and see."

By the time Kevin had followed me out of the house he caught me staring open-mouthed at the pink monster.

"That is not possible," I said, perplexed.

"Wow."

"How did you know about this?" The penny dropped. "Hang on a minute." I pointed an accusing finger towards the lumpen mess. "Did you do this?"

"Eh? No. Why'd I do that, uncle George?"

The car had been spray-painted once again, this time with

a list. Scrawled in white were the names of Tony, Margaret and Alan, each with a thick line crossing out the casualty in question. What made the graffiti most chilling was the addition of a final name – Jesus – at the bottom of the list. No one but Kevin and I had knowledge of what had happened on the mountain top that fateful afternoon four days ago.

"Have you told anyone?" I asked, panicked. "Come inside," I said before he could answer. "We do not want the whole street hearing this."

Once inside I repeated the question.

"I've been wi' you th' whole time."

It was true. He had.

"You have not emailed anyone? Or telephoned anybody?"

"No. I've got no credit anyroad."

"Then how is it possible that anyone knows this?"

Kevin's body went rigid and his face drained of colour. He felt blindly for the arm of the comfortable chair to prevent himself from toppling over.

"What is the matter with you?" I asked.

"I know," he said solidly.

"You know what?"

"I know who did it."

"Who have you told?"

"No one."

"Then who sprayed our car?"

Kevin's eyes turned imperceptibly towards Ambrose. He erected a wobbly arm with an outstretched finger in his direction.

"He," was all he said.

"What?"

"Ambrose did it."

With two fat thumbs he clutched his greasy forehead again.

"I'm gettin' it," he said in a shaken voice. "The spirits are tellin' me that Ambrose did it."

I gave him a sharp slap that seemed to tempt him back from his communion with the underworld, albeit temporarily.

"Think about it," he said. "Who was on that mountain? Me, you, Jesus...and the dog."

"Hay-*sus*."

"Jesus is dead. I didn't paint your car. You didn't paint your car." He narrowed his eyes. He was clearly about to deliver something of some import. "Once you've ruled out the impossible, the unpobable, no matter how unpobably, is all that's left."

"Arthur Conan Doyle would be proud."

He smiled as though I had been serious.

"Ambrose's out to frame us, uncle George. He killed that copper. An' now yer dog's scribbled his name on t' car to make it look like we did it. Like you did it. He won't be happy till we hang. An' I'll prove it."

"I would like to see that."

"I will."

"And yet," I said thoughtfully, "I have another explanation."

"What?"

"You have already mentioned it yourself. On that hilltop, there were four of us. Apart from Jesús, there was I, there was a beast with no known linguistic ability and there was Ambrose. So if I did not do it, and neither you nor Ambrose has the ability to do it, the only person who could have written it is...Jesús himself."

"Aaaaah," said Kevin, suddenly won over.

"Jesús is still alive."

"Yeah."

"And that is why we could not find him."

"Mmm."

"Solved," I said, rather proud of myself.

"Yes," said Kevin. "But...."

"But what?"

"You know you say I'm thick?"

"Yes. Frequently."

"I might be thick but even I can spell me own name."

"What do you mean?"

"Follow me," said Kevin.

Outside we went once again and looked at the paint on the car. My delusion of detective magnificence collapsed like a punctured lung.

"He ain't put that line over t' 'u'," he said.

"Yes, I have noticed."

"He has signed it as Jesus, not Hay-*sus*."

"I know."

"He didn't do it."

"Yes, shut up."

"So there's only one explanation."

"What is that?"

"Eminenty, my dear Watson. Ambrose did it."

"No, he did not," I screamed. "And it is 'elementary', you cabbage!"

*

Two hours of silence passed. Kevin had gone to my, his, bedroom I assumed for a sleep. Ambrose had disappeared, no doubt communing clandestinely with his band of canine assassins to decide whom next to butcher. The bedroom door creaked open. Kevin emerged looking unnervingly happy with himself.

"Allow me to present my latest detective..." he searched for an appropriate word..."thing."

"What now?"

"Ta-daaaah!" he said, his fat arm outstretched like a ringmaster about to introduce a cycling monkey.

Ambrose trotted out of the bedroom, a small camera

attached to his head.

"What have you done to my dog?" I shouted.

"It's a camera, uncle George."

"I know it is a camera."

"It'll let us know what he's up to."

"Will it?"

"Yeah."

"Well, if he can murder three adults in cold blood and write their names on my car in spray paint then he can certainly work out how to remove that camera."

"I doubt it," he said. "I've superglued it to his head."

Tuesday 10th December

"Uncle George?" asked Kevin tentatively. "What are you doin'?"

"Oh, hello," I said distractedly. "Good morning, Kevin."

I was standing at the sink filling the kettle with water.

"What are you doin'?"

His voice sounded uneasy.

"What does it look like I am doing?" I blurted. "I am making a cup of tea."

"In t' toaster?"

"What are you blathering on about, man?"

"You're pourin' water into t' toaster."

I looked at my hands and – god damn it! - he was correct. I could have sworn that I had picked up the kettle.

He attempted to put his arm around my shoulder.

"Go an' 'ave a lickle sit down, uncle George. I'll make t' tea."

"Yes, yes, thank you, Kevin."

I went to sit in the comfortable chair to empty my mind. Then two minutes later I jumped up having convinced myself that I was not in my chair but had actually climbed into the washing machine instead. I am going insane.

"Why is the front door open?" I yelled towards the kitchen.

Kevin's head popped from inside.

"Don't worry 'bout it, uncle George. You just sit there. I'll sort it."

"Well, do it quickly otherwise Ambrose will escape."

Ambrose was asleep in the corner, his head resting on his sole front leg. He had no desire to go anywhere and so I settled into my chair. I drifted off and dreamt of being trapped inside a well. Fortunately, after some deliberation, I used my thirty foot, bright green penis to escape only to have Kevin push me back down once I had reached the top. I was falling for what felt like hours but before I eventually hit the water at the bottom of the well I awoke with a jolt.

Ambrose had disappeared.

I leapt to my feet and ran into the front yard. There was something on the ground. In fact there were several of such items leading a trail out of my property. I followed it past Bar Wars and into the town proper before it dried up. I ran back to the house.

"What the hell is this?" I yelled at Kevin whilst holding a small piece of chorizo that I had gathered from outside.

"Ah," was his ineffectual reply.

"Well?"

"I needed to gather evidence."

"Evidence of what?"

"Yer dog's crimes."

"So you made a trail of sausage to lead him into town."

"Yeah."

"And what do you expect to learn from this idiocy?"

"We'll see if he has any accomplices."

"Oh, for god's sake. You do know that he has never been

out of this house alone?"

"That's what you think."

"That is what I know."

"But where's yer evidence?"

"I do not need any evidence. If I go out, I take him. Or I lock him in."

"You said yersel' he can teleport."

"I did not mean it."

Kevin looked confused.

"Really?"

"Really."

"Oh."

"Kevin, go and find my dog."

"Just lemme finish me Coco Pops," he said through a mouthful of chocolate rice.

"Now!"

*

Having the house to myself was blissful. I began to reminisce about what my life had been like before the human slug had arrived. I dug out some old copies of *Merla Now!* and read the beautifully constructed articles that I had submitted over the years. A copy from 2009 told the tale of my first ascent of Cabeza, the mountain that reaches to nearly two thousand metres just a few miles down the road. Although the article does not mention it, that was the occasion on which I sort of accidentally broke Very Terry's leg. The helicopter ride cost him a small fortune.

I flicked through to the classifieds at the back and something caught my eye, an advertisement for a doctor here in Merla. The accompanying photo showed a man in his late sixties. He must have retired by now put perhaps the advertised telephone number still worked. Since Vince was not going to help me to tackle my malady, maybe this old G.P. would.

"Hello, is that Doctor Bloomfield?"

"Yes," croaked a distant voice.

"I would like to make an appointment."

"What's that you say?"

"I would like to make an appointment."

The voice chuckled amiably.

"Sorry, son, I've been retired for six years."

"I do not care. I need to see you. It is urgent."

"I don't have a surgery. But what seems to be the problem?"

I explained about the CJD and about Vince's malpractice. The kindly old fellow took pity on my plight and said he would make an exception. He would perform some tests and then prescribe whatever he could. As it turned out he only lived about a quarter of a mile away. I popped around to see him.

"Hello, son. Come in," he said after spending ten minutes trying to unlock his own front door. He looked like Methuselah's grandfather. "Come into the lounge."

I followed him in.

"Do you want a cup of tea?" he asked.

"No, thank you."

He shuffled off and out through a door.

"Milk and sugar?" he shouted back to me.

I sat there waiting for ten minutes and then went to look for him. I found him asleep in a chair in his hallway. He had not made it as far as the kitchen.

"Doctor Bloomfield?" I said, shaking him gently.

He came to slowly, his eyes opening like the petals of a grey and scaly flower.

"What? Oh, yes. You wanted something."

"You said you would examine me. You said you would tell me how long I have left before my CJD kills me."

"Did I?"

"Yes."

"Oh yes. Come on then." He slowly raised himself from the deep fabric of his chair and we made it back into the living room. "Would you like a cup of tea?"

I grabbed his hand. He looked sternly at me for a second and then smiled a kindly smile.

"No, no tea," I said, "Thank you."

"Right then, please open your shirt, son."

*

Two long hours later we were done and the doctor had in his possession several vials of my blood. He had struggled to find a vein. He made some weak joke about my bloodlessness. Eventually the excitement had worn out the poor fellow entirely. I left him snoozing in his chair. I just hope that he remembers to take my blood to the testing clinic.

On my way back to the house I saw Kevin leading Ambrose towards me.

"You found him!" I shouted, overjoyed.

"Yep. He was in a bin."

"How did he get there?" I asked.

"Eminenty, my dear Watson. He teleported."

*

"Yep...OK...half seven...see you there, sexy. What? Oh sorry. See you in a bit."

I looked at him. He grinned from ear to ear before delving a hand into his underpants to rearrange himself.

"Janet?" I enquired.

"Yeah."

I shook my head sadly.

"Now to business," he said.

"What business?"

"Ambrose has had a big day. Let's see what he did."

"How?"

He flipped a memory card out of the camera glued to

Ambrose's head and stuck it into the side of my computer.

"Ready?" he said excitedly and clicked the mouse.

A dog's eye video appeared on the screen. A trail of chorizo was devoured as he made his bid for freedom. Once the sausage had run out he looked around and saw a Spanish mongrel across the street. What followed was forty-five minutes of close-ups of said mongrel's arse.

"It is a little disappointing, is it not?"

"Something'll happen in a bit."

But it did not. The video consisted of four hours of canine anuses and genitalia until near the end when an angry off-camera "Hey!" was followed by Ambrose's levitation and then close-ups of crisp packets, beer cans and a mouldy apple.

"Well done, Sherlock," I said.

Wednesday 11th December

We were in the living room having our morning argument.

"You have still not cleaned the paint off the car!"

"Why's it my job, uncle George?"

"You said you would do it."

"I don't remember."

"Well, I do. Go and clean it now."

"I've changed me mind. I'm not doin' it."

"Well, thank you very much."

"I'm busy. I have a mystery to solve."

"Is that the mystery of how many days you can go without bathing before your body simply sheds its outer layer?"

The telephone rang. Kevin grabbed it.

"Hello, Kevin speakin'. How can I help you?"

His face folded in concentration and confusion.

"Who is it?" I whispered.

"It's some sort o' robot," he said to me.

"Just hang up. They are merely trying to sell you something."

"DO NOT HANG UP!" commanded the electronic voice loud enough for me to hear. This was no pre-recorded message.

"Give me the telephone," I said.

He passed it to me.

"George Pearly?" said the electronic voice. It sounded an octave too low for a human and was distorted. I was being interrogated by a Dalek.

"Yes."

"The murderer George Pearly?"

"No. Who is this?"

"The George Pearly who killed a policeman in the mountains last Thursday?"

"I did not kill anyone. Tell me who this is?"

"I have information for you."

"What kind of information?"

"Information that will help you to defend yourself."

"Defend myself against what? Against whom?"

"The police have got their evidence. They have your diary. I can help you."

"Go on then."

"I cannot give you this information by telephone."

"Why not?"

"I cannot!" the voice barked angrily.

"But why not?"

"Others are listening."

"Which others?"

"Meet me in Manzano this afternoon. Three o'clock outside the tourist office and await further instruction."

"Alright then," I said. "Goodbye."

I was determined to finish this unnerving phone call as quickly as possible.

"Stop! I am not finished yet."

"Sorry."

"Do not bring any weapons."

"I do not own any weapons."

"I need to see that you do not have any weapons."

"I have told you. I do not own any weapons."

"But I need to see that you do not have any weapons."

"How?"

"Wear only underwear."

I laughed.

"No."

"This is no laughing matter, Mr Pearly. Wear only underwear or you will be going to prison for a very long time."

"I only have a few weeks left to live."

The voice went quiet.

There was a sudden crack, a high-pitched whistling past my ear and then the framed photograph of Ambrose on the wall behind me fell to the floor and shattered.

"What was that?" I said to Kevin.

He walked towards the window and noticed the hole.

"Shittin' hell. Someone just tried to shoot you. Duck!" he yelled.

We both slammed to the ground and scuttled like unlikely commandos behind the sofa, the phone still at my ear.

"Three o'clock," I said urgently into the telephone.

"In your underwear," said the robot voice.

"In my underwear," I said with the weariness of a man who had already humiliated himself before an international audience of several tens of millions. To make a naked fool of myself in a small Spanish village was all in a day's work.

The phone went dead. It immediately rang again. From my prone position I stabbed the receive button impatiently.

"Look, I have said I will be there in my underwear. Alright?"

"George?" said a female voice.

"Yes, oh sorry. Who is this?"

"It's Celia."

That was unusual. My sister-in-law had never called before.

"Hello, Celia. Is everything alright?"

"No. It's Richard."

She sounded pained.

"What is the matter?"

"It's horrible. He's in a coma."

This was the best news I had received in weeks.

"Oh dear," I said, smiling on the inside. "What happened?"

"Yesterday he was out near Holmwood. His car left the road."

Holmwood is where Edward lives.

"What was he doing in Holmwood?" I asked.

"I don't know."

"Is there anything I can do? I mean, I cannot come to see him. The police have my passport."

"Why's that?"

"It is complicated."

"No, George. I just thought...I just thought you would like to know."

"Yes, thank you."

There was a pause.

"Where are you going in your underwear, George?" she asked.

"What? Oh, that is complicated too," I said.

There was another pause.

"I hope things work out, Celia," I said.

I wonder if she could discern that I was lying. We said our goodbyes. The phone call had at least distracted me from our sniper.

"Who was that?" asked Kevin.

"Good news," I said. "Richard is buggered."

We remained behind the sofa for twenty minutes before crawling to the window and peering out. Measuring the angle between the hole in the window and the shattered photo frame, the gunman must have been on the roof of the house opposite. In fact, unless my estimations were inaccurate, he must have been several feet higher than the roof. Still, no one was visible there now.

"Do you think it is safe to stand up?" I asked.

"Not sure," said Kevin. "We could just close t' curtains."

"Of course," I said, feeling a little foolish. "I was just about to suggest the very same thing," I lied.

"That were a bit grim, weren't it, uncle George?"

"I think they are just trying to scare us."

"Well, it's workin'."

"I do not think I want to be in this house right now," I said.

After loading buckets and soap into the boot of our pink embarrassment we climbed into the car and drove into the hills, travelling aimlessly for an hour, twisting around the mountain roads that are the location of many a drunken, free-falling death.

"Stop here," I said. "There is a little stream."

We filled up the buckets with water and attempted to clean the paint from the car. What was normally a one-hour job for one man was a three-hour job for two. Whoever had painted this latest message had used a different sort of paint.

I looked at my watch. It was a half past two.

"We should head to Manzano," I said.

Kevin immediately stripped down to his underpants.

"What are you doing?" I asked.

"You said t' robot told us to wait in our underwear."

"Yes, but you do not need to be in your underwear until we get there."

"S'alright. I prefer bein' like this anyroad."

We climbed back into a car at least now devoid of incriminating information.

"It's a coincidence, i'n't it, uncle George?"

"What is?"

"Me mum, and now Richard."

"What do you mean?"

"And then someone tryin' to shoot us."

"What, you think these things are connected?"

"Just odd, uncle George, that's all."

"Richard came off the road," I said.

"Yeah, but there are different ways of comin' off a road."

"What do you mean? Someone forced him off the road?"

"Could be. An' me mum."

"She was using a microphone in the bath."

"Silly old sod. Yep, prob'ly just a coincidence."

"Yes."

"But why is someone tryin' to kill us? Well, you?"

"I do not know, Kevin."

"I know everyone hates yer, but still."

We rolled into Manzano at five to three and parked up in a space behind the tourist office.

"Underpants?" said Kevin.

"I really do not want to do this."

"Go on. You'll love it."

I removed my shirt, shoes and trousers and climbed out of the car.

"Wow," said Kevin. "What's wrong wi' yer arms?"

"There is nothing the matter with my arms, thank you

very much."

"There is. Where's yer muscles? An' how can you be so pale? You've lived here fer ages."

"Shut up."

We walked to the doorway of the tourist office. Three o'clock came. We looked around nervously. A car drove past with its windows down. Its occupants yelled out something obviously degrading in Spanish. I cannot be insulted in a language with which I am unfamiliar.

Five minutes later, an old Scottish woman came down the hill towards us walking her small dog.

"If you want some clothes we have a charity shop," she said.

"We do not need any clothes, thank you very much," I replied.

"You do. You look awful."

She prodded Kevin's belly with her withered finger.

"Too many sweets," she said.

Kevin looked miffed.

"Are you prostitutes?" she asked strangely.

"No, we certainly are not," I barked.

"Nah, you couldn't give it away," she muttered and disappeared around the corner.

It was quarter past three. Maybe this humiliation was a part of the deal.

In the end we waited for an hour. Our robot-voiced assassin did not materialise.

"I wonder if anyone's videoed this," said Kevin.

I shrugged.

"It might be on YouTube already." He thought for a moment. "You should set up yer own channel."

We skulked back to the car and I quickly got dressed. Kevin decided to remain in his underwear.

We left the mountains behind and Kevin pulled up

outside my tiny house. There had been too much excitement for one day. Kevin proudly trotted inside whilst I emptied the boot of the cleaning equipment. And that is when I saw it.

On the back seat of the car was a pair of red knickers, a pair of knickers that I had previously seen hanging from Janet's line. I dropped my head into my hands. Surely not. Never, ever mention this. Discussing it will only make it real.

Thursday 12th December

I woke up as usual on the sofa. I wish that the bank would resolve the issue of my stolen money. The sooner they can trace my funds, the sooner Kevin can remove his girth from my house and bed.

I had been awake for several hours when Kevin finally regained consciousness. He strode into the kitchen, one hand in his underpants and the other scratching his capacious belly. One half of his entire face was deformed after a night of blissful rest. Over the course of the next half an hour it slowly regained its more usual disfigurement.

"This is unacceptable," I said.

"What is, uncle George?"

"You, me, the bed."

"I need me sleep, uncle George."

"So do I."

He looked at me with his mouth gaping. No matter that Janet had said that the young blob thought the world of me, he was not going to give up his comfort for this weary septuagenarian.

"So do I," he said pointlessly.

I thought about our predicament for a moment.

"Maybe we could rent somewhere larger," I suggested.

"You don't have any cash."

"I know."

"Ah, you mean you want me to rent somewhere larger?"

"Well..."

"I were lookin' at a financial advice website t' other day and t' bloke there said not to rush in t' anythin'."

"I cannot live like this."

"Don't worry, uncle George, I'll sort it."

"You will?"

"Yeah, if you're good."

He winked. Did he imagine that he was effecting some sort of charm? Cheeky, little sod.

He disappeared into the bedroom and seconds later came out fully dressed in long shorts and a t-shirt that was already dampening in the region of the armpits.

"Are you going out?" I asked.

"Yeah, I'll be back in a mo."

I decided to make a cup of tea. The toaster had been locked away for my own safety.

"I'm back," he said.

"I did not realise that you had actually left yet."

"I have a pressie for yer, uncle George."

He handed me a large, blue box. On the front of it a child frolicked in a swimming pool.

"What is it?" I asked.

"It's a lilo," he said excitedly.

"A lilo? Am I expected to go swimming?"

"No, it's for you to sleep on."

This was his idea of 'sorting it'.

"Er...thank you."

"Now we don't need to rent anywhere bigger, do we, uncle George."

I looked at the photograph on the side of the box.

"No, from now on I shall sleep like a king."

He looked at me, trying to understand what he had just

heard.

"You bein' sarcastic?"

"Maybe."

"I can take it back, y'know."

"I am sure it will be more comfortable than the sofa. Slightly."

"Yeah."

"Could you possibly inflate it for me? I am not sure that I have enough puff."

He opened the box and removed the contents.

"Ooo," he said, "it's a black 'n' white one."

He placed his rubber lips around the air nozzle and blew until his forehead leaked some form of liquid cheese and his face went through various colours terminating in a violent puce. Eventually, however, the object was more or less fully inflated. And it was only then that we realised that what he had purchased was not in fact an airbed. It was an inflatable killer whale.

"Cool," he said. "It's a fish."

"It is a whale. And how am I supposed to sleep on that?"

"Dunno."

He threw the inflatable on to the kitchen floor and then mounted the killer whale in a manner that would have disturbed any animal lover, twisting his legs around the tail fin and resting his head where the blowhole would have been on any more accurate representation of the creature.

"Like this," he said, smiling. "Easy."

"I cannot sleep like that."

"Yeah, you can."

"No, I cannot."

"Suit yersel'. I'm not buyin' another."

"I wil

Summat bad as happened soz this is kevin writing. Uncle

george was on his computer typing summat probly this diary and then the front door were kicked in and it fell on the floor and nearly squashed Ambrose it were the police but speical army police with guns and stuff. They made us go on the floor with our hands behind our heads and they pointed there guns at us and shouted and one police said i am arresting you george pearly for the murder of antony hingston and the murder of margaret wells then they searched the house for a couple of minutes in the kitchen and the bedroom and then went to the drawers in the living room and opened a drawer and they took out a purse and they looked in it and they said this is margarets purse then they opened a different drawer and took out a wallet and then they said this is antonys wallet we have all the evidence we need now your going to prison for a very long time they picked up uncle george and took him outside and they said you fatty do not move or we will shoot you in that fat head of yours and they laughed i am sorry if i have not written this good and then they went and then after ten minutes i got up because ambrose came up to me and tried to do a we we on my head i am really confused how did uncle george have that purse and that wallet if he did not kill them and uncle george said so when he went out he said maybe i am sicker than i thought i do not know what to do i think i will go to bar wars and talk to the people their mr bullshit seems very clever and he will know what to do. no i will speak to janet first. no i will go to the police station and bale him out again but maybe i cant do that anymore because uncle george is two guilty. i hope they do not hurt him i know he can some times be a bit bad but he has bean kind to me and he has helped me and i do not want him to be hurt. i will go to janet now. i like janet i think i might love her she is fit and as really big boobs

Friday 13th December

i am even more confused than i was yesterday i went to the police station this morning with edith bobs daughter because she can speak spanish and russian and english. i asked her to ask them to ask if i could bale out uncle george but the police looked on his computer and said they had not arrested anyone called george i asked her to ask him to ask again but she said that she had done that already and would not ask again. i thought maybe he is at a different police station and so we drove to maleta and to herracar but the policeman their did not know anything about uncle george neither where is he maybe they have killed him. uncle george where are you

i went to bar wars tonight to talk to mr bullshit he was funny and said that is name is not mr bullshit but i said that is what uncle george said he was called and he just said that uncle george is a miserable old sod he told me that he invented the internet in 1980 but the americans stole it from him and he once had a disease were is head swolled up to twice its size. he as some funny stories i am not sure they are all true i told mr bullshit we had killed jesus and he said that were very seroius and that if the police find out they would get us and kill us and hide us in a wood and now i think that is what as happened to uncle george i think uncle george is in a wood. mr bullshit called that bean disappeared or summat. i hope uncle george is not bean disappeared but i said that we didnt kill jesus but ambrose killed jesus and so if anyone should bean disappeared it should be ambrose and mr bullshit told me about these greyhounds that they hang from trees in spain for being rubbish and they didnt even kill anyone and so ambrose will definately hang from a tree if they catch him and they will because i will tell them were he lives

anyways this is all too spooky and it is friday 13th and that is always spooky and now i think that uncle george is just a ghost and that he is dead so what do i do with ambrose who i hate because he wees in my shoes all the time and he did it again last night and i said he should not do that but he just looked at me and smiled without any teeeths i hate ambrose maybe i can put him accidently in the washing machine and accidently switch it on and see him spin round and round and i can laugh at him and point and say you shouldnt be weeing in peoples shoes. no i wont do that it is mean

i went to janets and she said she were tired and wanted to go to bed and i smiled and she said to sleep not to you know what and i told her about uncle george and she were worried because her husbands were all dodgy and they all died and she didnt want uncle george to die but maybe he is. i have run out of ideas i cant think any more uncle george is not in any police station but the police took him and I dont understand and maybe he is bean disappeared

Saturday 14th December

this morning i woke up and i thought uncle george wood be in the kitchen making a cup of tea with the toaster again and when i got up he wasnt their and i was sad and so i thought i should do summat to remember him and so i made a cup of tea with the toaster but then all the power went off and nothing worked anymore except for the laptop i think it is a sign of summat horrible like that uncle george is stone dead

Kevin, stop recording your moronic half-thoughts in my diary! As Kevin so poorly described, the last few days have been something of a trial for the both of us and I now realise that I have a second, more pressing death sentence hanging over me.

For the last forty-eight hours I have been chained to an old bedstead in a cortijo somewhere in the nearby hills. This morning, as the church bells struck seven, I was roughly unfastened and led outside with a bag over my head and my hands secured behind my back. Unbeknown to my captors the material of my headgear was gossamer thin, allowing me to ascertain the various shapes before me.

"On thee floor, gringo!" commanded one of the policemen in the style of a Mexican bandito, kicking the backs of my legs. I remained standing. I will fall on my knees before no one. I felt a gun in the small of my back.

"OK, 'ave it your way," he said.

"'Ave you dug thee grave, Antonio?" one policeman-bandito asked another.

"Si!" he replied.

"Muy bien. Then I will shoot 'im in thee head."

This was it, my death. Through my bag I could make out a small fence ten yards in the distance that appeared to safeguard passers-by from a steep drop down the hillside. It was my only chance. I felt the cold metal of an automatic weapon against the back of my skull.

"Any last requests?" the gunman asked.

"I would rather like to see my lawyer," I said.

"Lo siento, señor," he replied.

It looked like I would be required to take a different course of action. Mustering all my strength I raised the foot of my right leg sharply and connected my heel to the tender area between the legs of the policeman-bandito standing behind me. As he crumpled to the ground with an agonised groan I sprinted forward and leapt over the fence hoping that the fall would not be too great. I have no idea how far I tumbled but fortunately I appeared to land in a large collection of loose leaves. I shook the bag from my head and, still with hands behind my back, tramped down the hillside as fast as I could to a distant track. I looked behind me but no one was in pursuit. I had escaped execution on this occasion but no doubt they would hunt me down.

I stopped at the first house I saw, hoping that its owner would speak English, and who should answer the door but good Old Bob! It is quite a palace he has up there. I pointed out the distant house in which I appeared to have been jailed and asked him who lived there but he said that it had been vacant for years. He invited me into his workshop and removed the handcuffs without much fuss.

"Elena and Edith are out shopping," he said.

"Are they?" said I, wondering why he thought that such a fact would be of the slightest interest to me.

"Would you care to stay for a pint or two? I've got some John Smith's."

"No, Bob," I said. "I have to go."

"Please," he pleaded. "I just want to talk to someone."

"Sorry," I said and ran out of his front door.

Realising just how far I was from the coast I swiftly returned to his house and requested a lift home, a service that he duly provided. He may have been desperate to talk but his stories were of such a low quality that halfway down the hill I had to ask him to desist and we sat in a frosty silence for the remainder of the journey.

Kevin seemed delighted to greet me. I found it quite unnerving. I do not believe anyone has ever before missed my presence. Even Ambrose can be somewhat indifferent unless he has got himself entangled in a modern appliance.

Now I have a problem. I need to flee the country and yet I do not have a passport. Thanks however to European Schengen regulations I, or rather the human greasebomb, could drive to France and beyond without any border formalities. That said, the police will surely be aware of such an escape route and have set up numerous roadblocks.

I took a moment to survey my options. The truth slowly dawned: This is all pointless. There is no escape. Or, rather, there is only one escape: Death.

I held my head in my hands. My end could not come soon enough. I should have accepted the executioner's bullet rather than live life as a slowly disintegrating fugitive. I now had the choice of dying through mental deterioration or with a surprise assassin's bullet to the head. Neither option seemed particularly cheering. I sat in the comfortable chair and thought deeply. The sun set and room grew dark.

And why are none of the bloody lights working?

*

My mood had descended somewhere very dark indeed. The telephone rang. Kevin answered it.

"Hello, Kevin speaking. How can I be of service?...Doctor Bloomfield, eh?"

"Give me the phone," I said.

"You've got Uncle George's test results, have yer? To check his Mad Cow Disease?...Yeah."

"Give me the phone, you arse."

"I'll pass you over to him," he said officiously. I grabbed the phone from his oily fingers.

"Sorry about that, doctor."

He talked and my jaw dropped and he talked some more. By the end of the conversation I imagine my face was drained of colour.

"And you are absolutely sure about all of that?" I asked downheartedly. "There could be no mistake?...No...Thank you...Thank you, Doctor Bloomfield."

I ended the call.

"Go on then. How were it?" Kevin asked.

I looked him sadly in the eyes.

"It is bad news," I said.

"Oh."

Kevin was not one for sympathetic speeches.

"Yes, oh," I said.

"I've got some more bad news for yer," he said.

"Have you?"

Kick a man when he is down.

"Yeah. Do you want it?"

"Go on."

"The bank called while you were bean disappeared."

"While I was what?"

"The bank called."

"No, the other bit. Oh, forget it. What did they say?"

"I pretended to be you so they'd tell me t' details."

"Good. What did they say?"

"Your money's gone and they can't get it back."

Sunday 15th December

o no its terrible terrible i thought this might happen when i told him bout the bank and stuff and now hes gone and done it and uncle george is a ghost like me mum. he as topped himsel. i woke up this morning at half two and found this next to the computer

Dear Kevin,

I will keep this short. As you know, circumstances of late have been rather trying for me and so I have decided that it is no longer in my interests to remain on this foetid shithole of a planet. I shall now walk into the sea.

Piss off,
George

PS. It is perhaps of little interest now, but I know for certain that I did not write those first two additions to this diary.

terrible i have bean crying all day and even ambrose looks sad i know he knows. i like it here but i only like it because uncle george is hear and now hes gone and everything is rubbish

ive written this bit later ive understood what george said he did not write it and so he did not kill them and that means someone is trying to frame him for a crime he did not comit and so ill find em and take em to the police and maybe the police will bean disappeared them. ill make a list of all the things i need to do to catch the baddies

1. find out who added the words to the diary

thats it

ive written this bit even later no there is other things i need to find out like who was the robot and why did he shot us

thats really it now

and who wrote on the car

thats really really it now

ill get my silver kecks mended so i can find out who did these things

sorry if my writing is rubbish i didnt go to school much

Monday 16th December

i was worried cos id no clues to find the baddies and then a ghost helped me and i think that must be the ghost of uncle george hes going to help me solve the case even if hes dead. the ghost made me remember bout the video on ambroses head and when i checked the video it showed some good things an now ive got to write them down it was strange and ive worked out when it happened and it was the day we went to manzano and stood in our pants and nothing happened except that old woman said we was prossies. that day some shoes came into the house and walked to the drawers and then went away again and then bout an hour later some different shoes came in and went to the drawers and went away again and i think one of the shoes left the purse and the other shoes left the wallet and they could of put the wallet their before the purse i do not know and i dont know why the first shoes did not bring the purse and the wallet at the same time but they didnt so now i must find the shoes and who the shoes wearer is. one of the shoes is yellow and shood be easy to find and the other shoes is like a bit purple and like a boot. ill go in town now and look for them o no i was in town and i saw some shoes like the yellow shoes but not the same and i followed the shoes any way and then the shoes went down a alley and so i went down the alley but when i got to the end the shoes where not their and then their was a gunshot and it hit near the floor but i looked round and their were no one there i think this means im getting close to the baddies i hope they do not kill me before i find who wants to kill me

Tuesday 17th December

i dont like writing this diary it makes me head hurt

i looked for shoes and did not find none and so i went to bar Wars and spoke to mr bullshit and i told him bout the shoes and he said he will look for them an all then he said he were a expert on shoes because hes a close friend off jimmy shoe. i dont know who jimmy shoe is but mr bullshit says he does even if jimmy shoe dont sound like a real person

Wednesday 18th December

today was a good day and I have followed a clue and now i know who is the yellow shoes but i wont tell you cos it is a surprise and i the Silver Panthar wants to do this like a proper detective and i will and no one can stop me

i am still sad bout uncle george but i think he is now a happy ghost cos i have solved this thing well i know the yellow shoes and that is only lickle but when i do my detective thing i will be cunning and get them to be truthful

writing diarys is boring

Thursday 19th December

today a policeman phoned me and asked me to see if a body they found in the sea was uncle george and i went to the police station and i saw the body and i said yes that is uncle george and they said are you sure and i said yes so i went to bar wars and i said we shood have a good bye party for uncle george and i thought that if i invite everyone at the same time then no one baddy can shoot me and they said no one wanted to go and then they saw i were sad and said that they wood be really happy to have a party now that uncle george is dead and so tomorrow there is a party in uncle georges house and everyone is coming well some of them

Friday 20th December

they where all sitting there janet and vince and mr bullshit and malty mike and no one was saying nothing just drinking the beer id bought. i walked into the living room dressed in me Silver Panthar suit with the new kecks. id bean watching detectives on the internet all morning and so I knew what to do i waited till their were a bit of hush and then i says i suppose you wander why i called you all here and vince said cos george has pegged it and mike said he should show some respect and vince told him to button it and then mike started crying and he said something intresting mike said we shouldnt have pushed him and vince told him to shut up but he didnt shut up and mike said we killed him we killed george and janet asked him how but he just repeated that we killed him and then i said ta-daaaa and vince said ta-daaaa what and i said ive got a surprise and he said what sort of surprise and i opened the kitchen door

Thank you, Kevin, for your thoughtful, well-constructed prose but if you touch this computer one more time I will ram it so far up your massive arse that you will be typing email with your teeth.

I walked out of the kitchen to a symphony of gasps and found Morality Mike on his knees, weeping like a professional mourner.

"Good afternoon, Mike," I said.

He looked up at me and halted his blubbing.

"But...but...you're dead," he said, a look of utter confusion ravaged his face.

"Evidently I am not," I said suavely. I commanded the room with my charm. I glanced towards Janet, who was smiling broadly at me. I gave her a cool nod. It was unfortunate that this was the moment I belched inwardly, delivering a small amount of vomit into my mouth. Janet could not have known what had happened but the look in her eyes suggested that she was privy to some of my internal data and she swiftly turned her head as though trying to locate the exit. I quickly swallowed back down the semi-digested contents of my breakfast, but not without damage to the lesson in sophistication that I was delivering.

Janet turned back towards me.

"Glad you're alright," she said.

"Hang on a minute," I said. "Why is nobody wearing black?"

"Kevin told us not to," replied Bullshit Phil.

"And to be honest no one was that bothered that you'd snuffed it, John," added Vince.

Mike was still struggling to take in the vision of Georgeness he found before him.

"But," Mike turned to Kevin, "you said you'd identified his body, laddie. You said they'd found him in the sea."

"Yeah, I did. Clever, eh? I reckoned if he were officially

dead, people wouldn't keep tryin' to kill us."

"Who's trying to kill *you*?" asked Vince.

Kevin and I looked down towards his yellow shoes.

"I will come to that in a minute," I said. I cleared my throat. "In recent days I have had a little time to think, to ponder my predicament."

Whilst I was carefully setting up my stall Kevin jumped in with both feet.

"It's you, Vince! You were a robot an' then you shot us," said Kevin, excitedly dancing on the spot.

Vince looked to Bullshit Phil and twirled his finger at his temple.

"Mental. Fruit bat crazy," he said.

"You pushed them too far," said Mike to Vince. "I told you and you wouldn't listen."

"Interesting. Would you care to elaborate, Vincent?" I asked.

"He's lost it too," said Vince.

"Mike?" I said, hoping for a confession from the man who seemed most willing to spill the beans.

"What?" he said, still confused.

"Never mind. I think I have worked out most of it for myself – I have had a few days to investigate – but maybe you can help me fill in a few blanks."

Mike nodded dumbly.

"Look," said Vince, "it was only a bit of fun."

"Number one. Someone edited my diary."

There was silence.

"Aye, I did that," said Mike, regaining his composure slightly and seeming relieved to confess. "Your system was wide open. No password or anything. It's amazing no one has hacked your bank account."

"They have," I said sullenly.

"Really? Well, that wasn't me." He stared at me solidly.

"That definitely wasn't me. This was just Vince's stupid game."

"And you changed events to make it seem as though I had killed a number of people."

He started to whimper again.

"It was just a game. It's Vince's fault."

"How did ya work it out, uncle George?"

"For a while I doubted myself. But then I had the sudden realisation about a certain quality of my prose: You see, I never contract. Unless it is fundamental to the metre of a poem, obviously."

"Obviously," said Kevin as though he understood. Then his face crumpled into a mousse of confusion. "What you on 'bout, uncle George?"

"Those two paragraphs, and only those two paragraphs, in which I confessed to murder, contained contractions. I did not write them. I do not contract. I am better than that."

"So who did do it then?" asked Janet, clearly not a party to this scheme. "Who killed all those people?"

Vince sniggered. I continued, leaving the question hanging.

"Yes, for a while I doubted myself," I continued, "what with my having CJD."

I turned towards Vince, who burst out laughing.

"You don't have CJD, you turnip," he said.

"Yes, I know that now," I said. "A real doctor told me."

"You're not a mad cow, uncle George?" said Kevin with eyes full of wonder.

"I was never a mad cow, you dimwit. But I do not have CJD."

"That's wonderful, George," said Janet beaming.

"What I want to know," I said, "is why you went to the trouble of writing it up in my medical records when you had already refused to show me those very records?"

237

I felt the slim bristles on my upper lip curling into the moustache of Poirot.

"Well, it's not every day that you see a fat knob in a silver suit and top hat hiding behind the sofa in your reception, is it?" said Vince. Kevin's face collapsed. "I thought I'd write it up, leave the alarm off and let the Tin Man here take the good news back to base camp."

"So who killed Tony, Margaret and Alan?" asked Janet again.

"Yes, Vince, who killed them?" I reiterated.

"No one killed them, you silly sod," said Vince. "They were going back to England for Christmas so they decided to play along. That's why they disappeared."

"But if no one died, why did t' police bean disappeared uncle George?" Kevin asked Vince.

Vince frowned.

"What's he on?" replied the world's worst doctor.

"Why were he arrested by t' police?" Kevin repeated.

"He wasn't."

"I distinctly remember being hauled out of here by the Civil Guard," I said.

"Sod off," said Vince, scoffing. "They were builder mates of mine. Didn't you notice their Spanish accents were all over the place?" Yes, now that he came to mention it I did. "They're from the West Country." He looked at Kevin. "Your uncle was 'bean disappeared' by The Wurzels."

I could not believe what I was hearing.

"But their uniforms..." I said.

"Yeah, they came from *Party Hearty*," he added. *Party Hearty* is Merla's fancy dress shop, providing amusing costumes for birthdays, anniversaries and mock executions.

"You chained me to a rusty bedstead for forty-eight hours for a bloody joke?" I yelled.

"You deserved it!" said Phil suddenly exploding. "You've

made everyone's life 'round here a right misery. You've been denouncing people for fun, you bell-end. And what about poor old Mike?"

"What about me?" Mike said, still unhappy with his part in proceedings.

"How's the missus?" asked Phil.

Mike looked down.

"She still won't come back," he said sadly.

Phil glared at me.

"You did that, you tosser," he said. "We found out who started that rumour about Mike's affair. It was you! I'd have left you strapped to the bed for a month. I'd have done to you what I did to the gerries in Dunkirk."

There was a silence whilst everyone absorbed what he had just said.

"You were at Dunkirk?" I asked incredulously.

"Yeah. Caravanning holiday in '93, but I showed 'em."

"Oh," said Vince, "and you probably think you're all adventurous for escaping, don't you? They let you go. Jeff said it took you half an hour to get down that slope. He said he's seen tortoises make more effective bids for freedom."

I was silent. Regarding the denuncias I had merely sought justice where justice was to be found. I have to admit that I did feel rather bad about Mike's situation, but had Margaret not been such a high quality conduit of cheap gossip his family would still be together. As a whole I felt exonerated and did not feel I had anything for which to apologise.

"So none of them are dead?" asked Janet in thankful disbelief.

"No. Margaret's even on her way back," said Mike. "She felt rotten about what happened and wanted to be here for this."

"But I went to Tony's funeral," I said.

"It was staged," said Vince as though it were obvious.

"I saw his body."

"Eh?" said Vince. "No, you didn't. It was staged."

"His body was in a casket in the adjoining room," I added.

"No, it wasn't."

Mike chipped in.

"Y'know, I tried to call him a couple of days ago and didn't get a reply," he said.

"I hear reception is terrible in heaven," I said amusingly.

"He's not dead," said Vince firmly.

"I saw him. Either he was dead or he can hold his breath for an exceptionally long time."

"He is not dead," repeated Vince. "Mike arranged the funeral. Tell him Mike."

"What? No, I didn't," said Mike. "I thought you arranged it, Vince."

"I didn't arrange it," Vince said.

They looked at each other in horror.

"Oh shit," said Mike as the truth dawned. "I thought Trish was acting a bit over the top."

"Who's Trish?" asked Janet.

"Tony's missus," said Vince. His face suddenly went pale. "Oh no."

"What?"

"I gave her a wink and told her he'll be alright once he's had a good sleep," said Vince. "I wondered why she didn't laugh."

"Very tasteful," I said, "but no more medically inaccurate than the misinformation that you usually spout. But more to the point," I said looking around from face to face, "who killed Tony?"

Everyone thought for a moment.

"The same person who shot us?" yelled Kevin a little too excitedly whilst looking directly at Vince.

"Yes Kevin, I too thought that Vince had shot us," I said,

trying to put the pieces together, "and yet he did not even know Tony was dead."

I was, if I am being honest, baffled.

"Why do you keep saying I shot you? It was a game. I don't go around shooting people."

"Someone in yellow shoes phoned us up usin' a robot voice, shot at us, tricked us into standin' in our underpants in Manzano an' sneaked in here an' planted the wallet," said Kevin all in one breath.

He had to bend double to refill the tiny cheese and onion crisp packets that serve as his lungs.

"Yes, I planted the wallet – I saw the car was gone – but I didn't phone you and I certainly didn't shoot you."

"It musta been Phil then, uncle George," said Kevin. "There's no bugger else."

"Unlike Vince, I really would love to shoot you, professor, but I wouldn't have missed, mate," said Phil. "Sniper school and all that." He looked at his watch. "Isn't it time for another drink?"

"Ah," I said defeated. It clearly could not have been Mike. He was still wiping away tears of guilt.

There was a moment of silence.

"So well done, John," said Vince sleazily, "you've solved everything and you've solved nothing."

I stared into his eyes.

Slowly, through gritted teeth, I rasped, "My name is George." I waited a good five seconds, maintaining eye contact the whole time. "You stupid, little shit."

"I know that," he replied lightly, "but it screws with your head. Doesn't it, Johnny Boy?"

I made a mental note not to let him rile me in future.

"Well then," I said. "Perhaps we will never know."

My memorial seemed to be grinding to a disappointing climax. The torturers faced their victim in silence.

"Sod this. I'm going to the pub," said Phil, preparing to stand.

Before he could complete his movement there was a tumultuous crash, everyone looked from face to face unable to take in what was happening and finally my front door once again wrenched itself from its hinges. I stood tall, with hands on hips, observing the wreckage.

"Will people stop knocking my bloody door in?" I yelled. I looked at the two burly figures silhouetted in the door frame. "Who are you?" I asked.

They walked silently into the living room and filled entirely the only remaining space in front of the window. They both stuffed their black jeans and leather jackets with oversized muscles. Everyone stared at these imposing lumps. Janet was the first to break the silence.

"Julian?" she gasped towards the larger and older of the two men.

"I've told you before, Jan, don't call me faakin' Julian."

His voice was the solid bass of the opera star Feodor Chaliapin, if Feodor Chaliapin had been born in the East End of London.

"What are you doing here? Why have you kicked in George's door?"

"Who is this?" I asked her.

"It's my husband."

"I thought you said that your rugby team of former partners were all dead or remarried."

"Two of 'em got remarried to each other," sniggered Kevin to anyone who was listening.

"No, they didn't, Kevin" said Janet. "Yes, my ex-husbands are all dead or remarried. But my husband isn't."

"I've come for you, Jan," he said.

"When did you get out?" she asked.

"Wonderful! Is he another villain?" I asked, unwisely as it

turned out. The smaller of the men approached me.

"Yes, he is, sunshine," he said. "An' so am I."

He gave me a firm thump to the stomach and I went down, wheezing like a laboratory beagle.

"Leave him, Mario," said Julian casually. "You can't go 'round smackin' pensioners. You're here to smack whoever this little slut has been seein' behind me back."

Everyone stayed silent.

"Which one is it?" Julian asked the room but the room did not reply. "Cat got yer tongues? Well, I know a little loosener. Mario, fetch!"

Mario walked over to the drawers, opened the middle one and removed a gun. He walked back to Julian and handed it to him.

Janet turned to me dumbfounded.

"What's that doing there?" she asked.

"I have absolutely no idea," I said. "What is going on? Why is there a gun in my house and why do you know its whereabouts when I am entirely ignorant of the fact?"

The gangsters merely laughed at me.

"Purple boots!" shouted Kevin, jumping to his feet and pointing a stubby paw at Mario's footwear.

"Didn't want to get fingered holdin' a piece, did I?" said Julian. "Thought it'd be safer here, so Mario did his best robot voice to get you out the house."

Mario retrieved a small device from his pocket and held it to his lips.

"Exterminate!" he said in a distorted metallic tone.

"So it was you who shot us?" I asked.

"Gimme a chance," said Julian. "I only got out yesterday."

Julian turned to look at Kevin, who was gawping open-mouthed at him.

"What the faakin' hell at you lookin' at, pal?"

"Nothing," said Kevin meekly.

Julian moved towards my nephew and placed his nose one inch from Kevin's.

"I said, what are you faakin' lookin' at, you silver freak?"

Kevin attempted to dig himself out of his hole.

"Soz, you're t' spit of a mate o' mine."

"Really?" said Julian, turning up the aggression.

"Yeah, me best mate. He's dead now," said Kevin sadly.

Julian softened.

"Oh, sorry, pal. S'pose he was special to you."

He patted Kevin on his chest. Kevin smiled.

"Oh yeah, he were a legend. Everyone loved Ugly Pete."

Julian recoiled his massive arm and slammed a fist-shaped hole into Kevin's pillowy face. He howled and fell to the floor.

"Julian!" squealed Janet.

"Mr Bullshit, why don't you do somethin' wi' yer SAS training?" Kevin squawked through broken teeth.

"Now's not the time, Kev," Phil replied, sinking back invisibly into the sofa.

"What did I tell you about callin' me Julian?" he said, pointing the gun at Janet's face. "Right, enough faakin' about. Mario, which one of these tossers has she been knobbin'?"

"I'm not sure."

"What? But you've been followin' 'em for weeks."

"First I thought it was the old fella."

"Jesus! Well, it coulda been worse. She coulda been seeing the silver troll," he said, waving his gun towards Kevin.

"And then," replied Mario, "I thought she was seeing the silver troll."

"What? Faakin' hell. What's the matter with you, Jan?"

"I'm seeing no one," Janet said firmly.

"Don't believe you, love," he said, pressing his face up against hers. "Dave the Knife said he'd heard from his mate you were down on the Costa and you'd hooked up with someone." He looked around the room. "And that someone's gonna be eatin' a small snack from this little gun in a few seconds."

He waved the pistol casually around the room.

"Are you hungry, Julian?" asked Kevin out of nowhere. He hauled himself on to his knees. "Fancy a sandwich or summat?"

"What are you doing?" I asked him in an urgent whisper.

"Don't you ever, EVER, call me Julian, you little prick." He edged towards Kevin. "Or else I'll knock your other tooth out."

"Sorry, sir, but I were feelin' a bit peckish," said Kevin, standing unimpressively. "An' I thought you might be an' all."

"Sit down, Gollum!" Julian yelled. He surveyed the room as Kevin returned to the floor. "Someone in this room is knocking off me missus. Who is it?" He pointed the gun at each person in turn. It descended upon Kevin's broken face for the second time. Julian appeared to have come to a decision. "Y'know somethink, chubs, I *could* use a sandwich."

Kevin sprang to his feet.

"I'll make ya one," he said, turning and bouncing towards the kitchen.

"Stop!" shouted Julian. Kevin halted with his hands above his head. "Mario, go in and watch him. Make sure he don't do nothing stupid."

Mario followed Kevin into the kitchen.

"Hungry work, this," Julian said with a big, evil smile. He turned towards his wife. "Jan, do you still love me?" His voice dripped with pathos.

Janet shifted in her seat uneasily.

"Of course I do," she said unconvincingly.

"But you still knobbed someone, didn't ya, ya slag?" His face seemed to grow a shade redder. "Who was it?" He turned his gun towards me. "You're George, right?" I nodded apprehensively. "One question I was meaning to ask you.

Why did you kill that copper?"

"How do you know about that?"

"You killed a policeman?" asked Janet.

I shook my head.

"Mario told me," said Julian. "He said he saw him falling off the mountain."

"How?"

"He was following you, remember. Caused him a lot of grief that. He had to move the body 'cos it'd landed in the same place as that other fella."

"Which fellow?"

"I don't know. You'll have to ask him." He looked around and sniffed the air. "Thanks for the gun by the way."

Mario left the kitchen but still monitored its interior.

"Whose body did you move?" I asked Mario.

"Eh?" he said.

"Tell him," said Julian.

"You were walking with one fella," Mario replied, "the one who had the dog on his back, and then he disappeared and then you started going back down the mountain. Hang on, I thought. Where's the other bloke? I went to look and then outta nowhere he fell out of a tree on top of me. Shit me up, it did. What was he doing in a faakin' tree? I just lashed out and he went over the edge." He was pensive for a second. "Sorry about that," he added.

For a gangster he seemed unusually apologetic to have ended someone's life.

"You killed Scotch Tony?" said Mike, suddenly realising that his involvement in Vince's stupidity had ended in murder. He started to cry again.

"If that's who he was," said Mario. "Like I said, sorry. It all happened a bit sudden."

"Don't worry about it," said Vince casually. "His liver was goosed."

"I do not suppose you informed him of this condition," I said to Vince.

"As a matter of fact, I didn't. He wouldn't have stopped drinking – they never do – and he'd only have been miserable. I was doing him a favour."

I shook my head in dismay.

"And you moved Jesús, er, the policeman?" I said to Mario.

"Yeah, what happened? I saw him falling. I was at the bottom of the hill. I couldn't be arsed to keep walking up that same bastard mountain. What do you see in it? Rocks and trees and stuff. Boring! Anyway the copper fell off the top and landed in the same place as the first fella. I figured if someone found him they'd link the two deaths. And I wasn't going down for knocking off a pig, so I moved him."

"That explains a few things," I said. I thought I would use this opportunity to delve more deeply. Unconsciously I squinted one eye, a little like Columbo. "Are you familiar with the Russian contingent on this coast?" I asked.

"What?" he replied, confused.

"Do you know any Russians down here?"

"Yeah, I do a bit of work for 'em ev'ry now and again."

"Ah."

"Why?"

"It does not matter. And one final thing."

"Go on."

"Did you spray my car?"

He started chuckling to himself.

"Yeah, thought it'd be a laugh, seeing as other people kept doing it," he replied.

I looked towards Phil, who smiled sourly.

Kevin skipped from the kitchen and handed Julian a snack.

"Here you go, sir. I've made you a chorizo sandwich."

Oh, the little pug-faced genius! He had formed a plan.

Julian raised the sandwich to his lips with the gun still wandering the room in search of a target. Ambrose, who had been quietly dozing near the kitchen door, suddenly woke up.

The rest happened in slow motion. A white, furry rocket flew across the room, defying the laws of physics, heading towards the face of our assassin. A trail of smoke seemed to follow in his wake as he inched closer to his goal. Voices of an old 78 record were played at 33 rpm.

"Llllll-iiiiii-tttttt-tttttt-llllll-eeeeee ffffff-aaaaaa-aaaaaa-kkkkkk-eeeeee-rrrrrr!" slurred Julian.

Julian had finally seen our canine of mass destruction targeting his face and knew in an instant he was about to lose control of the situation, that he would be overpowered by a roomful of people and that he would be heading back to gaol.

He quickly raised his gun and shot Ambrose's upper body. My lovely hound fell to the floor bleeding and yelping pitifully and scuttled into a corner.

"You shot my dog," I said. He shrugged his shoulders. "You shot my fucking dog."

"Yes, granddad. Who's next?" I moved to comfort Ambrose. "Don't move a muscle," Julian barked.

This really was the limit.

"Tell him, Vince," I said.

"Tell him what?" he replied.

"About you and Janet."

"What?" she said, alarmed.

Julian levelled his gun at Vince.

"Well, he's much more her type. Come on, you big ponce. Talk!" he commanded.

"I don't know what you're talking about," Vince said with widened eyes. "Is this to get back at me because of our game?"

"No. Well, yes. But it is also true and that makes it all the more delicious," I said smugly.

"No, it isn't true," said Janet shakily.

"I found a chart in his reception scoring all the women with whom he had been intimate," I said. "Janet scored a ten."

"Did she now?" Julian's finger tightened on the trigger. "Sounds about right."

"It was all made up," said Vince with panic in his voice and holding out his hands in submission towards Julian. He turned to me. "I knew you'd go snooping. I was messing with your head."

"I don't believe you," said Julian in an eerily calm voice.

"I've only met him twice before today," pleaded Janet.

"I don't believe you either."

"How many rounds have I got, Mario?"

"It's full," he replied.

"Looks like there's a bullet for everyone who's pissed me off."

He pointed the gun directly at Janet's face.

This was my chance to impress.

"No, do not shoot her," I said boldly. "It was not Vince." All eyes stared in my direction. "It was me. I am her lover."

Despite the tension my attempt at gallantry was greeted with an explosion of laughter, which I found more than a little ungrateful.

"Don't worry, old man," said Julian. "You'll be getting a bullet too." He moved the gun closer to Janet's face. "It's been nice knowing you, Janet, love."

Julian squeezed the trigger.

There was a bang.

Followed by a squeal of brakes.

Followed by an even louder blast as a car crashed through my front window, crushing Julian and Mario beneath its wheels.

From within a dust cloud Margaret's head popped out of the driver's window.

"Sorry, I'm late," she said. She looked around the room. "Oh dear, I seem to have made rather a mess." She looked at me with a pair of crazed eyes. "George? I thought you were dead."

"I see your driving has improved, Margaret," I said.

Finally, with the opportunity to assist my tiny canine friend, I rushed towards Ambrose, who was breathing raggedly. I petted his little head.

"You brave, little soldier," I said. "You nearly saved the day." A hot tear spilled down my cheek. Kevin came and knelt beside me. I smiled a bitter-sweet smile at him. I turned to the others. "Thank you for all your help," I said sarcastically.

"It was nothing," said Phil.

"I know it was."

But unfortunately it was not over.

"Jorge Pearly, you are under arrest!" A distinctly dishevelled Jesús strode into the rubble of my house via the car-sized hole in my wall. "You are under arrest for the murder of Anthony Hingston."

"Will today never end," I said wearily. I turned to the police chief. "I did not do it. The murderer is the man trapped beneath the wheels of this car."

"Of course he is," said Jesús. "You are under arrest!" he repeated. "I have been waiting for two weeks to do this."

His previously calm demeanour had been replaced by something bordering upon insanity.

"It's alright, uncle George." He turned towards the policeman. "I've got summat to show you, Jesus."

Kneeling beside Ambrose, Kevin removed the memory card from the camera still fastened to his head. He went to the table and flipped open the laptop and inserted the card.

"Watch this," he said to the Jesús.

*

The others left, apologising for their part in the destruction of my house, if not my life. Janet did not seem in the slightest bit perturbed that her sixth husband was dead.

Jesús stayed to watch the video of this afternoon's events and reconsidered my arrest. He told us his story. He remembered regaining consciousness as a muscled fellow was dragging his body down the hillside. Then he heard distant voices. His captor quickly stuffed him in a hollow and raced off. He managed to summon the strength to call out. The voices had belonged to two of the hippies that live near the river. They kindly nursed him back to health, although he feared he would never again have the courage to face a mung bean. As a result of the fall he had lost his memory entirely but upon reading one of my fine walking pieces in *Merla Now!* and seeing my photograph he had remembered me and started to piece his own fractured life back together. Given the circumstances he decided not to press charges against Ambrose. My dog would not hang.

Jesús called the emergency services. They would not let me leave until they had cleared away the bodies of Julian and Mario and towed Margaret's demolished car, and left me with a huge hole for a front wall. I shooed Jesús out of the house as quickly as I could. I had my own emergency service to visit. Ambrose, hang on in there.

Saturday 21st December

For the first time in weeks I had been looking forward to waking up in a warm, comfortable bed. For the last few days, sleeping where I could whilst living off the last remaining twenty euro note in my wallet, the nights after my imagined suicide had been cold and lonely but no more uncomfortable than my usual sofa, which I assume was designed by a Puritan and then constructed by an alcoholic monkey with a broken saw.

With the house in disarray Kevin had organised a hotel room for us. Despite his enormous wealth he still had a parsimonious approach to spending and what he assumed to have been a twin room turned out to be a double. Sleeping beside his odour and the occasional accidental rubbing against his blancmange body was one of the most unpleasant events of my life. You might think that I should be more grateful but I am not. I would be more grateful if he had paid the additional fifteen euros and secured us a room each. No one wants to share a bed with a man who alternates between frenzied nightmares, thunderous snoring and clumsy fumblings, the nature of which I do not wish to ponder.

At nine I left Kevin in a vegetative state and returned to the veterinarian's. Tiny Ambrose was lying there on the vet's surgery table, unconscious, attached to a heart monitor. The bullet wound was in the top of his remaining front leg. Its size seemed to have increased overnight.

"This is very expensive," said the vet dispassionately.

"I do not care. I need him alive," I said. "At any cost."

This was easy for me to say. Kevin had reluctantly agreed to foot the bill on the condition that Ambrose would no longer urinate in his shoes.

"I can make that solemn vow on his behalf," I had said to him, knowing full well that if Ambrose did not rise to the challenge of polluting his boots then I surely would.

"It may be better if he is put to sleep," said the vet.

"Never. Let me know of any change in his circumstances."

*

I returned home just as my Spanish landlady, Dolores, and

a workman were striding through the rubble of my front yard. The workman looked around the building, yesterday's hole now covered in thick plastic sheeting. He rubbed his tanned, stubbled chin.

"Señor Pearly, this is big trouble for me," Dolores said.

"Yes," I said. "And for me."

"I will need to higher the rent."

"What?" I said in disbelief. "Is the rent inversely proportional to the number of walls a house possesses?"

"What?" she asked. She disregarded my question. "All this costs money," she said, rubbing her fingers together.

"You have insurance, surely?"

She laughed haughtily.

"No, I no have no insurance."

I had already enquired if Margaret had insurance for her car. She was not even aware of the concept.

Dolores was a witch. She had wanted me out for years but my original contract had only allowed her to raise the rent by five per cent per annum, a right that she had strictly enforced. Unfortunately the contract also had a disaster policy that allowed rents to be renegotiated in the case of a serious mishap. I assumed that she was preparing to exercise this option.

I looked around the remains of a house that symbolised what my desperate life had become: Marjorie's choosing gateau-enhanced spinsterdom over my urbane conversation, Janet's rejection of well-maintained if mature physical perfection, the pond scum betrayal by the inmates of my local bar. Back in 2008 I had hated this house. Now it was something much more visceral.

"You know what?" I said, looking her right in the eyes. "You can shove your house!"

She looked at me for a moment, her brow furrowed.

"I can shove my house?" she said.

I turned on my heel and marched away.

"Where can I shove it? *No entiendo,* señor Pearly!"

*

I returned to the hotel room. Despite its being mid-afternoon Kevin had only recently emerged from his daily coma. The room had a strange green tinge to its atmosphere and so in order to grab some bracing sea air we walked along the beach, beyond the hotels, and stopped at a lonely bar whose tables faced the Mediterranean. We each ordered a beer.

"We did pretty well I think," said Kevin.

"Mmm."

"I worked out 'bout Vince and his yellow shoes and you worked out you'd been set up. Grand, that."

"Yes."

"We should set up a detective agency, uncle George."

I laughed.

"You should be counting your lucky stars," I said. "If Janet's husband had discovered that it was you who had slept with her he would have murdered you."

"What 'bout me and Janet?" he asked with faux innocence.

"I found something of hers in the back of the car."

He sniggered and covered his mouth with the back of his paw.

"See," he said, "you'd be a good detective."

"I do not think so. There are still a couple of things we have not discovered."

"Eh?"

"Who hacked my bank account?"

Kevin looked blankly and shrugged his shoulders.

"And who shot at us?" I asked.

"Mario did. He were t' one wi' t' gun."

"I suppose."

"Except..."

"Except what?"

"The purple boots came in t' house on t' day we was in Manzano in our underkecks."

"Yes. The day we were shot at."

"Yeah. But, when you was dead, I were shot at five days later."

"So?"

"Mario's gun were in your house five days later."

I thought about this for a moment.

"Maybe he had a second gun," I said.

Kevin was quiet for a moment.

"Yeah, maybe," he said, seeming to have surrendered.

"Yes, I mean, who else would want to kill us?" I asked.

"Are yer jokin'? I know a townful of folk who wanna kill you."

We finished our drinks and walked along the beach, heading back to town. We were totally alone. A gentle breeze blew, chilling us now that the sun had sunk beneath the horizon. The sky was a palette of orange and maroon.

"Pretty, i'n't it, uncle George?" said Kevin.

"It is acceptable, I suppose."

"Nah, it's better than that. I love it 'ere."

"Good for you."

"You've gotta chance now to make life better."

"What are you prattling about now?" I asked.

"We're a team, uncle George. Wi' my money we can do stuff. We can do anythin'," he said. "An' you're not dyin'."

"Mmm."

"But I reckon you should make some friends."

"I do not need any friends."

"Everyone needs friends, uncle George."

"Not me."

"Well then, you should at least apologise for everythin'."

"What? They were the ones who kidnapped me, framed

me for murder and told me I was dying!" I said indignantly.

"Yeah, but only 'cos you'd bin an arsehole."

I pondered his words.

"Don't be an arsehole, uncle George. No one needs to be an arsehole."

"Mmm."

"Be nice."

I turned towards him. Towering above his squat body, I placed a hand on his dwarfish shoulder. We shared a smile. I believe I was on the point of uttering something deeply profound when the shooting started. It came from nowhere. We stood on an entirely empty beach.

"Run!" Kevin shouted, and we did, with impressive speed for a seventy year-old and an obese midget.

*

I had been more than ready to relinquish the hotel room given last night's hideous sleeping arrangements but no one knew that we were residing there and so it was at least a safe if awful haven.

I slumped on to the hotel bed.

"I find all this attempted murder quite depressing," I said.

"Yeah, it's no picnic, is it?"

"I need to cheer myself up."

"Bar Wars?"

"Are you joking? We would be sitting ducks."

"Yeah," was all he could say.

I looked around the room.

"There is not even a bloody mini-bar!" I moaned.

Kevin thought for a moment.

"I know how you can cheer yersel' up."

"How?" I asked, unconvinced.

He took out my phone that he had thoughtfully liberated from the house, pressed a few keys and threw it in my direction.

"See if Richard's still in his coma. You'll enjoy that."

He was correct. I would enjoy that.

"Hello? Hello?" said the phone before I had the opportunity to place it beside my ear.

"Oh, hello, Celia," I said.

"Ah, George."

She sounded cold.

"Yes, I just thought I would ring to see how Richard was getting along."

I had my fingers crossed.

"I thought you would have called before now."

"Yes, sorry. I have been a little busy." I paused. "I assume he has made a full recover."

Please, anything but a full recover!

"No," she said darkly. Oh what a tonic! "But he did come out of the coma this morning."

I pulled a face and gave Kevin a thumbs down.

"Well, that is…a development," I said.

"Yes, I'm at the hospital now," she said. "Would you like to talk to him?"

Before I had a chance to refuse, the old fraud was muttering into my ear.

"Hello, George," he said weakly.

"Yes, hello. Well, good to hear that you are on the mend," I lied.

"George?" he said before I had finished my sentence.

"What?"

"Are you listening to me?"

"Yes, Richard, I am listening to you."

He talked over me again, the disrespectful old cretin.

"I have something important to tell you about my accident," he said.

"What is it?"

"It's…"

"Yes?"

"It's your..."

My what? My mind whirred. My fault? My dog? No, I knew! It is my...I wanted to hear him say it.

"Go on."

I could hear a distinct rattle in his voice. He said nothing more. He completed his sentence with a fit of rasping coughs and further rattling.

I thought I would give him a moment to calm himself but just then the shrill alarm of a hospital monitor sounded. I could hear Celia frantically calling for a nurse. What appeared to be five or six pairs of feet raced towards Richard's bed shouting various medical commands.

"Richard!" I called, but in the commotion his phone was forgotten. I looked at my own mobile for a second. Realising that there was no way to extract whatever vital information that Richard had wished to present me I hung up.

Was I to be the last of the Pearlys? My siblings were all now dead or dying, one killed in a dubious boating accident, another the victim of a unfortunate game show debacle and Richard, with the most mundane death of all, a boring road traffic accident to match his boring poetry.

"So?" asked Kevin.

"Difficult to say," I said. "It all started a little pessimistically but in the end I think everything worked out just as desired."

"Feelin' better?"

"Absolutely!"

Sunday 22nd December

I turned over to see Kevin's bloated face turned skywards on the pillow beside me. His tongue lolled sloppily out of his mouth and vibrated as he snored. He gave a dry, hacking cough, licked his already over-moist lips and then heaved himself over in my direction, flapping a flabby arm violently across my face. Maybe it would have been better if I were dying.

"Arrrrrrrrrrgh!" I screamed with all the force I could muster.

Kevin sat bolt upright, his gut spilling on to the upper surface of our shared duvet.

"What's up?" he asked in a shocked voice. "Is someone after us again?"

"I cannot abide this for a further second!"

"What?"

"You! This bed! This...horror!"

I do not think that I overstated my case.

Kevin started smiling, scratching his saggy breast.

"You got me goin' then, uncle George. I thought there were summat up."

"Kevin, we need to talk."

"Do we?" he said wearily.

"Yes. Well, I need to talk and you need to listen."

We had a lengthy discussion about our living arrangements, about how we were now officially homeless and about how, if the situation did not remedy itself shortly, I would go out, purchase a gun and happily shoot him in the face myself.

"Well, we can't live in a hotel forever, can we?" he said.

"No. Or even for one more night."

"Yeah, this ain't ideal for me, y'know."

"What do you mean?"

"Your feet honk summat rotten."

"They do not 'honk'."

"They do. I think yer might have gangrene."

"I do not have gangrene." I checked inside my socks. I

definitely do not have gangrene. "Listen," I said, "this is getting us nowhere. We need to find somewhere to rent."

"OK."

"Today," I said.

"Yeah."

"Right now."

"What time is it?"

"Seven o'clock."

His face folded in confusion.

"In the morning," I added.

He shook his head as if he had never heard of such a time.

"Nowhere'll be open for hours," he said.

"Well, I am going to acquire for myself some breakfast."

"Suit yersel'."

He rolled over and appeared to be instantly asleep.

"I need some money," I said, prodding his gut apprehensively with my foot.

"Gerroff!" He slapped my foot away. "Me wallet's on t' side. Help yersel'."

"Thank you. I will be in the bar."

"Whatever."

*

After a croissant and two large espressos I was feeling much better. I had acquired a copy of this month's *Merla Now!* from the hotel's reception and discovered a number of suitable properties. At ten o'clock sharp Kevin appeared.

"I am impressed," I said. "You are up."

"Yeah, early."

"At the crack of ten," I said. "Well done!"

"Yeah, I'm doin' it for you. So you stop whinin'."

"Why are you dressed like that?" I asked.

"'Cos today I'm t' Silver Panther."

There can be few things more incongruous than a Creme Egg-shaped man dressed in a silver suit and top hat sitting in the bar of a cheap Spanish hotel.

"Why?" I asked.

"'Cos today we're sleuthin'. We need to find our assassin."

"Yes, we do. But I would prefer it if you did not attire yourself in such a fashion. You draw attention to yourself. And to me. And the last thing we need when being pursued by a gun-toting maniac is attention."

He ignored my statement.

"You know what t' oddest thing is?"

"What?" I replied wearily.

"Where did he shoot us from? You said t' first one was from above t' roof o' t' house across t' road. An' t' one who shot me when you were dead came out o' nowhere. An' yesterday's, well, there were no one about."

"I know."

"Maybe it's a ghost," he said.

"It is definitely not a ghost."

"I think it's a ghost."

"Then shut up."

There was a brief moment of blissful silence.

"You know," I said. "I think that you might have been on to something the other day."

"When?"

"When you linked the death of your mother to Richard's accident."

"Why's that?"

"Something Richard said yesterday."

"What did he say?"

"Something and nothing."

"Uncle George," Kevin said excitedly. "You have a theory!"

He rubbed his hands together with glee.

"I do."

"Are ya gonna tell me?"

"No."

"Are you at least gonna tell me t' motive?"

"Yes," I said. "It's simple. Your money."

He thought for a moment.

"Eminenty, my dear Watson."

He could see that I looked unimpressed. I was a second away from slapping his fat chops.

"Tell me who it is," he pleaded.

"No."

"Oh." He looked disappointed. "OK then. You write it down an' put it in an envelope an' when we've found who it is you can show me an' prove how clever you are."

"Alright. I will do that," I said.

After all, the identity of our assassin was by now self-evident.

*

"I think you'll like this next place," said Knut, the Dutch estate agent.

"I hope it is better than the last two places," I replied, and then I added sarcastically, "I know that my last home was hardly a paradise but I do think that windows are at least on my desirability list."

Knut looked at me with disdain.

"Thank you for coming out specially on a Sunday morning to show us some properties, Knut," said Knut.

Kevin looked confused.

"What's he doin'?" he asked me in a loud whisper.

"I think he is trying to insinuate that we are being ungrateful."

Knut smiled a sour smile of confirmation.

"Thank you for coming out specially on a Sunday morning to show us some properties, Knut," I said.

"You're welcome," he said coldly. "Now, if you can stretch your budget to another one hundred euros then you can have not only windows, but also a sea view."

I looked at Kevin. Despite not believing in any form of mind control I willed him to accept.

"Go on then," he said. "Those last two places were shit."

Knut showed us inside a not unreasonably proportioned apartment with two bedrooms and a lovely terrace overlooking the town's main Karma Beach. I was suspicious.

"What is the catch?" I asked with narrowed eyes.

"Catch?"

"Yes. Why is it so cheap?"

"We'll 'ave it," said Kevin to Knut. "Don't listen to him."

"I am only asking a sensible question," I said.

"We're havin' it."

Knut clicked open his briefcase and removed a printed contract and a biro.

"An' yer sure it's only four hundred?" asked Kevin.

"Yes. Here, have a read and then sign at the bottom."

Kevin looked quickly at the three page document.

"Borin', borin', borin'."

He took the pen from Knut, signed the paper with an illegible scrawl and handed it back to him. Even Knut was surprised by the alacrity of the transaction.

"Congratulations! It's yours," said Knut with a practised smile.

"It's ours, uncle George!"

Kevin bounced like a Space Hopper.

"Yes," I said warily, "along with the bodies in the basement."

"Bodies?" said Kevin.

"He is joking," said Knut. "There is no basement. The bodies are in the utility room."

He chuckled at his own quip.

"I need the deposit and the first month's rent," he said.

Kevin opened his wallet and removed sixteen crisp fifty

euro notes.

"Right then," said Knut, bringing an end to the formalities. "Any problems, you can see me in the office."

"What sort o' problems?" Kevin asked.

"I was only being polite. Now you've signed it I'm done. The landlady will be around on the first of each month to collect the rent."

I assumed Knut would make a hasty retreat but instead he strolled back on to the terrace, closely followed by Kevin and me.

"It certainly is a beautiful view," he said. He surveyed the sky. "The only person with a better view is him."

He pointed to a distant dot in the sky.

"What's that?" asked Kevin.

"It's a kind of petrol-driven paraglider thing," said Knut. "It has a big fan on the back. You fly around in the sky. You can hire them from a place in town. You can get anywhere with one of those."

I looked at Kevin and Kevin looked at me. We were entertaining the very same thought, an event I hoped never to replicate.

"The assassin!" said Kevin.

He danced a little jig on the spot.

"I think we have discovered how he could access such peculiar angles," I said, as though it was entirely my own solution.

"Come on then," said Kevin. "Let's go an' find out who's after us."

He headed for the front door.

"Where are you going?" asked Knut.

"To t' hanglider shop."

"It's Sunday," said Knut.

"So?" I said.

"Juan is closed on Sundays," said Knut. "Just like me.

Usually."

"Well," I said, pointing to the distant dot, "he appears to have rented out that contraption to someone, has he not?"

Knut was silent.

"A-ha!" said Kevin a little too smugly. "He got you there, didn't he?" he said to Knut.

His childish joy was infectious.

"A-ha!" I said, aping him. "Not so clever now, are you, my Hollandaise friend?"

He let us gloat for a moment.

"Have you both finished?"

Kevin and I looked at each other and then at Knut.

"Yes, I rather think we have," I said, still in the ascendency.

"Good," said Knut. He pointed towards the distant figure. "That *is* Juan, you English idiots!"

*

We ferried our belongings from the old, semi-demolished house to the shiny, new apartment. In the early evening sun we sat at my plastic garden table and necked a bottle of cheap *cava*.

Kevin was watching the sky.

"Oh, look at that," said Kevin.

"What?"

"Juan's comin' towards us."

"What?"

"He's comin'. Maybe we can flag 'im down an' ask 'im some questions."

"Give the man his one day off a week," I said. "We are safe. Our hunter has no idea of the location of his prey."

"No, look, he's comin'."

Kevin leapt to his feet and started to swing his highly reflective arms wildly in the air.

"Oi, mister!" he yelled. "Over here!"

The paraglider changed course slightly and headed directly towards the silver beacon.

"Sit down," I ordered.

Juan was close now.

"He's comin'. Oi mister! Oi!"

The paraglider whizzed overhead, we both looked up to see the device that had been haunting us and suddenly the crack of a bullet fizzed the terrace. We froze and then immediately defrosted before darting inside.

With the supposed safety of a concrete roof above our heads I grabbed Kevin by the lapels of his silver suit.

"You are an idiot!" I said.

"Why is Juan tryin' to kill us?" asked Kevin urgently.

"I am fairly certain that he is not Juan."

Kevin gulped.

"And the worst thing is that, thanks to you, he – whoever he is – now knows where we live once again."

"We could allus get another apartment?"

I pulled him closer to my face.

"I am sure that you would still find a way to invite him over for drinks."

He went quiet.

"I'm not an idiot, y'know," he said.

I let go of him and patted down the wrinkles I had made in his ridiculous suit.

"You are right," I replied. "You would have to get a PhD before you could work your way up to idiot."

Monday 23rd December

We spent the night with the apartment's rented furniture wedged against the doors. Fortunately, our windows are all installed with the traditional cast iron bars so beloved by

Spanish builders. I wonder how many locals have burned to a crispy death, peering hopelessly through the slender gaps in their home-made gaol, whilst the flames of some unfortunate, bed-based smoking accident licked their already tanned behinds.

Our first night was hardly an ideal way to christen our new dwelling but at least we were not murdered in our beds. Switching into survival mode at least distracted my mind from Kevin's imminent strangulation.

Around nine I received a less than heartening call from the veterinarian to inform me that the only sure way to save poor Ambrose was to remove his wounded leg. He advised against the operation but I do not wish to live in a world without his little, toothless face and his brave if ill-thought out, chorizo-inspired adventures.

Today was the day, the day this sorry affair would come to a head. After a visit to Juan's shop and discovering it to be closed — we assumed that if he only had one paraglider, which had itself been stolen by our assailant, then Juan probably had little reason to open — we formulated a plan. It was either him or us, the hunter or the hunted, the butcher or...the pigs.

For our plan Kevin's silver play suit was vital. We could use it to lure our attacker.

"An' that's yer plan, is it, uncle George?" asked Kevin uncertainly.

"Yes. Yes, it is."

Be firm, George.

"I walk 'round outside till he sees me," he said.

"Yes. You are the bait."

"But what if he takes t' bait?"

"What do you mean?"

"What if he shoots me?"

"Ah, do not worry about that."

"This is my life, uncle George!" he said as though that counted for anything.

"It is highly unlikely that you will be shot, Kevin."

A thought suddenly dawned upon him.

"Hang on a minute!" he said.

"What?"

"This i'n't a plan to catch whoever it is, is it?"

"Yes, it is."

"No, it's not. It's a plan to 'ave me rubbed out."

"Why would I want that to happen?"

Well, about from the three thousand reasons that I could reel off from the top of my head.

"If I die," he said with a raised finger, "then you'll get me money. Or at least some of it."

He had a point.

"That may be true," I said.

"See!"

"But I would rather have you alive."

He shook his head.

"Seriously," I said.

I do not believe that I delivered my response with the conviction that it deserved. In any case, although it was indeed true that I would be better off in virtually every area of my life if he were indeed lying slowly stiffening in the mortuary I was not going to be the one to effect such a life-death transition.

"Really?" he asked.

"Really."

"I dunno."

"Listen, Kevin. Only you can do this. You are, what I believe is called, the main man."

He liked that, the clot.

"You are very difficult to miss in that suit," I continued. "He will see you from a great distance, far greater than the range of his gun. He will follow you until you are somewhere that he can pick you off without witnesses."

"So whadda I do?"

"Wait until you know that he has spotted you and then proceed to the car. I will have parked it on the wasteground at the back of ¡*Ahorramos!*"

¡*Ahorramos!* is a typical Spanish supermarket chain, where wine is cheaper than water and where Hellman's Mayonnaise is not made with free-range eggs, or at least not advertised as such, since the Spanish do not give a stuff about animal welfare. If you want to adopt a puppy or a kitten in Spain, just pop to your local bins. You will find a bagful.

"Hey! Why am I goin' to t' wasteground? There'll no be witnesses. He'll shoot me."

"No, he has to see you get inside the car. If we do this in town then he might not realise where you have gone. And once in our car, our bright pink car, he should have no problem following us."

"Us?"

"Yes, I will be waiting in the car for you."

"And then what?"

"Leave that to me."

"No, really, what are we gonna do then."

"I have not worked out that part yet."

"D'you reckon you'll 'ave worked it out before I get there?"

"Yes," I said indignantly. "Well, I hope so."

*

At three minutes past three on a warm, clear, Andalusian afternoon I heard a lusty scream. I looked in the side mirror to see a sweaty silver ball rolling towards the car, his arms flailing independently, as though powering him across the wasteground. I regretted now having parked so far from the road. The chrome appearance of his suit set off nicely his bright purple face.

"He's comin'!" Kevin yelled. "He's comin'!"

I heard a ping. The paraglider was not far behind Kevin. He was taking pot shots at his admittedly easy-to-hit target.

Kevin swung open the car door.

"What are you doin' in t' passenger seat?" he screamed. "He's right behind me."

"You are the driver," I said. "You are always the driver."

"Yeah, but today I thought you was t' getaway man. Hurry up."

"No. I never said that."

"Hurry up!"

A metallic ping ricocheted off the bonnet.

"I am banned, remember," I said.

"So? I don't even 'ave a licence."

"Just get in and drive!"

He looked like he was about to spring across me.

"No!" I yelled. "Get in the other side!"

He ignored me and leaped across my legs, like the worst ever superhero, and landed painfully with the gear stick in his delicate regions.

"Owf!"

He went quiet and then seemed to be emitting a barely audible, high-pitched squeal.

"Are you alright?" I asked.

"I've 'ad it, uncle George."

"What do you mean?"

"Leave me here. Save yersel'!"

"Do not be a moron. Get in the driver's seat."

"I'll only 'old you back."

"Get in the bloody driver's seat!"

In a manner somewhat akin to a hedgehog, only with much greater effort, he curled himself up into a ball and then unravelled himself in the correct position.

"Well done. Very smooth," I said sarcastically.

He rubbed his testicles.

"I don't reckon I'll ''ave any kids now, uncle George."

"The odds were never stacked in your favour."

There was another metallic ping, this time from the overhead bars that held the jeep's pink canvas in place.

"Drive!" I yelled.

"What's t' plan?"

"Drive!"

"Yeah, but what's t' plan?"

"It is still in development."

"What?"

"Just go!"

He floored the accelerator and we roared off in a cloud of dust.

Dust!

Yes. That was what we needed. It would obscure his vision and keep him at a safer distance until I could figure out what to do next.

"Turn right here!" I said.

We took the quickest route to the mountain roads, the exceedingly dusty mountain roads.

"Look!" said Kevin. "Power lines! We can get 'im all tangled."

"Good idea! Drive towards them."

He accelerated as the paraglider ducked and dived behind us.

"Go faster," I said. "He is gaining on us."

"He's gonna crash," said Kevin, looking in the side mirror.

We passed beneath the lines.

"He's definitely gonna crash. Any minute now!" he continued.

The paraglider went into an immediate and daring ascent. The pilot clearly knew his way around these hills. He had in-depth knowledge of every last lane, line and bridge.

"Bugger," said Kevin. "What now?"

"I am still thinking."

"I've an idea," said Kevin suddenly. "But you'll have to drive."

"What?"

"I'm gonna go down here an' jump out. You get into t' driver's seat, reverse an' then come back down t' lane. I'll get into a tree an' leap out at 'im."

"Are you sure? That sounds awfully dangerous."

"Yeah, well, not as dangerous as bein' shot in th' head."

It sounded like a desperate plan but it was all we had. After a hundred metres with the paraglider still recovering from its earlier escape Kevin opened the door and rolled out of the driver's seat. I scrambled across and slammed the car into reverse, passing beneath the paraglider as something deadly ricocheted off the bonnet. The paraglider once again ascended to prepare another attempt at attaining a position from which he could blow out our brains.

I looked in front of me. Kevin had climbed a tree. He was remarkably agile for a man who looked less like a lemur and more like a blue whale. He waved a signal to me.

The paraglider was gaining from behind. I floored the accelerator, enjoying the feeling of being back behind the wheel. A jet of dust screamed from my wheels and I lurched down the lane, moving closer and closer to Kevin. The paraglider was almost on my canvas now. I looked out of the open window and could see him raising his rifle to have another shot.

I was near the tree. I slammed on the brakes and the machine flew overhead. Suddenly, through the air, leapt a creature, a silver creature. It reached out its arms and seemed to fly under its own power before catching the pilot's legs around the upper shins. The paraglider sank and wobbled as

Kevin held on with both arms. I watched as Kevin frantically tried to retain a grasp as he slid down the legs on to which he was holding. He was slowly removing the pilot's trousers. Down and down they went as Kevin's little legs flailed in the breeze until they were detached entirely from their owner and Kevin went into free fall, dropping the ten feet to the ground, collapsing in a heap in the road up ahead of me with a pair of trousers on his head.

The paraglider, with its recent load removed, inadvertently headed skywards again. I raced forward, swung open the passenger door and scooped up a battered Kevin.

"Well," I said. "You tried your best."

"We're never gonna shake 'im! Whadda we gonna do?"

"What can we do? Just keep going."

I ground my foot into the pedal as the paraglider had once again regained control of his machine. I knew these roads. We would soon run out of lane and the tight, three-point turn required at the end would give our gunman a fatal advantage. He swooped low above us. Once again, he raised his rifle and took aim.

We were screaming along at seventy miles an hour on roads that were better suited to thirty.

"You gonna have to stop, uncle George." He pointed ahead. "That's a sheer rock face."

It was the end of the line. We were undone. And so it came as quite a surprise when a happy-looking, little, black goat stepped out on to the lane ahead of us.

"Shit!" I said.

Before I could touch the brake we had rammed the poor thing and sent it arcing skyward. It flew through the air, spiralling over the car and into the fan of the paraglider above us. There was an awful metallic crunch as a tiny goat was shredded above us.

With the flying machine nobbled it fell out of the sky. The goat-based carnage had caused his machine to veer away from the road slightly but its parachute prevented him from gathering life-threatening speed. The rifle that he had released in the commotion fell more quickly. The paraglider followed the gun into an ancient, near roofless cortijo, cracking the remaining wooden slats that had once, many decades ago, provided shelter to some malodorous peasant.

We climbed out of the car and ran to the building's only entrance and peered quickly through. The man had landed in the far corner – he was invisible from the doorway – but his rifle was only a couple of feet in front of us.

Kevin smiled.

"That was fun, weren't it?"

"No."

"Now's a good time, by t' way," said Kevin.

"Sorry?"

"Now's a good time. To show me how clever you are."

"What are you talking about?"

"You said you'd worked out who were after us."

"Yes."

"An' now that person is trapped inside this shack. He ain't goin' anywhere."

"I will show you later," I said firmly.

"Aaaah. You haven't done it, have you? You didn't write t' name an' put it in an envelope."

"Yes, I did."

"Nah, you didn't work it out."

"Yes, I did!"

"Well, show me then."

"This is not the time."

He attempted to put his stubby arm around my shoulder.

"S'alright. We're safe. Can you hear owt? No, there's no sound. He's probably out cold or dead or summat."

"Well..."

"Show me."

What was the use in my arguing? Let him play his silly game.

"Alright then, you annoying, little turd."

I reached into my back pocket and pulled out an envelope.

"Ah, you lickle cheat," he said.

"What?"

I looked at my hand and realised I had extracted all three of my envelopes. To be honest, I had had doubts about my cast-iron culprit and so I wanted to hedge my bets. Each envelope contained a different name and I had planned to reveal the appropriate one when the time was right. I had been defeated by Inspector Clueless.

He tutted.

"Cheat."

I hung my head, scolded.

"S'alright," he said happily. "I did three diff'rent envelopes an' all." He held aloft a bundle of ragged paper. "We'll take turns."

I withdrew the envelope that I assumed to be my best chance and opened it. It was like a macabre awards ceremony to reward the world's most talented, or in this case most talentless, murderer. And the Oscar for Worst Assassin goes to...

"Right, listen," I said. "For me there was only one motive."

"My money."

"Your money."

"Eminenty."

"Shut up."

"If you and I were no longer around, your money would go to the family members left behind."

"Got ya."

"And so my number one murderer is..."

Kevin did a little drum roll on the door frame.

"Edward!" I announced.

"Edward? Your lad Edward?" he asked.

"Yes. He is always short of money. He hates me. Richard seemed to be trying to tell me something about him on the telephone. It all adds up."

"Mmm, not bad."

"Are you not impressed?"

"It's alright," he said. "'S not as good as mine."

"Go on then. Tell me yours."

He opened his first envelope.

"*My* number one murderer is..."

I stood waiting.

"Do a drum roll," he said.

"No."

"Do a drum roll."

"Just tell me."

"*My* number one murderer is..." He attempted an impression of a drum roll with his lips. It sounded more like white noise and sprayed me with spittle.

"Stop that, you filthy animal."

"Is..."

"Just tell me."

"Ambrose!"

Over this last month and a half Kevin has demonstrated an impressive talent for lunacy but I feared we had reached the nadir.

"How is it possible that a three-legged, sorry, two-legged dog, currently strapped to a veterinarian's table, can chase us around the countryside in a paraglider, shooting at us with a bloody rifle?"

"He's evil. I hadn't worked out t' details."

"I hope your others are better than that one."

He shrugged. Like me, I suspected that he had played his

strongest hand first.

"Go on, uncle George, do another one."

"Alright."

I opened the second envelope. He started his drum roll.

"This one is a little, well...alright, number two is...Charlie!"

"Charlie? My uncle Charlie."

"Yes. I know."

"He's been dead for ten years."

"I know." I felt foolish. "I always suspected that he might have faked his death for insurance purposes."

"But if he were dead, even pretendin' dead, he wouldn't get me money."

He had me.

"Damn it. Yes, you are right."

He jumped around excitedly.

"OK, me now, me."

"Go on then."

He opened his second envelope.

"Number two for me is..."

"Do not spray me again!"

"Is...a ghost!"

"A ghost?"

"Yeah."

"Whose ghost?"

"I dunno," he said. "Scotch Tony's?"

"Do we have to finish these?" I asked.

"Yeah, it's fun. Do your last one."

I opened the envelope reluctantly.

"I have to say that I am really not proud of this one."

"Just tell me."

"It is rather far-fetched."

"Is it?"

"Still, not as far-fetched as Ambrose or a bloody ghost."

"Tell me."

"Alright, number three is...Richard."

He felt about laughing.

"He's in a coma!"

"I know."

"If Ambrose is a rubbish culprit fer bein' in a coma, how is Richard bein' in a coma any better?"

"I know. It is just...well, the other day, when we talked on the telephone, he interrupted me a few times."

"So?"

"So I thought that perhaps his message was all pre-recorded, as though he had not inserted enough space in which I could respond."

"Pre-recorded? He'd pre-recorded talkin' to you."

"Yes."

"While bein' in a coma?"

"He is not in a coma. That was just a story."

"An' why'd he want me money. He's loaded."

"I entertained a fantasy that it was all a sham and he was on his last financial legs."

"He ain't. That one's worst than me ghost."

"No, it is not."

"Yeah, it is."

"Go on, just get it over with. Do your third one and then we can discover who it really is."

He opened his third envelope.

"Number three is..."

"No spitting!"

"Is...I didn't write a third one."

"Very good."

"OK then," he said, thinking as quickly as the mush between his ears would allow, "it's The Terminator!"

"What?"

"He's come from t' future to wipe out t' father of t' leader of t' resistance. Or summat. You never know."

"He is fictional, you clot."

A silly, little detail like that seemed not to bother Kevin unduly.

"So," I said, "our suspects in order are Edward, Charlie, Richard, Ambrose, a ghost and The Terminator."

"Why do yours get to go before mine?"

"I am not going to answer that."

"Go on then, see who it is."

"I will."

I hesitated.

I have to admit I was more than a little anxious. It had been years since I had seen Edward. And I am sure that he would blame me for his removal from the sky when it was, in fact, entirely the fault of a tiny goat.

"Go on," he said.

"I am nervous."

"After three then. Ready? One-two-three."

We both jumped into the house's single room. At the far corner lay a jumbled heap of blood-splattered arms, legs, ropes and silk. We walked slowly over to the body, cracking old pieces of broken bottle beneath our shoes. We stood now at his feet, his face still covered. There was a little movement beneath the silk. I reached down to where I imagined his head would be and gripped the silk tightly.

"Go on, uncle George."

Who would it be? Edward, I was sure. Or maybe Charlie. Definitely not The Terminator.

With a single swift tug I revealed his blood-soaked face. Kevin and I both wrinkled our faces in confusion and then looked at each other.

"Well, it ain't Ambrose," said Kevin.

"Who are you?" I asked.

The man rubbed his head.

"Argh! *Mi cabeza. Hijo de puta!*"

He grabbed the silk from my hand and re-covered his face.

"Who was that?" I asked Kevin.

He shook his head.

"I've never seen 'im before in me life."

We both looked at each other, perplexed.

"Whadda we do now, uncle George?"

"I will take the rifle and put it in the car. You keep an eye on him."

I picked up the gun, exited the cortijo and opened the back of the bullet-battered, pink car. What the hell was going on? Perhaps our Spaniard was a rogue element of the police who had not yet heard that Jesús was alive and well.

"I have been thinking," I said, as I marched back into the cortijo. "Perhaps he is from the pol..."

"Shut up, uncle George," Kevin said with terror in his voice.

"What did you just say to me?"

"Look at 'im."

Oh lord. Our blood-smeared parachutist had a pistol pointed directly at us.

"What do you want?" I asked.

"*Silencio!*" he said, moving the gun from head to head. He appeared to be waiting for something. There was a crackle of static and he raised a walkie-talkie to his ear. "I 'ave 'im," he said into it. The response was inaudible.

"I cannot tell you how sick I am of people pointing guns at me of late," I said.

Outside the cortijo a distant engine was increasing in volume. A car was approaching. Twenty seconds later there was a crunch of gravel outside the building as the car pulled up. A door opened and, after what seemed like an eternity, thunked shut again. Someone was walking on the chippings outside the house, someone walking very slowly.

Then it appeared in the doorway, an old woman, dressed

in a man's dinner suit. We both looked at her, unable to comprehend what we saw before us.

"Mum!" shouted Kevin.

"What the..." I tried to finish, but words would not come.

"See," Kevin said, "I were right. It were a ghost what's done it."

He tried to run towards her.

"Stop!" she shouted.

He halted mid-sprint and glanced back towards me with a look of confusion. Mary pulled a microphone from her pocket.

"Thank you. You're wonderful," she bellowed into it in a poor American accent. She began pointing to various members of a non-existent audience. "I love you. And you. Yes! Wow, and look at you. You're amazing. Thank you." She laughed falsely and then suddenly looked serious. "What time is it? It's show time!"

There was a sound behind me as our flying friend climbed to his feet, the gun still trained upon me.

"What's happenin', mum? This is weird."

"Now tell me," she said, ignoring the question. "What's the whole wide world's favourite television show?"

She cupped an ear in expectation of a reply.

"Spongebob?" offered Kevin tentatively.

She laughed again.

"Fool," she said. "No, it's..." She left a dramatic pause. "The Running Man!"

"Oh no," said Kevin.

"Please god, Mary, not another game show!" I said.

"And who loves you more than all the rest?" she continued with a cheesy grin and an upturned thumb pointing to herself.

She moved further into the house. The Spaniard edged closer, backing us into a corner of the cortijo. Noticing the state of her partner in crime for the first time seemed to bring her back to earth. She spoke with her own voice again.

"What happened to you, Juan?" she asked, seeing his blood-covered shirt.

"A-aaah," Kevin and I said simultaneously.

"So it *was* Juan," I said.

"See," said Kevin smugly. "I was right about that an' all. That makes me a better detective than you."

"I am not sure that your detective skills are going to assist us very much in the current predicament."

"And why aren't you wearing any trousers?" Mary asked the Spaniard.

"Eez a long story," said Juan.

"Mary," I said, "can I ask why you want to kill us?"

"Not both of you," she said. She pointed to Kevin. "Just him." She returned to her American impersonation. "Calm yourselves down, folks! We have one heck of a show for you tonight. Juan, please tell us who is tonight's guest runner."

"Kevin," he said meekly.

Juan took his gun off me for a moment and pointed it directly at Kevin's head.

"But why Kevin?"

"Because he is The Running Man," she said, as though it were obvious. "And he," she added, pointing to Juan, "is my stalker, Death Eagle!"

"Right, can we go back to the beginning?" I asked.

She was Mary again.

"That is not the format of the show," Mary said. "And you know it."

"Forget the show for a moment. Why did you fake your own death?"

"Because otherwise Kevin would have come home to me. And that would have ruined everything."

I knew how she felt.

"Ruined what?"

"This fantastic television show!" she yelled into the microphone again.

"You faked your own death for a television show. A pretend television show."

"I told you she were mental," said Kevin.

"It is much more than a television show!" she screamed madly. She once again transformed. "For the lord's sake, don't you get it? America *is* television. Our kids eat television, the sports, the violence, the game shows. We give them it all in one tidy package. I am television!"

I figured that the best approach was to ignore her.

"Alright then. But how did you fake your death? I was at your funeral."

Mary was back.

"I have friends, you know. Policeman friends, and coroner friends and even a priest. With a little palm-greasing nothing is impossible."

"A priest?"

"The priest was the easiest. He needed some money to pay off a few former choirboys."

"So now what happens?" I asked.

She raised her arms in the air before bellowing into the microphone with her Yankee accent.

"Let the execution begin!" she announced.

Juan's finger tightened on the trigger, the gun pointing squarely between Kevin's eyes.

"You are aware that all your money has now been inherited by Kevin?" I asked.

She was pensive for a moment.

"I did not know that," she said.

"You have no money. None at all," I said, to hammer the point home.

Juan shifted uneasily.

"And if you kill Kevin now, all of your money will go to Richard, Edward or me."

"No, uncle George. I made a will. It's all goin' to you."

She thought about this for a second and then raised the microphone to her lips once again.

"Let the execution begin!" she repeated.

Why was I even trying to talk her out of it? I stood to become a very rich man if I did absolutely nothing at all.

Juan stepped forward and pressed the barrel of the gun against Kevin's forehead.

"Now!" she yelled.

I am not particularly proud of what happened next. I still had the car keys in my hand. With my arms behind my back I threw the keys into the far corner of the cortijo. The resulting disturbance made both Juan and Mary turn to look. In the brief second that I had made available I grabbed one of the broken ceiling slats from the ground and walloped Mary squarely on the back of the head. She went down like a felled elephant in the sights of a poacher, only much less gracefully.

Juan looked at her unconscious body and it was clear that, in the absence of command, he was unsure about how to proceed. He pointed the gun at me.

"Juan, put down the weapon," I said.

He was clearly nervous.

"Juan, however much she has promised to pay you, she cannot. She has no money."

"No money?" he repeated.

"No. None."

"I've got some money," said Kevin.

He reached into his pocket, which sent Juan into a twitch. He removed his wallet and extracted a bundle of fifties.

"If you put down t' gun," he said. "I'll give yer this."

He offered it to Juan via an extended arm.

"We won't tell t' police or anyone," Kevin said. "I mean, I

don't wanna get me mum into trouble, do I?"

"You will give me the money?" Juan said slowly.

"Yes," said Kevin. "*Si, señor.*"

Juan smiled shyly.

"My boy, he needs an operation. I am sorry," he said.

"An' I'll buy you a new helicopter thing an' all," added Kevin.

The deal was sealed. He lowered the gun. Kevin handed over the money.

"There you go, Death Eagle," he said, patting him on the back.

Kevin and I expelled four lungfuls of tension.

We looked around at the wreckage, a blood-soaked and broken paraglider, a quivering Spaniard now sat on the floor with his head between his knees and the lumpen form of Mary flat out on her back.

"Well, all's well that ends well, uncle George."

"Yes, there is no more beautifully poetic way to end an ordeal like this than by battering unconscious an eighty year-old woman."

"Eminenty, my dear Watson."

Tuesday 24th December

I had picked Ambrose up from the clinic in the morning.

"I've also removed the camera from his head," the vet had said.

"Ah, thank you."

"Please don't glue anything to your dog's head in future."

I was about to protest my innocence but what was the use? Now, late at night, Ambrose lay drowsily in the new basket that I had purchased for him from the Chinese shop as a gift for his bravery.

The Chinese shop is a wonderful institution, now available, it seems, in every Spanish town and village. Its products are exceptionally good value for money provided that one requires one's purchases to fall apart, explode or otherwise malfunction upon first use. I felt, however, I was reasonably safe with a moulded plastic dog basket. It was unlikely to explode.

Ambrose could barely move, the poor, little dear. Maybe it would have been kinder to have had him put to sleep. I stroked his head and he gave me a weak, toothless smile.

We had been watching the usual cavalcade of shit that is presented on British television on Christmas Eve, the three of us, Kevin, Mary and myself. Vince had prescribed her some tranquillizers and she was dozing in my comfortable chair. Kevin was happily sipping a large glass of Vimto.

"Oo, uncle George, what's that?"

"I am celebrating," I said, carrying two glasses and a bottle from the kitchen. "Laphroaig. My favourite whisky."

I added a dram or two to both glasses and passed one to Kevin.

I sat down again contently. Our new apartment seemed to be ideal.

"I hope that you do not mind," I said. "I got the whisky with the change left over from breakfast the other day."

"No worries, uncle George. Anythin' for you."

He looked at me.

"We was a good team yesterday, weren't we?" he said.

"Not too bad, I suppose."

"Well, I mean, you was a bit rubbish until you lamped me mum but..."

"I would rather not think about that."

"You really whacked her. I don't reckon I'd have hit her that hard. But maybe it'll a knocked some sense into her."

I raised my eyebrows. I was not holding out much hope.

He grabbed the remote and turned over the channel.

"What are we watching?" I asked.

"It's one o' them Best Of clip things, the funniest things to happen this year. It's nearly finished."

I groaned wearily.

"And now in number one position..." announced the prepubescent presenter.

Kevin descended into a fit of guffaws as he saw my appearing from a pub toilet wearing nothing but bar towels.

"What's that racket?" asked Mary, awakening.

"Watch this, mum. It's uncle George."

She leant forward and focussed her medicated eyeballs.

"Oh my good god!" she said as my green penis exposed itself. "Is this the kind of filth you get up to down here, is it?"

Kevin was on the floor, rolling around like a hysterical beach ball.

"Stop it!" he said. "Stop it! I've wet mesel'."

We mercifully arrived at the end of my video.

"A worthy winner!" said the presenter. "So that was this year but before we go, we have an exclusive sneak preview of what will surely be a top entry for next year."

"This should be good," said Kevin, shuffling closer to the set.

"We have received an advance clip from next year's *X Factor*."

Kevin looked at me with a worried look.

"No," he said.

"Take it away!" announced the presenter.

What followed was, for me, the most difficult thirty seconds of my life, the pain of desperately needing to laugh but knowing that to do so could possibly destroy another individual irreparably. I bit the inside of my cheek repeatedly. In fact, I eventually ended up with a small piece of meat in my mouth. Each note of his audition, if indeed it was a note, was torn asunder and accompanied by an epileptic dance. Never have thirty seconds felt like a fortnight. Fortunately, at long last, the howling and the twitching eventually stopped.

"Have a good Christmas!" said the presenter as the credits began to roll.

I looked at Kevin expecting to see tears.

"Well," he said, "that weren't as bad as I thought."

"Was that you, boy?" said Mary.

"Yeah, mum."

She tutted.

"Where did I go wrong?" she said, falling back asleep.

"I don't think I wanna be a pop star any more, uncle George," Kevin said a little sadly.

"Probably very wise."

"I mean, I know I could do it – I could be ace – but I just don't wanna."

"Good."

"I wanna be a detective," he said, smiling.

I laughed.

"We should be detectives, uncle George. We could be."

"No."

"Well, 'ave a think about it."

"I do not need to think about it."

"Think about it anyroad."

The clock on top of the fireplace struck midnight.

"Hey, uncle George. It's Christmas!"

"Yes."

"Can we do presents?" he said excitedly. "Can we?"

"Can it not wait until the morning? Besides, I have not been able to buy you anything, what with having no money of my own any longer."

Kevin looked around the apartment.

"Just gimme that whisky," he said casually.

"Really?"

"Yeah, it's alright." I rather hoped that I could keep the whisky. "It's t' thought that counts."

At no point had I thought to give him my whisky.

I picked up the bottle.

"There you go," I said, presenting it to him. "I chose it especially for you," I added.

Kevin smiled.

"There is also a present for you from Janet," I said. "She came around this afternoon."

He picked up the small, soft parcel.

"I bet it's some of her knickers," Kevin said, shaking it beside his ear for some reason. Then he put down the parcel and looked at me. "I didn't sleep wi' her, y'know."

"Really?"

"I wanted to. But she weren't int'rested. Those pants you found in t' car, I sort o' stole 'em off her line."

Maybe she was not interested in Kevin because she lusted after George. I could but dream.

Kevin opened her parcel. It was a Pink Panther stuffed toy wrapped in a tin foil suit.

"Awww!" said Kevin, touched.

He put down the gift and was suddenly excited again.

"My present is somethin' that's for you but you're hard to buy for an' so it's mostly for Ambrose."

"Alright."

I could barely conceal by joy. I am being sarcastic.

He ran to his bedroom and returned with a large, brightly-coloured package, which he handed to me.

"Go on," he said. "Open it."

I looked at it.

"I'll open it for you if you want," he said.

He reached to tear the paper.

"No, it is alright," I said, slapping away his hand. "I can manage."

I tore off the wrapping, opened the box and took out a contraption, straps, metal struts and two wheels.

"What is it?" I asked.

"Dur. It's a wheelchair for Ambrose. See!"

He scooped up Ambrose from his basket and strapped him into the device, his former front legs replaced by two white, rubber wheels. Ambrose took to it immediately. Using his back legs as the engine he rolled forward and then did a little spin. He gave a triumphant bark.

"Hey, he's robo-dog!" Kevin said.

"Wow!" I said, genuinely impressed. "He is a new animal."

Ambrose wheeled into the kitchen and parked himself by the fridge.

"Go on, give him some chorizo then," I said.

They came back, with pink meat dangling from Ambrose's lips.

"That is a lovely gift. Thank you," I said. "Thank you very much."

"Yer welcome."

Ambrose rolled towards the trainers that Kevin had casually discarded in the corner of the living room, cocked a back leg and began to urinate copiously into them.

I looked at Kevin. He shook his head with a smile.

"Well, I am tired," I said. "It has been an exhausting few weeks. I am going to bed." I stood up. "Good night all."

I popped to the bathroom to brush my teeth.

"Night night, uncle George," Kevin shouted through the door as he shuffled off to bed.

"Good night, George," said Mary as she went past too. "And wash that green stuff off your Albert."

"Yes, good night. And merry Christmas!" I yelled joyously through the door. The whisky has obviously trickled through my veins and worked its magic.

I left the bathroom and walked towards my bedroom door, the door that had just that second been firmly closed. And then it dawned on me. I heaved a sigh.

I took a blanket from the bathroom cupboard and lay down on the sofa, the uncomfortable sofa that comes with every Spanish rental.

I twisted painfully, grimacing whilst trying to position myself. I cursed the world but then thought about the last few days and chuckled to myself.

"Merry Christmas, George," I said quietly. "Will you ever be able to sleep in your own bed, you miserable old sod?"

THE END

Also from Steven Primrose-Smith

NO PLACE LIKE HOME, THANK GOD
The #1 Amazon Bestseller

After a near fatal illness Steven Primrose-Smith has his 'best idea ever' when he decides that instead of finishing his degrees he will jump on a bicycle and take his university on the road with him, on a road that stretches 22,000 miles across the whole of Europe.

During his ride through 53 countries, climbing the equivalent of 20 Everests, he dodges forest fires, packs of wild dogs and stray bulls, is twice mistaken for a tramp, meets a man in Bulgaria who lives under a table, discovers if ambassadors really do dish out pyramids of Ferrero Rocher at parties, transforms into a superhero after being savaged by radioactive mosquitoes near Chernobyl and comes close to death in France, Norway, Ukraine and Russia.

Such a massive challenge requires calories and Steven gets his from the more unsavoury elements of European savouries: brains, testicles, lung and spleen stew, intestine sandwiches, sausages famous for smelling of poo, a handful of maggots and even a marmot. Nobody eats marmots.

But the distance, his studies and his culinary adventures are only a part of the mission. His real objective is much more difficult. Will he be able to confirm something he has long suspected or will he, after all his searching, eventually find somewhere in Europe worse than his home town of Blackburn?

Printed in Great Britain
by Amazon